MURDER AT
WHITEHALL

Center Point
Large Print

Also by Amanda Carmack and available from
Center Point Large Print:

The Elizabethan Mystery Series
  Murder at Hatfield House
  Murder at Westminster Abbey
  Murder in the Queen's Garden

**This Large Print Book carries the
Seal of Approval of N.A.V.H.**

MURDER AT WHITEHALL

AN ELIZABETHAN MYSTERY

———◆———

AMANDA CARMACK

CENTER POINT LARGE PRINT
THORNDIKE, MAINE

This Center Point Large Print edition
is published in the year 2016 by arrangement with
New American Library, an imprint of Penguin Publishing
Group, a division of Penguin Random House LLC.

The text of this Large Print edition is unabridged.
In other aspects, this book may vary
from the original edition.
Printed in the United States of America
on permanent paper.
Set in 16-point Times New Roman type.

ISBN: 978-1-62899-927-3

Library of Congress Cataloging-in-Publication Data

Names: Carmack, Amanda, author.
Title: Murder at Whitehall : an Elizabethan mystery / Amanda Carmack.
Description: Center Point Large Print edition. | Thorndike, Maine :
Center Point Large Print, 2016. | ©2015
Identifiers: LCCN 2015051415 | ISBN 9781628999273
   (hardcover : alk. paper)
Subjects: LCSH: Elizabeth I, Queen of England, 1533–1603—Fiction. |
Great Britain—History—Tudors, 1485–1603—Fiction. | Murder—
Investigation—Fiction. | Extortion—Fiction. | Large type books. |
GSAFD: Mystery fiction. | Historical fiction.
Classification: LCC PS3603.A75373 M877 2016 | DDC 813/.6—dc23
LC record available at http://lccn.loc.gov/2015051415

MURDER AT WHITEHALL

PROLOGUE

Summer 1546

"Oh, we shall all be killed! Your Grace, Your Grace, what should we do?"

Matthew Haywood heard the shouts and screams even as he climbed the stairs to Queen Catherine Parr's chamber. The messenger who had summoned him to the queen's side had vanished, and all he saw as he moved closer was a maidservant dashing past with something hidden in her apron, and a footman with an armload of firewood, despite the warm day outside the windows.

Rumors had swept around the palace corridors all day, but he had tried to dismiss them, tried to concentrate on the music lesson he was giving his little daughter, Kate. Rumors were always rife in King Henry's palaces, especially when the king was ill, as he had been of late. When his ulcerous leg pained him, he roared with anger, and everyone around him ducked and cringed. Everyone except his wife, that is. Queen Catherine was the only one who could soothe him, with her sweet voice and intelligent conversation.

But not lately, they said. Lately the king had become tired of her increasing devotion to the

7

new Protestant learning, impatient with her bookish ways, even envious of her success in writing. And the queen had many enemies, such as the king's conservative Secretary Wriothesley and his Bishop Gardiner. Both were men who did not like to be crossed. Had the queen's good fortune run out today?

Matthew glanced over his shoulder, thinking of his little girl, her dark head bent over her lute. He was devoted to the queen, but how could he protect his Kate if Queen Catherine fell? Her loyal household would certainly fall with her.

Another footman brushed past him, carrying more wood, and Matthew quickly followed him into the queen's rooms. Her chamber, an elegant room draped with fine silks and scattered with soft cushions and carved chairs, was usually a peaceful spot. Normally the queen's ladies read silently or quietly chatted as they sewed and played music. Today chaos reigned. A fire roared in the grate, and the queen's chief lady, her sister, Lady Anne Herbert, fed papers to the flames, her pretty face streaked with tears. Other ladies huddled in the corner, sobbing.

Suddenly Matthew felt an insistent tug on the hem of his robe, and looking down he saw a small dog growling playfully at his feet. He'd been so caught up in the somber scene he hadn't noticed. He fell back a step, then laughed once he realized it was only a lapdog.

"Gardiner, nay!" The Duchess of Suffolk, one of the queen's best friends and another great scholar of the New Church, cried out as she snatched up her naughty dog. It had seemed so funny when she named the dog after the bishop, admonishing "Gardiner" for growling and making a mess on the queen's fine carpets, but now the duchess's face was grim under her jeweled headdress. "I am sorry, Master Haywood. He is full of agitation today, as are we all."

"What has happened, duchess?" he asked quietly. "I was sent a message to come at once to the queen, but was not told why."

The duchess glanced around at the chamber, her arms tight around her dog. "I fear the queen learned that the king issued a bill of articles against her. Her physician, Dr. Wendy, found a copy of the vile document and brought it to her. One of her ladies, Lady Tyrwhit, has already been arrested, and we all fear we'll soon meet the same fate. The queen has ordered us to burn all her foreign books."

Matthew was appalled. He remembered the other queens who had fallen from favor, Anne Boleyn and Cat Howard, imprisoned in the Tower, executed. How could such a fate befall Queen Catherine, a lady of such gentleness and great learning? "On what charges?"

The duchess shrugged in bewilderment. "Heresy, I would suppose, though we do not yet know. The king does have a changeable temper, as we all know too well, but his fondness for the queen has always seemed so genuine!"

But Matthew knew fondness with King Henry turned too swiftly to indifference and hatred. He glanced quickly around the room, and at last glimpsed the queen. Catherine sat by the window, sorting through a small box of papers. There were books piled beside her, some of which she handed to her sister to be fed to the fire while she put others in a separate box to be kept. She looked calm, quiet, but her heart-shaped face was pale, her eyes shadowed with purple, as if she had not slept. Her raiment was usually impeccable, bright velvets and satins trimmed with furs and jeweled embroidery, her dark red hair brushed to a silken gleam and swept back into stylish headdresses, but today she wore a loose robe, her hair in a braid over her shoulder. Her hand trembled as she handed Lady Anne another book.

"Ah, Matthew, I am glad to see you," she called, and he hurried to her side. He gave her a low bow, but she shook her head at such formality. "I fear there is little good news today."

"So the duchess told me," he answered. He studied her face, and her eyes darted from lady to lady, as if she could read what was happening in their fearful expressions.

"Shall you desert me, Matthew?" she asked quietly.

"Never, Your Grace," he answered fiercely. "You have brought elegance and learning to the kingdom. Anyone would be honored to serve you."

She studied his face carefully, and nodded. "You must send your dear daughter away, though. If you are to stay by my side, she could be in danger. Those against us will do anything to harm someone loyal to me." She closed the box next to her and held it up to him. "Perhaps you would look after these things for me. I have put a few of my most treasured books and papers in here, and I need someone to keep them safe for me, if—if I must go away."

Matthew carefully took the box in his hand. It was small and rather light, but the weight of it felt strong in his grasp. He had come to work at the queen's court because it was a great honor for a musician, but also because he believed in what Queen Catherine taught, what she wrote of in her *Prayers or Meditations*. He believed in studying and learning for oneself, and he wanted such a life for his daughter. If all that was snatched away now . . .

He had to help the queen however he could.

"I will keep them safe, Your Grace," he said.

"I know you will, Matthew. I have great trust in you." She reached into the sewing box at her feet and took out a folded parchment. "And if you could keep this particularly safe for me . . ."

Matthew carefully unfolded the paper and saw it was a piece of music, the queen's own writings set into a song. Something about the notes did not look quite right, something strange about the arrangement of the bars, but he had no time to examine it closely now. The frantic atmosphere of the chamber had taken hold of him, and he knew as the queen did that time was growing short. He tucked the paper into his robe, and stepped back with a bow, the box in his hands.

"I will happily give these back into Your Grace's hands very soon," he said.

Queen Catherine shook her head with a sad smile. "Nay, Matthew, I think you must keep them safe for me for a long while to come. . . ."

CHAPTER ONE

The Christmas Season 1559
Whitehall Palace

"Holly and ivy, box and bay, put in the house for Christmas Day! Fa la la la . . ."

Kate Haywood laughed at hearing the notes of the familiar old song, the tune always sung as the court bedecked the palace for Christmas. Queen Elizabeth's gentlewomen of the privy and presence chambers, along with the young maids of honor, had been assigned to festoon the great hall of Whitehall Palace and its long corridors for the night's feast, the first of the Twelve Days of Christmas.

Long tables were set up along the privy gallery, covered with piles of holly, ivy, mistletoe, and evergreen boughs brought in from the countryside that morning, along with multicolored silk ribbons and spangles. Under the watchful eye of Kat Ashley, Queen Elizabeth's Mistress of the Robes, they were meant to turn all those random bits into glorious holiday artistry.

Kate sat at the end of the table with her friend Lady Violet Green, who was expecting another child after the New Year. They twisted together loops of ivy and red ribbon as they watched two of the queen's maids, Mary Howard and Mary Radcliffe, lay out long swags of greenery to measure them. The Marys sang as they worked, sometimes stopping to leap about with ribbons like two wild morris dancers, until Mistress Ashley sternly admonished them to "sit down again, and cease acting like children who have eaten too many sugary suckets."

Kate laughed at their antics. Surely Christmas was the time for *everyone* to behave like children again? To dance and sing, to feast on delicacies until one was about to burst, to tell stories by the fire until the night was nearly gone. She had always loved this time of year the best of all, those twelve days when everyone set aside the gloomy darkness of winter and buried themselves in music, wine, and bright silk ribbons—and then more music again. Always music for Kate, as she was one of the queen's principal musicians.

Kate snatched a ribbon from one of the twirling Marys and laughed. She might be missing her father, her only family, this Christmas, as she had last seen him two months ago in the autumn. But she was surrounded by such merriment that she scarcely had time to feel melancholy.

The queen's court at Whitehall was full to bursting for the holiday. There were groups from Sweden and Vienna, pressing the marital suits of their various princes and archdukes, as well as the Spanish under Senor de Quadra and the French, insisting on friendship from the queen's cousin Queen Mary of Scotland, now also the new queen consort of France. To make things even more complicated, a group of Scottish Protestant lords had also arrived, to ask the queen's aid in their rebellion against Queen Mary's mother and regent, Marie of Guise. It was enough to make every courtier's head spin to decipher who was against whom. And all this during Christmas, the season of banquets and dances and fun.

Nay, Kate thought, she could only miss her dear father very late at night, in the darkest hours when the rest of the palace finally slept and she was working on new music for the queen's revels. Then, in the silence as she bent over her mother's lute, playing old songs her father had taught her when she was only a child, she could miss him.

Kate reached for two bent hoops and bound them into a sphere for the base of a kissing bough. She picked out the greenest, brightest loops of holly and ivy from the table, twining them around and tying them with a length of red satin ribbon.

"Are you making a kissing bough, Kate?" Violet asked teasingly. She tied together her own twists of greenery into a large wreath for one of the great hall's fireplace mantels. She looked most plump and content in her new pregnancy, her blond curls bouncing and her eyes shining. "They say if you stand beneath it and close your eyes, you will have a vision of your future husband."

Kate laughed. "I think I would be too nervous to do such a thing. What if I saw a vision of an ancient gouty knight with twenty children? We can't all be as fortunate as you with your handsome Master Green."

Violet blushed, and laid her hand over the swell of her belly. "We are wondrously happy now, it's true, since my mother-in-law moved to her dower house. But that only makes me want to see my friends equally well matched! Have you had no suitors since I was last at court?"

"Nay, not a one. There is no one new at all. There is no more room at court for ambitious young lords. And if there were, they would all be in love with the queen herself."

As Kate snipped off the end of a branch with her dagger, she thought about Queen Elizabeth in the past months, as they had moved from Windsor to Richmond to Whitehall. After the frivolity of the summer progress, the queen's pale oval face had taken on a newly solemn expression, and she spent many more hours in meetings with her privy council and poring over her stacks of documents. Yet there were still days at the hunt and nights dancing, still suitors and sonnets.

And still Robert Dudley, richly arrayed and ready to pour lavish gifts at Elizabeth's feet.

"What of the delegations visiting now?" Violet said as she tied off an elaborate bow. "There are so many here. The French are so charming, so well dressed, and they say the Swedes are most generous with their gifts to anyone who will help them in their prince's suit. Or the Scots! Some of them are quite handsome indeed. Very tall, such good dancers. You could marry one of them!"

Kate laughed. Violet was right—some of the Scots lords visiting Elizabeth's court, asking for aid against their Catholic regent, *were* rather exotic and dashing. But . . . "And be carried off to some drafty old castle beside an icy loch? I don't think that would be enjoyable at all. They seem rather quarrelsome for my taste, as well. If they aren't fighting a duel with a Frenchman, they're glaring at the Spanish over the banquet table, or even arguing amongst themselves. I would prefer a more . . . harmonious household."

"Very well, no Scotsman, then," Violet said with a giggle. "What of that actor who was at court in the autumn? I vow he was the *most* handsome man I have ever seen, except for my own husband, and he did seem to like you very much."

"Rob Cartman?" Kate frowned as she thought of Rob. He was indeed very handsome, with his golden hair and sky blue eyes, full of laughter and poetry. But also full of secrets. "I haven't seen him for many weeks." Though she *had* received a letter from him, telling her of how he and his theatrical troupe fared as they toured the country again under the patronage of the queen's cousin Lord Hunsdon. She didn't want to admit how her heart beat just a little faster whenever she saw his handwriting on a missive.

Or how she wore his gift, a tiny jeweled pendant in the shape of a lute, beneath her gowns.

"Oh, well. If you don't fancy a cold Scottish castle, I daresay a traveling actor's life wouldn't be good, either. You should find someone who would keep you here at court. You would not want to live with a mother-in-law like mine, anyway," Violet said with a dramatic shudder.

Kate laughed. "I told you, Vi—I don't care to marry yet. I suppose I am like the queen in that way. And I am much too busy right now."

Violet pursed her lips. "I know, Kate. It is just as I said—I want all my friends to be as happy as I am. And I owe you so very much. If you had not saved my life at Nonsuch last summer, I would not even be here. Nor would my little Catherine or this one, who will make his appearance next year."

Kate swallowed hard at the terrible memory of what had happened to them at the fairy-tale Nonsuch Palace, the fire—and the murderer—that had almost ended both their lives. She reached for a branch, trying to banish the dark thought of those days beneath the brightness of Christmas. "Anyone would have done the very same as I did, Vi."

"I do not think that's true. Few would have been as brave as you. So, if you will not let me matchmake, you must at least be a good god-mother to little Catherine."

"That I am most honored to do," Kate said with a smile, thinking of the gift she would get her goddaughter Catherine for Christmas—a child-sized lute.

"Good! Now, you should put mistletoe into your bough. It is the most important element, otherwise the magic won't work."

Kate laughed, tucking a thick branch of glossy green mistletoe dotted with lacy white berries into the center of her circlet. Surely there *was* some kind of magic floating in the icy winter air. She felt lighter already, with the holiday upon them. After months of worrying over the queen's safety, it seemed the perfect time to have a bit of fun.

"Holly and ivy, box and bay," she whispered. "Put in the house for Christmas Day . . ."

But her laughter turned to a rueful sigh when she returned to her room later that afternoon and saw the stack of books and papers waiting for her. As promised, the queen's chief secretary, Sir William Cecil, had sent her volumes on codes and languages. She loved studying codes, especially the work on musical mysteries to be found in Plato's *Republic*, symbols hidden in the twelve notes of Greek musical scales which Cecil believed had once been used in hidden letters for the Tudor court—and could be used again. Kate loved learning of the strange mysteries there, but sometimes a Christmas dance was just more alluring.

"Fa la la la la," she whispered, and sat down to her studies.

CHAPTER TWO

"You shall all be the death of me! If I cannot leave these rooms soon, I shall—I shall . . ."

Queen Elizabeth's furious words ended in an incoherent shout that sent ladies-in-waiting, lapdogs, and parrots fleeing to every corner of the royal bedchamber. She jerked her royal arms away from the ladies who were trying to tie on her silver-brocade-and-sable sleeves, and kicked her velvet shoe at a hapless footstool.

"Now, lovey," murmured Kat Ashley, the only person who would dare to speak to Elizabeth that way. Kat shooed the younger maids away and stepped up to tie the sleeves herself, clucking over the slippery satin ribbons and the loops of pearls clicking over the queen's shoulders. "You know it is far too cold today for you to go outside. They say it may even snow later. And you are supposed to meet with the Spanish ambassador."

"Senor de Quadra can kick his heels about all day for all I care," Elizabeth cried. Her pale face, with its high, sharp cheekbones and pointed chin, was flushed a bright pink. Despite the angry roses that bloomed in her cheeks and the sparkling anger in her dark Boleyn eyes, she stood still for Mistress Ashley to adjust the sleeves. "This palace begins to feel like an overheated mouse-hole,

21

all of us scurrying to and fro to no good purpose. We have had no fun in weeks. It is much too quiet here."

Kate had to agree with the queen about the feeling of being mice in a maze, even though she kept her head bent over the ivory keys of the virginals in the corner. She continued to play her song, as if she was oblivious to any storms that broke over the luxurious chamber.

After almost a year at Queen Elizabeth's royal court and her whole life of nearly twenty years spent in palaces of one sort or another, she had certainly learned the value of standing firm, smiling, and staying inconspicuous in any tempest. One learned so much more while going unnoticed.

And when the queen had one of her Tudor fits of temper, the most outspoken ladies and gentlemen generally received the brunt of it and had shoes thrown at their heads.

But the queen *was* right. Whitehall Palace, that vast edifice of winding corridors, long galleries, hidden chambers, and sparkling treasures, began to feel very crowded in the cold, short, gray winter days. The groundsmen kept the windows firmly fastened against the icy winds that howled past off the river. Fires crackled all the time in the marble grates, struggling to send any warmth into the rooms, but always sending plenty of smoke. The press of people everywhere, in their fashionable glossy satins and furs, made the air humid and heavy.

And the queen's bedchamber felt the most close-packed. It was not the largest chamber, but one with a view of the queen's privy garden below. Elizabeth's desk, piled high with documents that waited for her attention, was placed by the one window. The huge edifice of the bed, carved in fanciful patterns of vines and flowers, hung with red and gold brocade curtains and draped with velvet blankets, was set on a dais at the far end of the room, opposite the fireplace. Cushions were scattered across the inlaid floor for the ladies-in-waiting, amid workboxes, lutes, and baskets for their little dogs.

Kate glanced quickly out the window, near where the virginals sat behind the queen's desk. She could see the queen's garden, brown and gray under the winter frost. Beyond the high brick wall, she could see a small sliver of the river, a pale blue ribbon frozen at the edges. The meager daylight was fading, night closing in around them.

For just a moment, she let herself remember winters when she was a child. Her father had taught her to ice-skate when she was seven, and when he lived at Chelsea with Queen Catherine Parr, Queen Elizabeth's stepmother and Matthew Haywood's first royal patron, he would take her out on the ice whenever he had a moment from his duties.

She was not a graceful skater, always too afeared of falling on the hard, cold ice, but she loved the feel of her father's hand holding hers, so strong and steady, always the greatest certainty in her life. But then she grew older, and found out he kept secrets from her—secrets about her mother, Eleanor, who had died in childbirth. Eleanor had been the illegitimate half sister of Anne Boleyn, and thus Queen Elizabeth's aunt, but Matthew had not been the one to tell that to Kate.

Kate shook her head. She wondered what her father did now, in his country cottage next to his cozy fire. Now he finally had all the time he desired for working on his music, cooped up with all the little luxuries the queen sent him. In his letters to Kate, he told her of the music he was writing, of a friendly widow who brought him fresh butter and milk and fussed over his gout. But she hadn't been able to see him for herself since the autumn.

What would it be like if Kate could sit with him there now, the two of them working on their music as they so often had when she was younger? Both of them lost in their own worlds, yet still so close. Always understanding.

She thought of what Violet had said about marriage, and for just an instant Kate wondered what it would be like to have her own cozy hearth with a husband. A husband who understood her . . .

"Nay, not that cap! The black one," Elizabeth

snapped, pulling Kate out of her memories and daydreams and into the present moment in the royal bedchamber. Kate glanced over the fine inlaid top of the virginals to see that the queen was pushing Mary Howard away as the lady tried to offer her a red velvet cap. But the queen's tone had lost some of its fire, and she stood still while Mistress Ashley finished dressing her.

Elizabeth even bent her head to let Lady Catherine Grey carefully place a black satin pearl-trimmed cap on her coiled red hair. Relations between the queen and her cousin, the beautiful lady so many whispered should be named as Elizabeth's heir, had certainly not always been cordial. Kate knew Elizabeth suspected that Lady Catherine was not entirely loyal. She had been friendly with the previous Spanish ambassador, the Count de Feria, and his English wife, who had been lady-in-waiting to Queen Mary. Lady Catherine was young, headstrong in the Tudor way, and Elizabeth had sometimes seemed to snub the Greys.

And Lady Catherine had not been seen so much with the handsome Lord Hertford since she returned to court after the death of her mother, Lady Frances, a few weeks before. Could she have finally learned some sense?

"What think you, Cousin Catherine?" Elizabeth said. "Is it too quiet at my court?"

Lady Catherine smiled, but it was not quite the

25

bright, flashing, laughing smile she had before her mother's death. She was still as pretty as ever, with a heart-shaped face, bright blue eyes, and golden hair, beauty that was set off even better by her black mourning gowns than by the scarlets and blues she usually seemed to love. "It is the Christmas season, Your Grace! Surely we should have a bit of merriment?"

A wave of murmured agreement moved over the ladies gathered around the fireplace. Excitement for the holiday had been building for weeks. Banquets and dancing, decking the halls, sleigh rides and spiced wine, and especially stolen embraces under those carefully made kissing boughs, would be a welcome distraction from the cold winds and the foreign embassies gathered around to press their suits on the queen.

Even Elizabeth smiled at her cousin. "So it is, Lady Catherine. I can smell the evergreen boughs from the ladies' decorations even in here, and it is a most welcome bit of the fresh outdoors. What else of the season shall we have, ladies? A boar's head feast? Sugarplums? Games of snapdragon?"

"Oh, all of that!" Mary Radcliffe cried. "It has been so cold and gray for so long."

"I do well remember when I was young, and Christmas was the time for so much merriment," Mistress Ashley said, her usually brisk tone wistful as she slid jeweled rings onto the queen's long white fingers. "Mumming plays, Yule logs . . ."

"I remember those, as well," Elizabeth said. "My stepmother, Queen Catherine Parr, always saw to it that Christmas in my father's palaces was most grand. And we have so much to celebrate now. I proclaim *this* holiday we shall make merry as they did in the past! We must have a Lord of Misrule to oversee the Twelve Days, with theatricals, games, dances, everything."

The ladies laughed and clapped their hands, twirling around happily at the prospect of a grand Christmas.

"It will be just like when you were a little girl, lovey," Mistress Ashley said.

Elizabeth squeezed her hand and smiled. "Except when I was a child I did not have to meet with the Spanish ambassador, who will no doubt plague me with the Archduke Charles's suit again. Go, all of you, and let me gather my thoughts for a moment."

Immediately, all the ladies gathered up their little dogs and their embroidery, their books and lutes, and hurried out of the chamber, their silken skirts rustling like a sweep of dry autumn leaves blown into the sky. Mistress Ashley hovered behind them, but Elizabeth waved her away as well.

Kate quickly lowered the inlaid lid over the keys and rose to make her own curtsy.

"Nay, Kate, you stay for a moment," Elizabeth said.

Kate watched as the queen hurried to the window, and, against the instructions of her physicians and of Mistress Ashley, unlatched it and pushed it open. An icy breeze swept into the velvet-lined stuffiness of the room and carried out some of the heavy scent of woodsmoke and floral perfumes. Elizabeth closed her eyes and drew in a deep breath.

The noise of London, the constant roar of voices, shouts, laughter, clattering cart wheels, carried on the wind over the slate roofs and chimneys of Whitehall. Kate peered past the queen's shoulder to see night closing in quickly around the garden below. She wasn't entirely sure what to do, or why Elizabeth had asked her to stay, so she just waited. She knew the queen always revealed her purpose eventually.

Elizabeth turned away from the window with a smile. There was no sign of her earlier burst of stormy temper. It had passed as swiftly as such fits usually did, and now she looked—excited. Her dark eyes sparkled.

"You have been working on new music for the Christmas season, have you not, Kate?" Elizabeth asked.

"Aye," Kate answered. Indeed she had. Every night, after the queen's feasts and dancing and the quiet banquets in her privy rooms were done, Kate would return to her own tiny chamber under the eaves of the vast palace roofs, and would write until she was so tired that the notes would not sound in her head any longer.

"That is good, for if we are to have an elaborate Christmas we shall need much new music," the queen said with a laugh. "Our court is going to be busy this year, with all the foreign ambassadors closing in on us. We must impress them all."

Kate couldn't help but laugh, too, thinking of how busy every day was at Whitehall. Everyone was always running from one place to another. "Is it not always thus, Your Grace?"

Elizabeth laughed, and as always her laughter was as wondrously alive as her temper. "True enough, Kate. The life of a monarch is never an empty one. There is always someplace to be, someone who wants something. Yet it seems all my plague of suitors thinks Christmas is the time to press their cases for matrimony."

Kate thought of the presents that piled up daily for the queen, portraits and jewels and bolts of fine cloth from Vienna, Sweden, Spain—not to mention the English-grown suitors. "The chance to outdo each other with the splendor of their gifts?"

"Exactly so. Not that I mind that . . ." Elizabeth held up her wrist to examine the pearl and ruby bracelet that shimmered there, and counted off her would-be fiancés on her beringed fingers. "Archduke Charles, Prince Eric, a French prince—take your pick of them. Then there are those closer to home, like Lord Arundel and Master Pickering." A frown flickered over her face. "And then there are those who desire things more complicated."

People such as Robert Dudley? Kate thought of the queen's face when he was near, her radiant smiles—and the rumors that were spreading of the queen's affection for her Master of the Horse. Or did she think of something else, something more political in nature? "Your Grace?"

Elizabeth shook her head, as if trying to clear her thoughts. "Can you organize a masque quickly, Kate? Perhaps with some of the music you have already written?"

Kate nodded eagerly. This sort of challenge was assuredly one she could meet. Music, even complicated pieces that kept her awake until the small hours, was never as confounding as the doings of courtiers. Not all of the queen's requests were so easy to fulfill.

"What sort of theme, Your Grace?" she asked, her mind racing over sets and costumes in the Office of the Revels that could be easily used. "Something for the beginning of the Christmas season, like one of the old mummers' plays?"

Elizabeth stared down at the frozen garden below, her gaze very far away. "I told you a few days ago we are expecting a new arrival very soon. Well, they are a party from Scotland, and they must have a proper welcome."

"From Scotland?" Kate was wary. Everyone knew England's northern neighbor had long been in upheaval, with Protestant lords rebelling against Queen Mary's mother and regent, Queen Marie of Guise. "Queen Mary's ambassador is surely already here."

Elizabeth smiled, a small pursing of her lips as if she held a secret. "Monsieur de Castelnau. So he is, and always so insistent on his mistress's great love and friendship for England. Though even he cannot properly explain why Queen Mary still insists on quartering the arms of England on her engraved plate. Nay, these new arrivals will be no Frenchmen, Kate, but real Scots who declare they have vital business here at Whitehall. We must show a friendly face to everyone in these most changeable days, don't you agree?"

Friendly to everyone—and true friends with none, it seemed. "'Tis surely always better to have as many friends as possible, Your Grace," she answered carefully. That was one lesson she had learned well in the last year.

"So, I am sure you will organize the perfect welcome for our new friends from the north, Kate." Elizabeth returned to her Venetian looking glass, and smoothed the tendrils of red hair that had escaped from her cap, as slow and careless as if the Spanish ambassador was not waiting for her. As if she was not, as Kate feared, contemplating aiding rebels who sought to overthrow

Mary, Queen of Scots, and her mother. It would mean war, which was something Elizabeth had been so carefully avoiding.

"I will do my best, Your Grace," Kate said.

"Perhaps you could use some assistance," Elizabeth said, with a new, brighter smile, a teasing smile. "What of that handsome Rob Cartman? His strutting upon the stage is always amusing—and most diverting. I could send for him to help you."

Kate was startled. Did Elizabeth somehow know about her conversation with Violet, about the tiny lute pendant hidden under her bodice? The queen *did* seem to see everything at her crowded court. "Rob Cartman?"

"Aye." Elizabeth spun around, her smile more open, teasing. She suddenly seemed younger, as she had last summer at Nonsuch, with Robert Dudley at her side for every hunt and every dance. "I know you do like him, Kate. Fain to deny it."

"He is my friend," Kate said carefully. "He understands my love of music, and is indeed a talented actor."

"He rather reminds me of my own Robin," Elizabeth said musingly.

Kate couldn't help but laugh. "Of Sir Robert Dudley?" Rob Cartman was blond and blue-eyed, fair and golden as a summer's day. Sir Robert was often called "the queen's gypsy" for his darkness, his swarthy skin, and black, curling hair.

"Oh, aye. There is an adventurous spirit about them both, a bold attitude. Do you not agree?"

Kate *did* agree. Rob's adventurous spirit was always intriguing—and sometimes trouble. "There is certainly much boldness about Master Cartman, Your Grace."

"Too much so sometimes? Just like Robin— such men do sometimes need to be put in their proper places by women of equal adventurous spirit," Elizabeth said, picking up her feathered fan and silver pomander. "So, it is settled. We shall send for Master Cartman to assist with these Christmas revels. I understand he is employed by my cousin Lord Hunsdon."

Kate glanced over her shoulder, making sure they were alone. "Yes, Your Grace. Lord Hunsdon has asked him to form a troupe at his estate at Eastwick."

"Henry does love a good play. A Boleyn trait, I think. He will not mind if we borrow his prize player for a time."

And Kate would not mind seeing Rob again. Nay, not at all. "I will be glad of the help."

"Just remember . . . ," Elizabeth said, suddenly stern. She could go in an instant from playful intimate to distant monarch. "Now is not the time to be distracted by romance, Kate. I need people I can truly trust close around me, and those are so very few. I must not lose them, not now."

"I will always be Your Grace's most loyal

servant," Kate said. It was Elizabeth who had saved England from darkness, Elizabeth who promised a glorious, prosperous future. Elizabeth alone who stood between the battling claimants to be her heir. Kate would always do all she could to preserve that.

Elizabeth nodded, her eyes closing for an instant as if in weariness. "I know you are, as your father has always been. But right now there is work to be done that is far less pleasant than an old-fashioned Christmas for Mistress Ashley. Will you come with me to meet with the Spanish ambassador?"

"To meet with Bishop de Quadra?" Kate said, surprised.

"Aye. You knew the bishop's predecessor, the Count de Feria. Perhaps you will have some opinions on their differences? Things I cannot see, things they will keep carefully hidden from me. You do have an actor's eye."

Kate *did* recall the count—and what happened to her in the cold halls of the Spanish embassy at Durham House. "I daresay you also have a fine actor's eye, Your Grace. But I will do what I can."

Elizabeth nodded. A knock sounded at the door, and she sighed impatiently. "Enter!"

It was the queen's chief secretary, Sir William Cecil, who pushed open the door. Though Cecil was only in his thirties, he already seemed older, bowed by his long hours of work for the queen and for England, gray threaded through his brown beard, a walking stick in his hand. The silver trim on his black velvet garments glinted in the light. "The Spanish ambassador awaits, Your Grace," he said, his tone so endlessly steady. "He is becoming rather impatient."

"Does he press his master's latest prospect for our hand in marriage?" Elizabeth said with a laugh. "Ha, but surely he must know how busy our court is this time of year. How many suitors we must answer. These things must be carefully considered. Look what happened when my father did not properly think over his matrimonial prospects."

Cecil frowned. "It is never wise to antagonize the King of Spain, not when England needs allies. And the Archduke Charles would not be a poor choice as consort."

Elizabeth waved off his words with her fan. "I do not intend to *antagonize* anyone, dearest Cecil. King Philip is, as ever, my dear brother-in-law—even though he certainly married his French princess with such haste after declaring undying love for me."

"We must keep the Spanish and French balanced, Your Grace," Cecil said. "With Queen Mary the queen of France now, Philip must stay our friend."

"Quite right, my dear Cecil. We shall keep de Quadra waiting no longer. Kate, bring me that box on my desk. A small Christmas token for King Philip."

Kate nodded, and hurried to fetch the small ivory-and-gold box atop a pile of papers on the queen's desk. As she picked it up, she glanced out the window and noticed a lady in a black cloak rushing down the path, a gentleman in bright green behind her. She shook her head, and he held out his hand beseechingly.

"Kate," the queen called, pulling her attention from the garden. Elizabeth took Sir William's arm and swept out of the room, with Kate rushing to follow. The chambers outside the bedroom were crowded with courtiers waiting to catch the queen's attention. They all bowed and curtsied, hoping for a royal nod, a word.

One of those was the queen's cousin, Lady Margaret Lennox, who had once been given precedence over Elizabeth when Mary was queen. She hovered there with her tall, pale son, Lord Darnley, who merely looked bored to be dragged along by his mother to seek favor with the queen. Elizabeth sighed to see them, but gestured to Lady Margaret to follow her.

Kate fell into her place at the end of the queen's train of courtiers, watching the faces around them carefully. Everyone smiled, laughing and making merry with the spirit of the festive season, but she had seen all too often how quickly the laughter turned to fury, and danger to Elizabeth lurked around every tapestry-draped corner.

CHAPTER THREE

The queen processed from her privy apartments and turned toward the great waterside gallery, where the Bishop de Quadra waited. As always, knots and crowds of people hovered just beyond the doorway, their smiles strained as they longed to catch the queen's precious attention, their petitions held in trembling hands. Elizabeth just smiled and nodded, sailing forward on her way. There was not time to linger now.

Kate followed closely in the path of Elizabeth's black and silver velvet skirts, the box held in her hands. She moved quickly, quietly, trying to be unobtrusive as always in her simple dark blue silk gown, her hair drawn up under a plain net, watching what happened in the queen's colorful wake. That was always the great advantage of her position as the queen's musician. She was one of the few female players at court. She was always there, at grand feasts and in quiet chambers, yet few took any notice of her.

They were far too busy jostling for attention with the queen and her favorites, such as Robert Dudley. She could learn much of importance to the queen—see the expressions they tried to hide behind courtly smiles and hear the whispers they thought no one heard.

The great gallery was a long, wide passage running along the side of the palace that over-looked the Thames. One wall was made up almost entirely of windows, sparkling panes of the finest Venetian glass that revealed the vista of the river and let in whatever gray winter light could be gleaned. Fine tapestries covered the opposite wall, a series of summer picnic scenes woven in vivid reds and greens, shimmering with hints of gold thread. The hangings struggled valiantly to keep the cold drafts from the windows at bay.

The vaulted ceiling was painted blue and gold, with the beams carved and gilded, like a summer sky. Vast fireplaces at either end were laid with crackling flames all the time, giving the grand space at least an illusion of intimacy.

It was one of Kate's favorite spaces in the meandering warren of the palace, and she liked to linger a bit whenever an errand took her there. She loved to peek out at the river and the city beyond, glimpsing the church spires and bridges. A few times, she had put on her boy's breeches and doublet and gone out into those streets herself, amid the jostling crowds, the shop windows and taverns and houses. At court, she was usually kept much too busy to think much beyond her work for the queen, but in snatched moments she sometimes dared imagine the freedom of those streets.

The great gallery was also a gathering place for

so many courtiers in their idle moments. They played at cards near the warmth of the fireplaces and whispered in the light of the windows. All sorts of interesting tidbits could be overheard.

But not when the queen was there. When she took her strolls along the gallery, everyone flocked to her.

Bishop Alvarez de Quadra, the Spanish ambassador at court since the Count de Feria left in the summer, waited with his followers near the farthest fireplace. Where Feria had been handsome and sophisticated, yet never quite able to hide his dislike of England's new Protestant queen, de Quadra was older and always calm and ponderous. He looked like a plump, dark crow in his black bishop's cassock, and his shiny brown eyes watched the English world from under thick graying brows. He seemed affable, friendly, and especially enjoyed conversing with Cecil.

Kate could not quite decipher the man. She had grown up in staunchly Protestant households, starting with her childhood in the household of Queen Catherine Parr, who had led studies of the writings of the new religion with her ladies and written her own works, and later with Princess Elizabeth at Hatfield. Kate had learned to speak some Spanish, as so many popular songs came from Spain, and had studied their ways when Mary was queen. But she still found them rather labyrinthine.

Elizabeth sailed toward the bishop, smiling serenely, nodding to some of her favorites as everyone curtsied and bowed in a rustling satin wave when she passed. Kate studied the Spanish as they moved closer.

The bishop wore his usual black, austere in color but, like Cecil's, made of the richest velvet and lined with glossy fur, and a ruby-and-pearl cross on a gold chain hung from his neck. Behind him stood a knot of older gentlemen, whom Kate had seen several times. They were de Quadra's constant advisers; some of them had been in England with King Philip when he was king consort. There were also two new men, younger than the others by several years, and, she couldn't help but notice, rather handsome.

"Bishop de Quadra," the queen said, smiling easily as if she was not at all late. "We must give our Yuletide greetings to your master, our good brother King Philip. I hope he is settling happily into his new marriage. They say his French princess is uncommonly charming, for all her great youth."

"Your Grace," the bishop said, bowing as he leaned heavily on an ebony walking stick. Kate noticed that its handle was a golden serpent with emerald eyes, winking in the gray light. "The king is indeed most content with his marital state. He sends his best wishes that you, too, might find such felicity very soon."

Elizabeth laughed merrily. "King Philip swore he was most devoted to courting me, and then he abandoned me most precipitately. Now he presses me onto someone else?"

The bishop, too, just kept smiling. He had heard the queen's words often, ever since King Philip abandoned his suit of Queen Elizabeth, which everyone knew was futile anyway, and wed Princess Elisabeth Valois. "King Philip speaks most highly of his kinsman, the Archduke Charles of Austria, Your Grace, and declares he knows you two would be of compatible natures."

Elizabeth waved his words away with her fan, even as Cecil nodded at her side. It was well-known that he, too, favored the archducal match. That, at least, was something Cecil and the Spanish ambassador seemed to agree on—according to Cecil, Archduke Charles was much preferable to no manly consort in England at all. But Robert Dudley scowled, as he always did at talk of the queen's many suitors.

Out of the corner of her eye, Kate noticed Lady Catherine Grey slipping away from the other ladies and out a side door, her black skirts a shadow.

"It is too fine a day for such talk, Bishop," Elizabeth said. "We are much too merry thinking about Christmas. You must present these two young men to us. We haven't seen their handsome faces at our court before."

For an instant, de Quadra looked as if he might like to disagree, to go on pressing the archduke's case, but of course he never would. He bowed again, and waved the two young men forward.

Up close, Kate could see that they were indeed quite handsome. They looked so alike they could surely be brothers, with glossy dark hair and fashionably short beards, and they were clad in stylish brown satin and black velvet, slashed and puffed, sewn with pearls.

Yet Kate could see that one of them looked as if he might burst out laughing at any moment, and his eyes were a lighter brown, almost amber. The other looked most solemn indeed, like so many of the priests she had once seen around Queen Mary. He shifted on his feet, as if he longed to flee the crowded scene. His smiling friend tugged him forward.

"Your Grace, may I present my new secretaries, who have lately arrived from Madrid," the bishop said. "Senor Sebastian Gomez and his cousin Senor Jeronimo Vasquez."

They made elaborate bows, and Kate heard the queen's ladies giggle.

"Secretaries?" Elizabeth said. "Then I do hope they will be of much help to you, Bishop—and help liven up our court for the holidays, as young men do. Do you bring us the new Spanish dances, senors?"

The solemn one, Senor Jeronimo Vasquez,

looked as if "dance" was an unknown word to him, and certainly an unknown action, but the merry one laughed, and gave the queen an even more theatrical bow. "A *branle cope*, Your Grace? Or mayhap a *baja danza*? They are most lively."

"I do like a lively dance the best," the queen said, giving him an appraising glance. "You must also teach them to my ladies. And perhaps some Spanish songs to my chief musician, Mistress Haywood." She held out her bejeweled pale hand and gestured for Kate to step forward. "Now, my dear bishop, we wish to give King Philip a token from his English sister on his marriage."

Kate curtsied and handed the box to Bishop de Quadra. As he lifted the lid to reveal a gold-chased timepiece, Elizabeth leaned closer to Kate and whispered, "Did you see my cousin Lady Catherine talking to the handsome Senor Gomez when we came in, Kate?"

"I did, Your Grace," Kate whispered back.

"She has been rather too friendly with the Spanish of late," Elizabeth said, the merest whisper of a frown rippling over her smiling mask. "Would you keep watch on her?"

Kate remembered Lady Catherine at Nonsuch Palace the summer past, how she crept into corners with Lord Hertford, rumored to be her lover. Lady Catherine seemed to have lost some of her lively, flirtatious ways in her mourning, but she had indeed seemed rather animated in her

43

conversation with Senor Gomez. And de Quadra's predecessor, Feria, had seemed most intent on keeping Lady Catherine's friendship.

Kate nodded. "Keeping watch" on Lady Catherine Grey with her flighty ways, while also organizing a masque and composing the music for dances and feasts, made her want to sigh. But Lady Catherine was the queen's cousin, her nearest relation at the English court, and some whispered she was the best possible heir to Elizabeth's throne. What she did was always of import to the queen.

As Elizabeth took the bishop's arm to stroll with him along the gallery, followed by his new secretaries, Kate slipped away to look for Lady Catherine.

Lady Catherine was usually to be found at the center of her large groups of friends, almost always with Lord Hertford's sister, Lady Jane Seymour, at her side, laughing and whispering.

Until now. To Kate's surprise, Lady Catherine was not with her young friends, playing cards or chasing their lapdogs, giggling at the fashions of everyone who was not part of their circle. She was sitting by herself next to the fireplace of one of the small withdrawing rooms beyond the great gallery, her hands folded in the lap of her black skirts. One of her many little dogs, who always seemed to follow her around, peeked out from under her fur-trimmed hem. She stared into the crackling flames, her pretty heart-shaped face very still and pale.

Kate suddenly felt uncomfortable, and glanced back over her shoulder to see if any of Lady Catherine's friends were near. Such solemn sorrow, especially from a lady who was usually so light, tugged at Kate's own heart. She knew how that time of year, meant to be so merry and joyous, sometimes pulled forward too many sad memories, too many lonely hours.

But Lady Catherine glanced up and saw Kate in the doorway, so it was too late to back away. "Mistress Haywood?" she called.

Kate was rather surprised. She wasn't sure Lady Catherine knew her name, though they were often in the same room at court. They had never spoken before.

"I didn't mean to disturb you, Lady Catherine," she said. "I just wondered if you were quite well."

"I am well enough. It was just very crowded in the gallery. Please, do come sit with me for a moment," Lady Catherine said. Her face looked rather hopeful, as if she much desired some distraction from whatever her sad thoughts were. "If my royal cousin can spare you."

Kate nodded, and slowly walked toward the fireplace. "She is with the Spanish ambassador right now, of course," she said, thinking of how Lady Catherine had just been in conversation with the ambassador's secretary.

Lady Catherine laughed, an echo of her usual distinctive silvery giggle that had often sounded in the privy chamber. She jumped up to tug another stool closer to the fire, disturbing the dog at her feet. "Everyone is always so very busy this time of year. I never really noticed it before. It's so difficult to find a quiet spot like this one."

Kate carefully lowered herself onto the stool, watching Lady Catherine as she settled back onto her seat. She still smiled, but her sky blue eyes were shadowed. "Do you not enjoy the Yuletide, Lady Catherine?"

"Oh, aye. It's usually one of my favorite times of the year! When I was a girl, at our house at Bradgate, my parents would have the loveliest parties. Dancing all night, with games for all the children, sleigh rides, fireworks. My sister Jane always berated us for having such elaborate celebrations, I fear. She was always buried in her books, and wanted only to think of churchly doings. But I loved the parties, too. My mother was always so elegant, the house so bright and full of noise and warmth. . . ." A flash of pain suddenly creased her brow, and she shook her head. "We were all so merry then, my parents and my sisters, our whole household. Now there is only Mary and me, and my poor stepfather, who is sunk into grief. How is that possible?"

Kate thought of her own father, of how they had always been their own small family, and yet there had been so much loss for them both. Though not as much as Lady Catherine had endured. "There is your cousin the queen, Lady Catherine."

"Ah, yes. The queen." Her smile turned brittle, and she shook her head again, as if driving away the past—or the painful present. A lock of golden hair fell from beneath the gilded edge of her black headdress, and she tucked it back. "I know *you* must know something of what I feel, Mistress Haywood. I hear it so often in your music, such emotion, so very many things we poor humans can't say in mere words."

Lady Catherine had surprised Kate yet again. "If I could not write such things in music, pour them out in the notes, I think my heart would burst. It would be much too full," she said honestly.

Lady Catherine nodded eagerly. "My sister Jane, she was immensely clever. She could express herself in her writing, using words as I never could. But I fear my heart is not as wise and cool as hers was. As cool as the queen can be. Sometimes I feel I will start screaming with it all, and never be able to stop. A song can help me hold it all in. But now . . ."

Kate swallowed hard. Lady Catherine, who had always seemed so impetuous, so very conscious of her high rank and all it entailed, had captured so many of her own feelings about music. "You must miss your mother now, Lady Catherine."

"I do, so very, very much. No one understood

me as she did. The worst of it is, I know I shall never have another friend as my mother was to me." Lady Catherine's eyes shimmered brightly, and she blinked the tears back. "Tell me, Mistress Haywood, do you perchance have a sweetheart?"

And there was that surprise again. Kate had certainly not expected such a question. "I fear I am too busy for such things."

"As are we all." Lady Catherine's smile turned teasing, her tears dashed away. "And yet I think you must have felt a passion, for I do hear it in your songs."

"Nay, not as yet, my lady. But all music must speak of romance, as in poems." Kate felt her cheeks turn warm, as she thought of Anthony Elias, her friend from Hatfield days who was studying to be an attorney, and his calm, serious green eyes, and Rob and his laughter, and once again felt caught between the two men in her life. "I only imagine it all."

"Then you must find yourself a *real* love! It is quite unlike anything else. It is what life must be for, I think. What we are all made for." She suddenly turned away, as if she realized she had said too much. Her back stiffened, and the royal Tudor expression Lady Catherine so often shared with the queen returned.

"The queen has asked me to compose a masque to welcome a Scots delegation to court," Kate said quickly. She could see why so many people flocked around Lady Catherine; her attention was dangerously charming. Plus Elizabeth had asked her to keep an eye on her cousin. "Perhaps you would be kind enough to assist me, Lady Catherine? It is a large task at the last moment, I fear, but perhaps it could be a small distraction for you."

The sunny smile returned. "Oh, yes! I would enjoy that very much. I have some poetry of my own written, only small fragments, but perhaps they would be of some use?"

"Cat?" someone called from the doorway. "There you are! We have been looking everywhere for you. You promised to play primero with us."

Kate glanced over to see that it was Lady Jane Seymour, Lady Catherine's best friend and Lord Hertford's sister. She looked rather like him, with her sharply carved features and pale brown hair, but Lady Jane had grown thinner in the last few winter months than her robust brother, her fine gowns too large. She studied them with her dark blue eyes, also like her brother's.

"I shall be there in only a moment, Juno, dear," Lady Catherine called back. "Shall we practice the masque tomorrow, then, Mistress Haywood? Do you need help casting the parts?"

"That would be most welcome. Thank you, Lady Catherine."

Lady Catherine nodded, and hurried off to join

her friend, her little dog leaping in her wake. Kate turned back to the fire, completely bemused. What game was Lady Catherine playing at court? Did she covet her cousin's throne—or quite the opposite?

And why was she so cozy with the Spanish? Kate couldn't help but think that once the Scots arrived, the whole balance at court would be quite overturned yet again, and all the pieces on the chessboard would move. But where would they all end up?

CHAPTER FOUR

"Mistress Haywood? This letter has just arrived for you."

The page boy knocked at Kate's door just as she was preparing to return to the queen's chamber after the night's supper. Elizabeth liked to hear soothing music as she made ready to retire, but Kate's own small room, tucked up at the highest level of the palace, was so far from the royal apartments that it was a journey to get there. She felt fortunate to even have her own room, when so many courtiers had to share or even find lodgings away from court, but more than once she had become rather lost.

Even though she was late, she opened the door eagerly. A letter! Who could it be from? She thought of how she had remembered Rob and Anthony while talking to Lady Catherine, how that lady's words of romance and passion had brought them both too vividly to mind, but she pushed them both away now. There was no time for such silly thoughts!

But she was still very curious.

The boy in the queen's green-and-white livery handed her a thickly folded missive, and she saw at once it was no love poem—but no less welcome. The shaky handwriting, the tiny lute-shaped seal pressed into the red wax, was her father's.

Kate broke the seal as she brought her candle closer, eagerly scanning the message. It had been too many weeks since she last heard from her father. As Matthew Haywood grew older and his eyesight faltered and his gout worsened, he used much of his energy on his compositions, sending Kate quick word of how he fared by the returning messengers who took him the queen's own gifts of fresh meat and sweet wines. Kate knew he was most content in his cozy cottage, with a friendly widow who lived nearby to keep him some company and his work to keep him busy, yet she missed him.

Especially after seeing Lady Catherine's sorrow for her lost mother.

My dearest daughter, she read,

> You must be so very busy at court this time of year—how I remember Yuletide in my younger days! The dancing and feasting and the glorious music. I hope to show you some of the work I have finished soon, and hear your thoughts on it. Mayhap the queen can use it at her Christmas in the coming years.
>
> Winters of the past have been much on my mind of late, and with a very good reason. Perhaps you remember my friend

Master Gerald Finsley? Or perhaps you do not, for you were very tiny when he served with us at the court of Queen Catherine Parr, of blessed memory. His sister Allison was your godmother, and most fond of you, though sadly she has now left this world. Gerald has arrived most unexpectedly to visit me, and we have spent many an evening by my fire talking of those days. I confess, I have also boasted a wee bit about your work now, at the court of another fine and learned queen, and Gerald remembers you most fondly. He has listened to my tales of you with great interest.

Gerald Finsley. Kate closed her eyes and tried to remember. Aye, she *did* recall him, and his sister. Allison Finsley had been so pretty and patient when Kate was barely out of leading strings, teaching the little girl to play her first notes on the virginals, and Kate felt a great pang of sadness to hear of her passing. Her memories of Gerald were more hazy—a tall, handsome, stern-looking man who played for Queen Catherine Parr in her chapel.

The Finsleys had been two of a small circle of musicians she remembered surrounding her father when she was small, along with a husband and wife, the Parks, who were famous for their sweet duets. After King Henry died and they all left the royal court, her father went with the Dowager Queen to her dower house at Chelsea, and the Finsleys joined them for a time. The others scattered to new positions.

A burst of laughter from the corridor outside her chamber pulled her back from the hazy memories of the past to the present moment—a moment when she realized she needed to hurry to the queen's chamber. She quickly folded the letter and tucked it into the embroidered purse of her kirtle to finish later. She wrapped a warm knitted shawl over her satin evening bodice, and felt the weight of Rob Cartman's lute pendant tucked away on its chain. As Kate hurried into the royal bedchamber, most of Elizabeth's ladies were leaving, among them Lady Catherine Grey and Lady Jane Seymour, the two of them whispering together. Lady Catherine gave Kate a small nod as she passed.

The queen herself sat at the virginals, her long, pale fingers skimming over the keys. She was dressed to retire, in a tawny brocade robe trimmed with sable, her red-gold hair loose over her shoulders, but she showed no signs of being tired at the late hour. Unlike everyone else at court, the queen never seemed to grow weary, despite her days of privy council meetings and hunting, meetings with ambassadors and hearing petitions. She would still be dancing while everyone else was drooping where they stood.

Elizabeth did seem pensive that night, though, playing a soft, sad song while her chamber was nearly empty. Only Mistress Ashley was still there, mending by the fire.

"You're late, Kate," Elizabeth said, not looking up from the keys.

Kate dropped a hasty curtsy. "I am sorry, Your Grace. I just received a letter from my father, and was distracted."

"From Matthew?" The queen glanced up, a small smile breaking through her reverie. "How does he fare? I hope he is not ill."

"Not at all. He says an old friend has arrived to stay with him. Perhaps you remember him from Queen Catherine Parr's household? Master Gerald Finsley?"

"Master Finsley." Elizabeth frowned in thought. "Aye, I do recall him. A most solemn man, almost puritanical, yet he had a surprisingly deft touch with a madrigal lyric. Did he not have a sister, too, who waited on my stepmother?"

"Mistress Allison Finsley, my godmother, though my father says she is now gone. You remember more of Master Finsley than I do, Your Grace, though I do recall the black clothes."

Elizabeth laughed. "Somber clothing can hide much, as I learned when my brother was king and praised me for my plain dress. You were very small then, Kate. But those were lovely days indeed, when my stepmother came to my father's court and transformed our lives. She acted as a mother to me in truth, which was something I had never known until then. She was a kind and sensible lady, and I learned much from her when she served as my father's regent for a time. Music was always an important part of the day with her."

Kate moved closer, thinking of her childhood days, when she had hidden behind her father as he played for the queen. She, too, had learned much then, listening to the ladies talk of their books. Watching their courtly manners. "I do well remember Queen Catherine, though. She was so pretty, with such lovely clothes, and I had never heard a lady speak in such a learned way as she did before."

"Indeed she did. Perhaps you will recall more of life at her home in Chelsea, after my father died?" Elizabeth said, her tone revealing a small strain under the light words.

Kate hesitated. She had indeed grown a bit older by then, and remembered the house where Queen Catherine had retreated after she was widowed— and where she quickly remarried a few months later. It had been a pretty house, elegant redbrick and white stone, with beautiful gardens. "I was not there long. My father sent me to the country before Queen Catherine moved to Sudeley." Before the downward spiral of Catherine's life with Thomas Seymour.

"That was wise of him. You did grow up very

fair, Kate, and my stepmother's husband had a keen eye for a pretty young face, as I am sure you have heard." Elizabeth's fingers crashed down on the keys, sending out a discordant note, and she stared out the window with a defiant frown.

"I remember Lord Thomas a bit," Kate said carefully. "He was very large, and very well dressed, I think. I think of him always laughing."

Elizabeth smiled. "A man of much wit and little judgment, I do fear. Though I was a girl of little judgment then, too. I learned it quickly, but I would have been better served to have followed more of my stepmother's example. She was wise and serene—until love felled her, as it does so many."

The queen stared out the window into the black night, dotted only with the light flurries of snow falling to the garden below, and Kate wondered what she really saw there. Sunny days at Chelsea? A man who was long dead—and who had almost taken Elizabeth with him when he was beheaded for treason? Or Queen Catherine, a beautiful, intelligent woman killed in childbed of the dreaded fever? The lost little baby daughter of Queen Catherine?

"But, aye," Elizabeth said suddenly. "Life at court was grand for a time with my stepmother, especially at Yuletide. It was the first time I remember being at court with my brother and sister for the holidays, like a true family. And there was dancing and mummeries, just as I intend to have this year. Perhaps your father and Master Finsley would care to visit our court now, and see how our holidays compare?"

Kate almost clapped her hands in excitement at the thought of seeing her father again. To sit by the fire with him, to look over their music, to play duets on their lutes—to have him see her now, with such a fine place she was building for herself. "I am sure they would be most honored, Your Grace."

"If it would not tire Matthew too much, of course," Elizabeth said. "We are meant to be celebrating the festive season as they did in olden times, aye? I should love to remember what it felt like when I was a girl, and they can share their memories of Queen Catherine and my father. In fact—did your father not have other friends who played for my stepmother then? I remember them always together."

"Yes. There was Master Finsley and his sister, who was my godmother. And the Parks."

"Aye, I do remember them. We shall find them, and bring them all to court!" Elizabeth's earlier sadness over the thought of Thomas Seymour seemed to be drowned out in fresh eagerness. "Yes, indeed. I want music everywhere this Christmas, and no more dark memories. What think you, Kate?"

Kate laughed, swept up in the queen's excitement. "I should dearly love to see my father again, Your Grace. And you know I like there to be music everywhere, all the time!"

Elizabeth gave her an indulgent smile. "How fortunate you are, Kate, to have a father you are so eager to see. I always prayed for a summons to court when my own father was alive, but it frightened me to tears at the same time. I shall write to Matthew, and all of our old friends, this very night. But for now, come here and play this song for me. I want to learn it to play for the Bishop de Quadra, and cannot quite decipher this section . . ."

CHAPTER FIVE

"Oh, cupids, Kate! There must be cupids."

Kate laughed at Violet's eager words. They were working on the queen's new masque for the Scottish visitors, and the scribbled pages of all their ideas were scattered across the table in the great gallery. "Flying cupids, Vi?"

"Of course. I am sure someone could devise a way for them to ride on the clouds above the gods and goddesses. Tiny children in white draperies and golden curls. Singing as they float across the heavens . . ."

"As delightful as that would be, I can't think which of the courtiers would loan us their babes to use as flying cupids." Or of any who had their children at court at all. Elizabeth wanted all her nobles to have their full attention on their business—which was *her*. There was no room in the crowded, noisy palace for children underfoot. Even favorites like the queen's cousin, Lady Catherine Carey, had to leave her many babies in the country.

The thought of families made Kate remember her father's letter, and the past when she herself had lived as a child of the court. It had all been so wondrously colorful and exciting then, but she had known nothing of the dark currents that always swirled beneath the merriment.

Violet laid her hand gently over the small swell of her belly beneath the dark green silk of her surcoat. "You are quite right, of course, Kate. Perhaps some painted cupids, then?"

"I'm sure that can be done, if the scene painters in the Office of the Revels won't scream too loudly about having yet more work pushed on them for the Yule season." Kate scribbled a note to herself to visit Sir Thomas Benger, the new Master of the Revels, in person to ask about the new scenery and which costumes to borrow. He did seem much easier to charm into helping when confronted with a rueful, beseeching smile than with a note.

Kate laughed at herself. S'blood, but she was surely becoming as adept at being a courtier-performer as Rob Cartman! He would laugh at that. The queen had said he would be summoned to help with the holiday revels, and she was excited and nervous to think of seeing him again. What if he regretted giving her the necklace?

Kate pushed away the image of Rob's smile from her mind. There was no time for such daydreaming now. There was much work to be done in preparing the masque, waiting for her father to arrive, and keeping an eye on the flighty Lady Catherine Grey for the queen. There was not a moment to be lost. And Kate still had to pick the play.

"It will have to be only grown-up gods and

goddesses, then, and they must stay earthbound," Kate said. "And it shall have to be a tale every-|one already knows, with so little time to practice. But which one?"

"The queen always loves tales of Diana, the virgin huntress," Violet said.

Kate bit her lip uncertainly. The queen *did* like Diana, but Kate couldn't help but recall what had happened when they were rehearsing a tale of the virgin goddess at Nonsuch Palace last summer.

Yet Violet was right. Everyone always liked such stories, with gods and tempests and feuds and happy endings, and there would be plenty of roles for the ladies-in-waiting to show off in their goddess draperies. "I suppose we could do Diana and Niobe, two goddesses who end up living in royal amity like Queen Elizabeth and Queen Mary."

"And you could use that fanfare you wrote for 'The Coronation of Juno' last spring, when Queen Elizabeth welcomed the French ambassador," Violet said.

They made a list of other songs that could be refashioned and costumes that could be cobbled together. As they were finishing, there was a burst of laughter at the end of the gallery, and a group of some of the younger courtiers went tumbling past, a jumble of velvets and furs and plumes. Kate glanced up to see Lady Jane Seymour, arm in arm with another maid of honor, the two of them giggling with their handsome suitors.

Catherine Grey trailed after them with one of her dogs in her arms and another at her heels. That was rather strange—she was usually leading them toward whatever mischief they sought. Now she followed, looking as if she would rather be somewhere else, a dark blue cloak over her black gown and a fur cap on her pale hair.

"Mistress Haywood," she called as she walked past and glimpsed Kate's desk. "We are to go ice skating, since Will Percy says the river is finally frozen through. Would you care to come with us?"

Kate sensed Violet's astonished gaze on her, and she herself was scarcely less surprised. She had had only one chat with Lady Catherine; was it so easy to keep an eye on her for the queen, then? "It's been so long since I've skated, Lady Catherine. I fear I would slow you down."

"Oh, nay!" Lady Catherine cried. "It is wondrous easy, I promise, and the fresh air seems much needed of late. I will help you with your work when we get back, if you like. Perhaps you would come too, Lady Violet?"

Violet laughed. "Oh, I am in no condition to skate, Lady Catherine. But I agree you should make Kate go with you. She has been working much too hard today."

Kate glanced at the window. It was a gray day, but clear, no snow or ice, and she had to admit it would be nice to take some time away from the stuffy great hall and play in the fresh air. And the queen *had* asked her to watch over Lady Catherine. . . .

"Very well," she said with a laugh. "I will go skating."

The cold air snapped at Kate's cheeks, whipping her cloak around her as she wondered if this was such a good idea, even to keep watch on Lady Catherine. Whitehall was warm, with lots of fireplaces to huddle next to, music waiting to be practiced, mending to be done. Surely if she had been sensible, she would have stayed there?

But at the palace there wouldn't be the fresh, powdery snow, the faint sunlight peeking through the pale gray clouds, and free, easy-sounding laughter. Here, away from the constantly watchful eyes of the court, everything felt lighter. Simpler.

She listened to Lady Catherine and her friends laughing, watched two of the gentlemen throwing snowballs at each other, and she realized how solemn her days had become of late. Music was wonderful, but it was also work, and Whitehall was a confusing place at times. The cold wind and carefree laughter seemed like a delicious, secret little escape. They left the crowded streets of the city behind to find a quiet spot around the bend of the river.

Lady Catherine glanced back and waved at Kate. "What think you of this spot, Mistress Haywood?"

Kate studied the small clearing they had found, downriver from the palace and London Bridge, beyond the most crowded lanes but still full of people seeking just the same sort of winter escape. The river was a pale silvery blue, frosted with white at the edges, and she hoped it really was quite frozen through.

She sat next to Lady Catherine and Lady Jane Seymour where they perched on a fallen log covered by an old blanket. At their feet was a hamper, filled with purloined delicacies from the palace kitchens, which Lady Catherine sorted through and laid out on a napkin.

"Ah, marzipan!" Lady Catherine cried. "And cold beef pies, manchet bread—even wine. Very well done, Juno."

Lady Jane laughed nervously, and dabbed at her pinkened nose with a handkerchief. "I did feel so terrible filching them. But no one seemed to notice, so I suppose all is well."

"Surely they are all too busy preparing for tonight's feast to notice one or two little things, or a few courtiers, missing," Lady Catherine said. She popped a morsel of marzipan into her mouth. "Here, Mistress Haywood, have some wine. It will soon warm us."

"Thank you," Kate said. She sipped at the goblet Lady Catherine handed her, careful not to gulp down too much. Comfortable and informal the outing might be, but it would never do to lose

65

her head around people like Catherine Grey and her friends.

The men had finished building the fire on the frosty riverbank, and it crackled and snapped merrily as they laughed together and slapped each other on the back before fetching their skates.

"Hmm," Lady Catherine scoffed, even though she smiled, "they act as if they were the first men to discover fire."

"Better than letting us freeze here," Kate said with a laugh.

"Will you skate today, Mistress Haywood?" Lord Hertford asked.

"I think I would only be in your way, my lord," she answered. "And besides, is our role not to watch and admire?"

He laughed. "I will always be grateful for any scraps of admiration you ladies throw my way." Lady Catherine blushed at his words.

The other men called for him, and he launched himself onto the ice beside them in one long, smooth glide that Kate had to admit was rather adept. He looped around in long, lazy-seeming patterns, backward and forward again. He left smooth scores in the ice, unbroken lines and circles that showed the precision and grace of his movements.

"Such show-offs," Lady Jane said. She and Lady Catherine leaned against each other as they giggled. Kate definitely agreed with that—but at least today they were *amusing* show-offs, well away from causing trouble for the queen.

The ladies nibbled at the pies and ginger cakes as they made bets on the men's races, the wind still catching at their hair and hems. Kate watched them, laughing, as the passersby stopped to see who was skating on the ice in such finery.

Kate glanced over her shoulder as one group paused on the shoveled pathway, and was startled to see a familiar face among them. Anthony Elias, whom she had not seen in many weeks, walked with them, a lady on his arm. She was very pretty, small and birdlike in her blue velvet and pale fur, with dark auburn hair and blue eyes in a freckled, dimpled face. Anthony laughed at something she said, but the sound died on his lips as he glimpsed Kate sitting there.

For an instant, she remembered other days. Walking down country lanes near Hatfield with Anthony; searching for clues to finding some of the queen's enemies in dusty libraries and hidden alchemical labs. His gentle laughter. He had been such a good friend to her.

But then she remembered the words of his employer, the lawyer Master Hardy, who had stated that the right wife was essential in building a career in the law. A wife such as Master Hardy's own, who could run a fine London house and host gatherings that advanced her husband's friendships. A quiet, supportive, elegant wife—a woman Kate feared she could never be, not with her new taste for usefulness to the queen and the court.

And yet her heart still gave a pang when she saw Anthony give a gentle smile to the lady on his arm.

"Kate," he said as he made his way to her side to give her a bow. "How good to see you again. You are looking very well."

Kate stood up shakily from her place on the log, aware of Lady Catherine watching her with interest. "And you, Anthony. It has been too long."

"You no longer need my help, I am sure," he answered. The lady tugged at his arm, and he smiled down at her. "Kate, this is Mistress Anne Derwood, niece to Mistress Hardy. She has come to stay with her aunt and see a bit of London. Mistress Derwood, this is Mistress Haywood, who is a musician to Queen Elizabeth."

"To the queen!" Mistress Derwood cried, her eyes sparkling. "How very exciting. I long to see her. They say she is most astoundingly beautiful."

"So she is," Kate answered. "She is to go out to a hunt at Greenwich in a few days. I am sure she will pass the Hardys' home in her procession, if you care to watch for her."

"Oh, Anthony, aye! We must," Mistress Derwood said. "I would so love to hear more of your life at court, Mistress Haywood."

"We are to meet your aunt soon," Anthony reminded her. "And Kate is obviously occupied with her—friends." His gaze swept over Lady Catherine and her friends, the plumed and bejeweled men on the ice. "We must not take up her time."

"Of course not," Mistress Derwood agreed quickly. "Good day, Mistress Haywood. I hope we shall meet again."

"Good day, Kate," Anthony said. "It is wonderful to see you looking so happy."

Kate watched them stroll away, a bittersweet feeling falling over the brightness of the day. She had always known that only friendship was possible for Anthony and her; why would it make her feel so wistful now?

"Is that a friend of yours, Mistress Haywood?" Lady Catherine asked as she rose from the log and moved carefully to Kate's side. Her eyes were wide, and much too sympathetic.

Kate made herself smile brightly. "He used to live near us at Hatfield. He is an attorney, or will be soon. The lady is a niece of his employer's wife."

"He is handsome enough, but there are many men at court who would far outshine him," Lady Catherine said. "Come, shall we make a small wager on the skating race? Then we must find a nice, warm tavern before we go back to Whitehall, I am quite longing to dry out my poor feet. . . ."

• • •

The public room of the Rose and Crown Inn was crowded and noisy with prosperous-looking travelers, a warm haven against the frost of the day, with a fire crackling in two grates and a large bowl of spiced wine warming over the flames.

Lord Hertford quickly found them an empty table, or rather a table was quickly cleared for them, at the far end of the room near the warmth of the fireplace. A maidservant brought pitchers of spiced wine and platters of warm beef pies and ginger cakes, which everyone snatched up amid much laughter and declarations of how hungry they were after the exercise.

Everyone but Kate. She slid onto a seat at the end of the bench and tried to let the cheerful fire warm her, yet the heat of it wouldn't quite reach her numb fingers and toes. The merry scene around her couldn't erase the image of Anthony and that pretty young lady on his arm.

Kate took a deep drink of the wine, hoping it would wash away her foolish feelings. She hadn't seen Anthony in months; certainly she had no claim on him, nor he on her. They had been friends once, when they both lived near Hatfield House while Elizabeth was a princess and Queen Mary on the throne, and he had often helped Kate when she needed to find documents to help the queen. His law studies took him where she could not go. Once, she had even imagined . . .

But nay, that could not be. Anthony needed the right sort of wife to help him. Someone quiet and pretty, who knew how to run a fine house and entertain patrons. A wife like Mistress Hardy, in fact.

Or like Mistress Hardy's niece.

Kate had always known *she* could not be that sort of wife. She liked the changing scene of the royal court, the excitement and movement, and even the intrigue. She loved her music, and the chance to play it for the queen and her courtiers, people who knew and appreciated the art of it. She had never learned how to run a household, as most ladies did. Nor did she really want to learn.

But sometimes—just sometimes—life was lonely, and someone to laugh with next to the fire after a long day would be nice.

She took another sip of her wine, and the warmth at last began to seep into her heart. She listened to the laughter around her, the chatter about the Christmas season at court, and it made her laugh, too. This was the life she had been raised to, the life she had chosen. She just needed to remind herself of that sometimes.

She suddenly felt a gentle touch on her arm, and turned to find Lady Catherine smiling at her. Lady Catherine had scarcely taken her gaze from Lord Hertford since he arrived, and her eyes still glowed with a happiness she couldn't conceal when she was with him, yet her smile was concerned.

"Are you quite well, Mistress Haywood?" she whispered.

"I am very well," Kate answered. She made herself laugh again, a careless laugh she had learned from the queen, and hoped she was becoming better at courtly concealment than Lady Catherine was. "Merely cold, I think."

Lady Catherine frowned. "But that man we saw by the river, the one you spoke to. I thought he might be your—well, he was very handsome."

"I told you, Lady Catherine, he is an old friend. I knew him when I lived at Hatfield House. I haven't seen him in a long time."

"Are you sure that is all?"

Kate nodded firmly. "Quite sure, Lady Catherine."

Lady Catherine looked as if she wanted to say something more, but Lord Hertford claimed her attention. "I fear the wine is gone, my dear Lady Catherine," he said. "How shall we play a game of snapdragon without it?"

"I will go fetch more," Kate said quickly. Her concealing smile could be held for only a few moments longer, she feared. An errand would give her a quiet moment.

Before Lady Catherine could stop her, Kate slid away from the table and made her way through the crowded room. She heard snatches of all sorts of languages as she passed the crowded tables, German, Spanish, French, Dutch. She found the maidservant in a long narrow dark hallway leading to the stairs. The girl seemed rushed and red-faced, but she cheerfully stopped to take Kate's order for more wine.

"Of course, mistress, right away," she said. "I do like it when the queen's own courtiers come here—their clothes are always so lovely."

"Do they come here often?" Kate asked.

"When the queen is at Whitehall Palace, mistress. We are near to there but not so far, especially for the gentlemen, if you know what I mean," the maidservant said with a laugh and a wink.

Kate nodded. The queen encouraged flirtation at court, but only if it was centered on her own royal person, and she always watched everyone around her with the keen attention of a hawk. At an inn, lords and ladies could laugh together freely— and the men could look for other distractions, as well. Kate had glimpsed such things often enough, in the darkened corners of the palace and at places like the Cardinal's Hat in Southwark, run by her friend Mistress Celine.

"It should make things quite interesting," she murmured.

The maid studied Kate's fur-trimmed red cloak and fine Spanish leather boots. "But you're from the queen's court yourself, aren't you, mistress?"

"My father is a musician to the queen," Kate answered. She often found it was much easier to say that than explain how she came to be a court musician herself.

The maid's eyes widened. "Music? We do love a good song here, though we don't get to hear it as much as we like, unless you count it when the customers get ale-shot and sing bawdy chants. The Spanish gentlemen seem to like that sort of thing more than anyone."

Kate laughed, trying to imagine Bishop de Quadra and his black-clad retainers singing bawdy songs. She could almost picture the new secretary Senor Gomez doing that, but not his solemn friend Senor Vasquez.

"But we do have a lady staying here now who plays the lute very finely," the maid said. "I like to stand outside her room and listen when I can. I would get my ear twisted by the landlady if she knew, though."

"A lady who plays the lute?" Kate thought of the crowd she had passed in the great room, the prosperous-looking travelers with their cacophony of languages. "Is she the wife of one of those merchants I saw in the great room?"

"Nay, that is the odd thing, mistress." The maid glanced over her shoulder, as if to make sure the inn's ear-twisting landlady was nowhere in sight. When she saw they were alone in the dim corridor, she leaned closer and whispered, "She is dressed very fine, but she stays all alone up there in her room. A gentleman brought her here almost a fortnight ago, and left a large purse to pay for her keep, but we haven't seen him since."

"How very odd." Kate was rather intrigued. It sounded like a poem or a play, a fine lady left in distress, waiting for a knight to ride to her rescue. Perhaps she was a kidnapped princess, spirited away from her home, or a runaway bride. Most interesting.

"We do have the wives of lots of foreign merchants stay here, since the palace is so near. Dutch, and French Hugenots, people of that sort. But this lady is *English*. We take her meals up to her, and she says very little. All I know is that she is called Mary. I think it must get lonely there."

"I daresay it must be," Kate murmured. She wondered who she could be, an English lady called Mary who played music all day. It would be interesting to meet her. Kate was with people all the time at court, and everyone there had to play music to one degree or another to please the queen. But there were few she could speak to freely, and fewer still whose secrets were quite so intriguing.

"Hester! There you are," a woman shrieked. She was a portly, red-faced lady dressed in fine green wool and a lace-trimmed cap, but she was scowling under its frill as she rushed toward the maid and grabbed her arm. "What are you doing standing about here when we have so many customers? Take the wine out immediately!"

"Of course, Mistress Fawlkes. Right away." The maid gave Kate a quick smile and hurried off, closely followed by the landlady. Kate was left alone in the corridor. She could hear the echo of the laughter from the great room, and she knew she should go back as well, but somehow she couldn't quite make herself move. The quiet was so welcome for a moment. She leaned back against the plastered wall and thought of the lady hidden in her room. What would it be like to run away for a while, to lock a door behind her, pick up her lute, and not have to move? It would be lovely for a day or two, but maybe not for a whole fortnight.

The sound of a door closing at the top of the stairs startled her. She pushed herself away from the wall and glanced up the narrow staircase. A girl stood on the landing above, and even in the dim, dusty light Kate could see that she was pretty, with a pale oval face crowned with a wealth of dark auburn hair worn loose over her shoulders. She was rather tall for a woman, but coltishly slender, a girl on the cusp of being a lady.

She wore a fine gown of peach-colored taffeta trimmed with gold ribbons, and Kate realized she must be the mysterious lute-playing lady. She looked rather familiar, with that burnished hair and pointed chin, but Kate couldn't be sure she'd seen her before.

The girl, like the maid, looked back over her shoulder uncertainly, as if she feared someone followed her. One of her delicate hands hovered at her throat uncertainly. To Kate's surprise, a narrow gold wedding band circled her finger. She seemed rather young for such things. Lords and ladies at court, especially the ones who commanded large estates, often married in childhood, but most people did not.

"Are you Mistress Mary?" Kate called.

The girl gasped, and her attention shot to Kate. There was only a glimpse of wide, bright green eyes, and then the girl spun around and fled. There was the sound of the door slamming and the click of a lock sliding back into place.

Kate laughed ruefully. "I didn't realize I was so very fearsome," she whispered. She turned to make her way back toward the great room. It would soon be time to return to Whitehall to prepare for the night's dancing.

Before she could get there, she glimpsed the white fur-trimmed hem of a dark blue cloak rounding the corner of the corridor that led down into the kitchens and vanishing into the warren of rooms behind. It looked like Lady Catherine's cloak, and Kate could hear the soft, musical murmur of her voice.

Kate tiptoed to the corner, careful not to be seen. What was Lady Catherine doing there? Surely she was not going to the kitchens for a bit of cookery advice.

But Lady Catherine was not there alone. Kate

heard a deeper voice answer hers—Lord Hertford's voice.

"Can we not wait until we return to the palace to talk, my sweeting?" he said. "A public inn is far too crowded."

"Not as crowded as Whitehall would be! There are ears in every wall there, I vow," Lady Catherine cried. Her voice sounded thick, gasping, as if she was on the verge of tears. "And we have not truly spoken since you came to Sheen to see my mother before she died."

"There has been no chance to speak, as you well know," Lord Hertford said impatiently. There was a rustle of cloth, the sounds of a kiss.

"Nay," Lady Catherine said after a long moment. "I must know what is happening, Ned. I can wait no longer."

"Happening, my sweet?"

"I know my mother gave you permission for us to wed, that it was her dearest wish. Yet you have not spoken to the queen."

"You know that matters are not so simple as that."

"Are they not?"

"Of course not. You are no mere maid, but the queen's cousin. Perhaps one day you will be her declared heir. We must tread softly."

"I am sick unto death of treading softly!" Lady Catherine cried. "We have been in love for so long. I want us, need us, to be truly together."

"And so we shall be," Lord Hertford murmured soothingly. It didn't seem to work, as Lady Catherine gave a choked sob. There was a thud, as if she hit him on the shoulder. "Your stepfather advised me to wait to approach the queen until I can gain the support of the privy council. I think he is right."

"That will surely take ages."

"But it would be worth it, if we could be properly wed. We must preserve your station, for our children's sake."

"It is always thus with you, Ned," Lady Catherine said fiercely. "So cautious. Station and rank. But what of our love? The days are just slipping away, days when we could be starting our own family. Yet now you must curry favor with every peacock on the privy council!"

"I am not the only one seeking favor," Lord Hertford said, his tone hardening. "You spend all your time whispering with de Quadra and his so-called secretaries."

"I must talk to those who would pay me some heed," Lady Catherine hissed. "You say yourself we must preserve my rank, but the queen cares nothing for it. She dislikes me and my sister, and wastes no opportunity to make that clear. The Spanish ambassador treats me as my family name deserves. And his friends are amusing."

"They do say all the ladies at court find the

new Spaniards, Senors Gomez and Vasquez, most handsome."

"Why, Ned," Lady Catherine said with a laugh, "are you jealous?"

"Certainly not. A Seymour jealous of a Spanish lackey?"

"I declare you *are* jealous. Just as you once were of Lord Herbert."

"You were married to Herbert."

"Not really. I was but twelve when my father arranged the match, and not much older when it was annulled. I never cared for him, or anyone, as I do you. But I must be wed soon! I refuse to molder away my youth, as the queen does."

"And mayhap if we cannot wed soon, you will encourage a Spanish match?"

"I never said that. I merely enjoy their conversation. If they presume more, I cannot help that."

"And do they presume more?"

Lady Catherine laughed. "Ned, how can I know? I have no interest in politics, you know that. Look where politics got my father and my sister, Jane. To the block. And if we have so little time together, we should not waste it arguing."

"Now that I truly agree with, sweeting."

Lady Catherine giggled, and their words were lost in the sound of kisses, the rustle of fabric. Kate carefully backed away and made her way toward the great room again, hardly daring to breathe. Lady Catherine's marriage, as the queen's cousin, was subject to the permission of the queen and her privy council, or it could be treasonous. Elizabeth was obviously right to keep watch on the Greys.

And yet—Kate could not help feeling sorry for Lady Catherine. Nothing there could possibly end happily for everyone involved.

Mary leaned back against her locked chamber door, and pressed her hand to the nervous flutter of her stomach. She had been seen. If he found out, he would be so angry.

You must speak to no one but the servants, Mary, and let no one into your chamber. It is of the most vital importance that you listen to me now.

She *did* listen. What choice did she have? But it grew so lonely sometimes! Her room was so small, so stuffy with the smoke from its one tiny fireplace and the candles that did so little to pierce the wintertime gloom. She could hear the laughter from the great room below, and she longed to join in. It had been so long since she had talked to anyone.

Music was a lovely thing, but after hours and hours of practicing on her lute she longed for something else. Anything else. Maybe even just a new book of songs to learn.

In a small fit of rebellion, she shoved a stack of books off her table and kicked them out of her way. She stalked to her one small window and nudged the curtain open to peer outside.

Below her was the snow-dusted courtyard of the inn, where she could see some of the servants huddling together in the cold wind in order to laugh for a moment without the landlady shouting at them. Beyond the gate she could glimpse the spires and chimneys of the city, looking golden and enchanted in the gray light of day.

When she had lived in the country, she would pore over maps and engravings of London and dream of the day when she would see the great city for herself. She would envision shops full of silks and books and ribbons, the people she would meet, even the queen herself. She had glimpsed such things on her journey, peeking out from her litter to see the sparkling shop windows, the grand palaces along the Strand, the ladies in their beautiful gowns, the handsome young men. She had even gawked at terrible sites, like the heads of traitors staring down sightlessly from the top of the bridge.

But ever since then, London had been only this room.

As she watched the courtyard below, a large group came out of the inn and hurried toward the street. They wore beautiful cloaks of fur and velvet, embroidered doublets and plumed caps. Ice skates gleamed on ribbons tossed over the men's shoulders, and they were all laughing and merry together. One of the ladies seemed to slip on the snowy ground, and her escort caught her up in his arms.

With them was the lady who had called out to Mary on the stairs, her cloak a distinctive red in the gloom of the day. How Mary had longed to answer her, to ask her questions about life at court! But she had become frightened and run away, and now the lady was gone.

The woman in the red cloak glanced up, and Mary instinctively drew back into her room, letting the curtain hide her from the world outside. She was going to have to be much more careful now. She did not want to get into trouble, not again.

CHAPTER SIX

Kate heard the most wondrous sound coming from some distant place in the palace, a music that sounded almost like that of a lute, but not quite. It was lighter, higher, more resonant, almost like a summer cloud.

She followed the sound as if drawn by a magical spell. The queen was in a meeting of her privy council, so the privy and presence chambers were not as crowded as usual. But the room from where the sweet music emanated, one of the smaller sitting rooms off the waterside gallery, *was* full—mostly with ladies who had obviously gathered to watch the song's player.

It was one of Bishop de Quadra's handsome new secretaries, Senor Gomez. He balanced an instrument in his hands that looked almost similar to the Andalusian guitar Kate had seen a few times, but this instrument was smaller, with a curved body and longer neck. From its six double strings, he coaxed the most amazingly sweet sounds.

Kate lingered in the doorway, listening to the bittersweet song. It sounded like a slow, warm summer's day, and seemed to push her out of the chilly, drafty winter palace into some distant, sunny grove, filled with the scent of oranges and a balmy, salty sea breeze. It captured what she always hoped to find in a song, a certain mood, a place, a feeling. It was ever elusive, and she longed to reach out and grab it in her hand. She closed her eyes, hoping to hold on to it.

The magical song ended in a long, curling note, and her eyes flew open. She was startled to find herself still in Whitehall, and even more to find Senor Gomez looking directly at her.

He was indeed handsome, in an almost unreal way, like a painting, or like his own song. His eyes were dark and lustrous, unreadable even as he smiled. That smile widened, and she could see why the ladies gathered around him—and why even Lady Catherine Grey, who never lacked for admirers, might enjoy his company.

"Hola, senora! ¿Cómo te va todo?" he said. "Won't you come in and join us?"

"That is Mistress Haywood, one of the queen's musicians," Mary Howard said.

"Ah, then you definitely must join us," Senor Gomez said, his smile sparkling. "I am very curious about your English style of music. I want to collect some new songs to take with me back to Madrid."

Kate smiled in return. Music was something she *could* talk about, while courtly flirtation was still something she could not quite master.

"I can show you an English song or two, senor," she said, making her way into the room. She could sense some of the others watching her curiously, but she could only see that intriguing instrument. "If in return you will tell me about that song you were playing. It was beautiful. It took me away from the cold winter day entirely."

"Then it has done its job, I think. It is by Luis de Milán, one of our finest Spanish composers."

"I have a book of his compositions, but I don't think it includes that song." Kate sat down on the stool next to his, studying the guitarlike instrument in his hands, its fine inlaid decorations of strange, pale woods.

He held it out to her. "Have you played a vihuela before?"

Kate shook her head. "A guitar once or twice, but this appears different."

"It is, a bit. Here, I will show you."

Senor Gomez leaned close to show her the inlaid frets, the double-strung strings. Up close, he was even more handsome, despite his somber Spanish fashions. He smelled sweetly of cloves and orange, just like the atmosphere of his song. If Lady Catherine was trying to distract herself from the capriciousness of Lord Hertford, she could certainly choose worse. But Kate found herself oddly distanced from him, that feeling of observing a painting growing even stronger.

The vihuela, though, was fascinating. She ran her fingers experimentally over the strings and tried a chord. She got lost in the song.

When she glanced up, she was surprised to see that the light beyond the room's window had turned brighter. Some of the ladies had drifted away. Senor Gomez's friend, the other secretary, Senor Vasquez, sat near that window, his head bent over a book. Despite the music and chatter around him, he seemed completely absorbed by whatever he read.

"Does your friend not enjoy music, too, Senor Gomez?" she asked.

He laughed. "He is my cousin, senora; our mothers were sisters. But I fear he inherited a tone deafness from his father."

She studied Senor Vasquez, whose face looked like an austere, thinner, paler version of his cousin's. He seemed very withdrawn from everything around him. "I am sure London must be very different from Madrid. But can he find nothing to distract him here?"

Senor Gomez leaned closer to say quietly, "I did think perhaps he had found a fair lady to distract him. I saw him walking with a woman by the river. He had a disappointment in romance at home, I fear."

Kate smiled. If either of the Spanish cousins looked likely to find an English romance, it was this man. But she had learned at court that everyone could have a secret. "Queen Elizabeth does like to keep a young, lively court around her."

Senor Gomez smiled. "So I have found, much to my delight. And when I saw Jeronimo with a lady. . . ."

"One of the queen's ladies?" Kate whispered. She thought of Lady Catherine Grey, and the queen's suspicions that her cousin kept too much Spanish company.

"A very pretty red-haired lady."

Not the blond Lady Catherine? "Red like the queen?"

"Nay, darker red than your queen. Queen Elizabeth is like a dawn, I think; this young lady was like a deep, rich wine. Changeable, as if someone could be lost in the depths of the color."

"You sound as if you write music yourself, senor."

"I do, once in a while. But I fear my cousin would never be a fit subject for the hero of a romantic madrigal."

"And why is that?"

"When I asked him about the lady, he denied any knowledge of her. I think he would rather go home and become a priest."

Kate studied Senor Vasquez closer, the pinched contours of his face above his high white ruff. "And then come back to England as ambassador, like the bishop?"

Senor Gomez laughed. "My cousin would make a better cloistered monk than a bishop-ambassador. But I find I would be happy to come back to England again and again."

"And why is that, senor?"

He gave her a puzzling smile. "It seems a land where a man can make a new fortune, *sí*?"

"Mistress Haywood," a maidservant cried as she hurried into the room. "There you are. Her Grace sent for you to meet her at the privy river stairs."

"Her Grace?" Kate said, surprised. Had so much time passed already, that the queen was done with her privy council for the day? She reluctantly gave the beautiful vihuela back to Senor Gomez, and stood up to shake out her forest green skirts and smooth her hair beneath her cap. She had no idea why the queen would need her at the privy stairs, but she knew she had to hurry. "Thank you for showing me the song, senor."

He gave her a charming smile. "Perhaps we could play together again soon, Senorita Haywood? I know many Yuletide songs from my homeland you might enjoy."

Kate nodded. If Senor Gomez was as open as he seemed, he might have interesting information from the Spanish faction. "Perhaps indeed, senor."

As she hurried out of the room, Senor Vasquez at last glanced up from his book and nodded at her. Kate curtsied, turning her head for a glimpse of the volume's title. *Libro de musica de vihuela.* No clue to Senor Gomez's romantic life or political ambitions at all.

She made her way down the winding stairs and out the gate that led to the queen's privy stairs, where she usually boarded her own barge and greeted official guests. Elizabeth's pale-blue–and-silver gown blended into the icy river beyond, the pearls in her hair gleaming like the snowflakes that drifted around them. Robert Dudley stood next to her, also in blue and silver, whispering into her ear as she laughed and pushed him away with the ermine muff on her arm.

"You sent for me, Your Grace?" Kate said with a curtsy.

Elizabeth glanced toward her with a smile. "Ah, Kate, there you are. Good. We have a surprise for you."

"For me?" Kate said. She looked around, but could see nothing except the stone walls of the palace, the boats slicing past on the river.

Elizabeth laughed, and pointed her gloved hand upriver. "Just coming into view there."

Kate shielded her eyes against the gray glare of the light, and saw one of the queen's barges sliding into view. It was not the royal barge Elizabeth herself used to navigate the river, but one used to transport her court from palace to palace. It was very fine nonetheless, painted gold and white, with royal green banners snapping in the cold wind. The oars cut through the icy waters with slow, laborious movements; soon they would be too frozen for vessels to pass at all.

She glimpsed a figure standing in the prow, a tall, stooped man wrapped in a fur-trimmed cloak, leaning on the gilded railing. There was something very familiar about his posture, and Kate caught her breath, hardly daring to hope.

As the barge came closer, sliding toward the moorings of the privy steps, Kate saw that it truly was her father who stood there. She cried out with a surge of happiness, and completely forgot the dignity of palace etiquette to jump up and wave at him.

Matthew Haywood waved back, and as soon as the barge docked he hurried up the steps as quickly as his walking stick would let him. Kate ran to throw her arms around him, to hold him close enough that she knew he was really there.

"My Kate," he whispered, pressing a kiss to her cheek with his cold lips. He still smelled of parchment and ink, of dusty, fire-warmed rooms, and a hint of cinnamon from his favorite cider drink, just as she always remembered from when she was a child and he would tuck her in as she begged for one more song.

Yet when she drew back to look up at him, she saw that he was not quite the same man he had been when she last saw him in the autumn. He was paler, his face more heavily lined beneath the edge of his velvet cap, his eyes shadowed. She knew she had to take care of him now, as he once did her.

"Oh, Father," she said, going up on tiptoe to kiss his cheek in turn. "How wonderful it is to see you! I didn't think you would be here for days yet."

"Her Grace sent her own barge for us, as you see, and insisted we had to be here to celebrate a royal Christmas," Matthew answered.

Kate glanced back at Elizabeth. The queen laughed and clapped her hands, her dark eyes shining, as she did always love surprises, both ones given to her and ones she bestowed on her favorites. "I need all my best musicians around me at this time of year, especially with so many foreign ambassadors who must be impressed with the glories of the English court. There is not a moment to be lost."

"And I longed to see my dearest girl again," Matthew said. He laid his gloved hand gently to Kate's cheek, and to her surprise she found he trembled. She looked up into his eyes, the same grayish blue as her own, and thought she saw the shimmer of a tear. "You have become such a grand, elegant lady here at court, my Kate. Just like your mother."

Before Kate could answer, three other passengers came down the barge steps behind Matthew, an older couple and a gentleman in a brown woolen cloak. Kate had not seen them since she was a child, but she remembered them right away, and the sight of them brought back all her old memories of hiding under tables to hear them playing music late into the night.

"Kate, do you remember Edward and Hester Park? And Gerald Finsley? They were in Queen Catherine's household with us. You have not seen them since you were about ten years old," Matthew said. Mistress Park, who had been golden blond then, now had whorls of luxuriant white hair beneath the hood of her cloak, and Kate recalled her exquisite voice. Her husband was still much shorter than she, with a merry smile, and Master Finsley still sported a luxuriant salt-and-pepper mustache. His eyes were pale gray, taking in everything around him with quick, darting glances.

Master Finsley and the Parks came hurrying over to make their bows to the queen, and to kiss Kate's cheek.

"Your father was quite right, my dear," Mistress Park said, her voice still resonating like a golden bell. "You have become most elegant indeed. Why, I remember when you would steal comfits from my sweet bowl! But you were too adorable for anyone ever to be angry with you."

"And too talented with your lute," Master Finsley added. His eyes, bright blue under bushy silver brows, sparkled with laughter she well remembered. But he had been quick to lose his temper then, too, as she recalled. Quiet and rather puritanical, except when he played his music.

"We knew you would go far with your lute."

"I do remember Christmases when I was a girl and you all served my dear stepmother," Elizabeth said. "How Queen Catherine loved this time of year! I never remember it being so merry before her. I hope we can re-create something of those days this year."

Master Finsley bowed, and held up a rolled leather case. "We have brought many of those old songs with us, Your Grace, just as you asked. We also love to talk of those days with Queen Catherine."

"I am glad to hear it," Elizabeth said. "Now I must go. I am to meet with the Swedish ambassador. But I hope you will all dine with me this evening, so we may talk more about the old days."

"We would be honored, Your Grace," Matthew said. He tried to bow again, but Elizabeth stopped him with a gentle hand on his arm and a smile. She swept back into the palace, leaving the rest of them to follow.

Kate took her father's arm with one hand and Master Finsley's with the other. She felt a sudden wave of contentment wash over her, with her father and their old friends nearby. She had not quite realized how very alone she sometimes felt until that feeling was gone. There would be glorious music now! "Come, let us find a fire where we can sit and talk. I have missed you all so very much!"

"As we have missed you," Mistress Park said. She and her husband followed as Kate led them into the warmth and noise of the palace. "We would never have expected such a very gracious welcome to court, by the queen herself! I am most overcome."

Her husband patted her arm with a fond smile. "We have certainly lived very quietly in retirement these last few years, Kate, at a cottage our patron Lord Melville gave us. It is a comfortable life, but not a grand one, and only ourselves to make music for. I know Hester has missed some of the glitter and fashion."

"I don't miss it so very much—not certain parts of it, anyway," Mistress Park protested. She turned her head to watch as the Duchess of Stratfield hurried past in a pearl-embroidered scarlet gown, followed by her pet monkey in a matching jacket. "But I admit I have missed the clothes. How very wide skirts have become of late! And tell me, Kate, do all ladies keep monkeys?"

Kate found that the chamber where Senor Gomez had played his vihuela was now empty, and she hurried to find cushioned stools and chairs for her father and his friends. "What of you, Master Finsley? Have you missed court life?"

Gerald Finsley gave her a smile, and in it she could see a glimpse of his sister, who had been her godmother. A sweetness, combined with courtly wariness. His eyes were bracketed with deep lines, as if he had spent much time outdoors of late, and she wondered where he had been since leaving Queen Catherine's employ. "I like my quiet life, Kate, but I have missed the company certainly. There is a certain satisfaction to knowing one is part of something so important, is there not? I am sure you have found it so. I did during our days with Queen Catherine. She was a great lady indeed, and commanded the loyalty of even the lowliest of her servants. There was a nursemaid who insisted on staying with her since her days as Lady Latimer, I remember. I am sure the new queen commands just such loyalty."

Kate nodded warily. "I enjoy serving the queen. She is what is important here."

"Of course," Gerald said with another smile. "She has certainly always thought it thus—even when she was merely the Lady Elizabeth. Things change so quickly at court, do they not?"

"I prefer the country now," Mistress Park said, not entirely convincingly. "A person always knows where they stand there."

"And sometimes they must stand far too long," Matthew said with a low groan. He leaned heavily on his walking stick, and Kate took his arm with a start of guilt.

"Let me show you to your chamber, Father," Kate said. "The queen made sure you have a nice, warm spot with a large fire."

"That was most kind of Her Grace. I well know how space is more precious than gold at court this time of year," Matthew said. He leaned on her arm and let her help him make his way along the corridor. It had grown quieter, as everyone went to change into their finery for supper and dancing. The light from the windows had turned to slate gray, ice creeping to coat the glass. "You are certainly doing well here, my Kate."

Kate laughed. "Thanks to you. The queen enjoys Haywood music."

"Nay, not on my account. You have built a life here for yourself, my dearest. I am so very proud of you, and your mother would be as well. You have come to resemble her so much."

Kate swallowed hard at the sudden press of tears in her throat. She was glad that they had reached the chamber Elizabeth said she was setting aside for Matthew, glad of the distraction of settling him in, as a page led the Parks and Master Finsley to their lodgings nearby. Thoughts of her mother, especially at Christmas, made her feel too wistful. She pulled a cushioned cross-backed chair close to the fireplace, and made sure her father's lute case and the boxes of his music were away from the chilly windows. "Would she truly?"

"Of course." Matthew sighed as she stretched his swollen legs to the fire. "You do have so much of Eleanor in you. She was of such a sweet nature, willing to do anything for those she loved. But there was a core of steel in her, as well."

Kate thought of the things her friend the elderly Lady Gertrude Howard had told her, finally the truth about her Boleyn heritage. She'd spoken of Eleanor's musical talents, her beautiful dark eyes and lustrous dark hair—Boleyn hair. But of the Boleyn temper, Eleanor had none. Kate feared sometimes she had more of her aunt Anne Boleyn's vinegar in her than her own mother's sweetness.

She sat down on the stool next to her father's chair. "Do you think of her very much, Father?"

"All the time. Especially at this time of year. How she loved Christmas! The dancing, the laughter. Long evenings singing and telling stories by the fire. This season has me thinking much of days past."

"And seeing your old friends again?"

"Aye. 'Tis good to see Gerald and the Parks again, and talk of life in Queen Catherine's household. Those were heady days indeed."

"The queen has been speaking much of Queen Catherine lately, as well."

"Has she?"

"Indeed. She says Queen Catherine also loved Christmas, that it was the first time she could recall being part of a true family."

"It is truly the season for families—of all sorts." Matthew frowned into the fire. "I do sometimes regret I did not marry again and give you siblings. Mistress Park used to try to play matchmaker for me with her lady friends at court, and for Gerald. I think she might want to try it again, even now that we are old and gray and set in our lonely ways."

"Father, no!" Kate cried. He had never said such a thing to her, of wanting more children. "I could never have been happier than I have with our little family—unless we still had my mother, of course. But if *you* have been lonely . . ."

"Never! You made me so happy, and I've had my music, and memories of Eleanor. But I have been alone for a long while, my dearest, and seen much. That doesn't come entirely without regret."

Kate thought of their life, of moving from palace to palace, years of sparkle and royal palaces, but also years of uncertainty and danger. "What are your regrets, Father?"

Matthew gave her a small smile and patted her hand. "Would you hand me that small box there, Kate?"

She hurried to fetch the small chest that sat with her father's trunk and lute case. It was surprisingly light, but inlaid with fine mother-of-pearl work and set with a lock.

"I have long wanted to show this to you," he said as he unlocked it. It was filled with papers, and as he sorted through them, Kate saw that most of them were musical notes. "And now that

I am growing older, I know I must do it now."

"What is it, Father?" Kate said, curious. "A secret?"

"Aye, it seems so. But not mine."

Kate was most puzzled. Aside from the truth of her mother's parentage, she thought her father had never kept anything from her. "I do not understand."

Matthew took out a scroll in leather wrappings, much like the one Gerald Finsley had carried from the barge, and unfurled it to hand it to Kate. It was also a musical score, the ink faded and the parchment slightly yellowed, and as she glanced over it she saw the lyrics were from one of Queen Catherine Parr's own published writings, *The Lamentation of a Sinner*. The music seemed to be slow and stately, as such solemn and contemplative words deserved.

"Did you write this, Father?" Kate asked, but she could see it was not his handwriting.

"I did not. Queen Catherine gave it into my safekeeping on a terrible night, long ago when you were just a child, and she never took it back. I have kept it safe since then, as she asked me to." He quickly told her a strange, nightmarish tale, of a queen in danger of her life from her own husband, of powerful men arrayed against her, and only her wits to defend her. Of a piece of music pressed into Matthew's hands, on a long, dark night, that only slowly faded into day.

"Oh, my Kate," Matthew said wearily, rubbing his hand over his bearded jaw as he stared into the fire. "I am glad those days are over. Queen Catherine was a grand lady, and I am proud to have served her. But I do grow tired now. I am relieved to give this into your hands. Look at it, see what you think."

But what did it *mean?* Kate studied the music closer, but she could decipher nothing in those faded notes. She could almost fancy she smelled a whiff of Queen Catherine's rosewater perfume on the paper, but surely that could not be, it was so old. But in the curls and lines of the music she fancied she could see the mark of the late queen and see the lady sitting up into the deepest night, scribbling her song in haste by candlelight as she tried to save her life and those of her family and allies. Kate thought of her studies of Plato's musical codes, and longed to compare the ideas to this newer piece of work.

She glanced up and saw that her father had dozed off by his fire. She quickly tucked the music back into its hiding place, and wrapped a blanket over his legs. There would be time for more questions, more remembrances of the past, later. The queen had bade them to supper.

The small room just beyond the queen's bed-chamber, where Elizabeth took many of her meals in private when there was no grand banquet to attend, was laid out with platters of venison and sliced beef complemented by honeyed vegetables and dressed salads, steaming at the far end of the table along with pitchers of spiced wine. To Kate's surprise, that was where she was led by Mistress Ashley when the queen summoned her for supper before the night's revelry began. The table, covered with a fine white damask cloth embroidered with Tudor roses and six places, was yet empty.

"Are you quite sure this is where Her Grace wants me, Mistress Ashley?" she asked.

Mistress Ashley gave a puzzled frown, as if she actually wasn't quite sure, but she nodded. "The queen asked if you would have a small meal with her before playing for the dancing. Your father and his friends have been summoned as well."

Kate nodded, stunned by this show of favor.

"Well, I have much work to do, and have not the time to be standing around here," Mistress Ashley said briskly.

"I will wait for the queen, then. Thank you, Mistress Ashley," Kate answered with a little curtsy.

As the Mistress of the Robes hurried away, Kate suddenly found herself somewhere she had seldom been before—alone in one of the queen's private chambers. She scarcely knew what to do.

She turned in a slow circle, taking in the small space. It was shaped in an octagon, with one window along one of the sides, intimate but lavish in its appointments, as all the queen's rooms were. Instead of rushes, a carpet lay over the floor; silver oil holders in the corner scented the air with lavender; and portraits of the queen's parents and Queen Catherine Parr watched from the shadowed walls.

Kate had been in there before, of course—the queen liked music even when she dined alone. But now the perfect silence was striking. Royal palaces were always anything *but* silent. There were always people crowded around, gossiping, laughing, whispering, always dogs barking, servants hurrying past on errands. It was often only very late at night, alone in her own small chamber, that Kate could quiet her mind enough to work on her own music.

The quiet in the queen's private dining chamber, when no one else was there to rattle the serving platters and wine goblets, to whisper with the queen, was astonishing. Sound seemed swallowed up by the rich green velvet hangings and the carved paneling.

Or perhaps not *entirely* swallowed up. As Kate contemplated filching one tiny candied grape from a platter on the table, she heard a sudden flurry of murmurs, indistinct voices that seemed to come from the very air itself.

Startled, she jumped back from the table, clasping her hands behind her back. She quickly realized that it was *not* one of Whitehall's many ghosts warning her from stealing the grape, but real voices.

She peered out the window, yet in the dying daylight she could see no one in the frozen garden below. The sound seemed to be coming from the other side of one of the walls. But which one?

Curious, Kate made her way slowly around the chamber, studying the panels of the octagonal walls. At last she found one that seemed to stand out a fraction of an inch, and she slid her fingers through the tiny crack to pry it open. Beyond the open space was a winding, narrow staircase, one she realized must lead down to the kitchens. A quick, hidden way for meals to be delivered to the queen. There was even a white-draped table on the landing where the queen's ladies could fetch the platters that the kitchen servants left there, so they could properly serve her.

Yet it did not seem to be scullery maids and cooks who were whispering somewhere down there in the stair's hidden coils. The men's voices were deep and rich, distinctly aristocratic. She couldn't hear all their words, but some were echoed by the whitewashed twists in the staircase walls.

". . . are caught?" one man hissed.

"We will not be," the other man said contemptuously. His voice sounded familiar, though not the sneer in it. "Meg and her friend are most—

accommodating, once their work is done. We will not be even an instant late for the queen's dancing later."

Kate listened closely, trying to remember where she had heard him before. She was startled to realize it was Lord Hertford, his voice shorn of the sweetness and laughter he used to address Lady Catherine Grey.

"And if the beauteous Lady Catherine finds out?" his friend said.

"She would not care a whit," Lord Hertford said with a laugh. "Cat knows very well how the world works. Male needs have naught to do with—shall we say—higher considerations."

Kate had the distinct feeling that if Lady Catherine knew her "Ned" was off in tawdry pursuit of kitchen maids, she certainly *would* care. Her Tudor temper would surely fly then, if her romantic, poetical thoughts were tarnished. It made Kate rather glad she herself would remain in a single state, as she served the queen.

"Besides, I do tire of this endless waiting," Lord Hertford said. "Come, we must finish our business here and be gone."

Kate slid the panel shut and went back to the window. She could see now why the queen liked to take her meals in this little room. Perhaps there were even more hidden doors scattered around, where unwary words could be overheard? But Kate found that she didn't always want to know such sordid truths that lurked behind bejeweled smiles. It made it difficult sometimes to sing romantic madrigals with much conviction.

The wry thought of songs reminded her of Queen Catherine's music, which her father had shown her after keeping it in such secrecy for years. It seemed far from romantic, of course, being a prayer and statement of the queen's strong conviction in the new faith, but surely it had to conceal something?

Kate frowned as she thought about the secrets of courtly life, layers and layers of them, folded back and tucked in on themselves. Everyone who clustered around the queen had them; some had held on to them for years. Nothing was ever as buried as people would like to think.

Who would know what was concealed in the queen's song? Who would want decades-old secrets to stay hidden?

The chamber door opened, and Queen Elizabeth appeared, a flash of bright green satin springtime against the dark walls, topaz ropes threaded through her red-gold hair. Kate's father was on her arm. She matched her always quick steps to Matthew's slower pace, and Master Finsley and the Parks trailed behind them.

"Ah, Kate, good—you are here already," Elizabeth said. "I have left orders we will serve ourselves, so we can get lost in memories of the old days. Matthew, shall I pour you some wine? It is a very fine sort from Burgundy. Queen Mary sent it herself through her ambassador. Monsieur de Castelnau, though wretchedly closemouthed about so many things, does know a good wine."

"Your Grace, you must not serve us yourself!" Matthew protested.

"Of course I shall," Elizabeth merrily. She was obviously in one of her happier moods. "Now, Mistress Park, tell me what you and your husband do now! I remember your lovely voice from when I was a child. I do hope you have all brought new music to perform for us at our Christmas revels."

Kate helped her father find a footstool for his leg, and passed around a plate of the queen's favorite candied fruit suckets as Elizabeth herself poured out goblets of wine. She laughed as Mistress Park told tales of Christmases when Elizabeth was young, and Queen Catherine arranged all the lavish feasts and mummers' plays. Soon they were all laughing at memories of Queen Catherine and King Henry, and the pranks his favorite fool, Will Somers, would always play on holiday merrymakers.

And Kate realized that if anyone would remember Queen Catherine's secrets, especially secrets hidden in music, surely it might be her father and his friends. . . .

CHAPTER SEVEN

"La Virgen a solas piensa qué hará cuando al Rey de luz inmenso parirá . . . ," Senor Gomez sang, his voice low and sweet. He was teaching the ladies some of the Spanish songs of the Yule season as they worked on finishing the queen's masque. The long table in the great gallery was littered with papers and quills, bits of ribbon and tinsel and silk, and ladies hurriedly sewing or writing.

"That is a beautiful song, Senor Gomez," Lady Catherine said with one of her gleaming, silvery laughs. "What is it called?"

" 'No la devemos dormir la noche sancta,' " he answered, smiling at her as most men did with Lady Catherine, as if he could see only her. "Perhaps you could use it for your masquerade? It is a song everyone sings at this time of year where I am from."

"If only ancient goddesses could sing of Christmas," Kate said.

"Can they not? Surely even goddesses, even *English* goddesses, do enjoy the Yule season," Senor Gomez said. "What is your scene about, then? What are you writing?"

Before anyone could answer, the door to their chamber opened and Queen Elizabeth swept inside like a cloud of white-and-silver satin shimmering with pearls. To her right was her constant escort, Robert Dudley, also clad in bright white that set off his dark good looks, and on her left . . .

On her left was Rob Cartman.

For an instant, Kate thought she was imagining him. It had been so long since she had seen him, months since the summer warmth of Nonsuch Palace, and yet he looked just the same. Possibly even more handsome, with a new beard the same sunny gold as his hair, tall and lean, his smile glinting like that lost sun. He was fashionably dressed, as befitted the leader of Lord Hunsdon's Men, in gray and black silk, with a white cloak embroidered with exotic birds and fanciful trees.

His attention fell on Kate, and he gave her a dazzling smile.

Everyone jumped up from the work-table to bow and curtsy. Elizabeth nodded graciously, but she frowned a bit as his gaze swept over Lady Catherine.

"Everyone is hard at work, I see," Elizabeth said.

"The masque should be completed in plenty of time, Your Grace," Kate said, gesturing to the papers scattered over the table.

"I am glad to hear it. But perhaps now it can be finished even faster, Kate, for Master Cartman has come to assist you," Elizabeth said. She laid her hand lightly on Rob's silk sleeve and smiled up at him, making Robert Dudley scowl. "I hereby declare Master Cartman shall be our Lord of Misrule for this royal holiday!"

Rob laughed, his golden beauty dazzling. Even the queen had to smile back, flirtatiously tapping his arm with her fan. "Lord of Misrule, Your Grace?"

"Aye, 'tis an old role, one I remember from Christmases when I was a girl," Elizabeth said. "My father's favorite fool, Will Somers, took it on at the Christmas season, directing the revels. The custom fell out of favor at my brother's court, he was so austere in his celebrations. But I do like the idea of it. Someone must lead us in our merriment."

"I should be most honored indeed to be your Lord of Misrule, Your Grace," Rob said with an elegant bow.

"If Your Grace wishes to revive such a custom," Robert Dudley said, his tone underlaid with strain through his smile, "should it not be taken on by your Master of the Revels?"

"Or mayhap by my Master of the Horse?" Elizabeth said teasingly. She tapped Sir Robert's hand with her fan, and laughed when he scowled. "Nay, I have seen Master Cartman's antics onstage many times. He is most capable of such a task. And since my cousin Lord Hunsdon was kind enough to lend us Master Cartman's services for Christmas, we must make the most of them."

"When should I begin my duties, Your Grace?" Rob asked.

"When we bring in the Yule log tonight," the queen said. "But for now you must help Mistress Haywood with her music. I'm sure that is one duty you will not mind at all."

Kate felt her cheeks turn warm, despite the distance from the fireplace, and she ducked her head as Rob bowed again.

"Show me what you have done so far, Kate," Elizabeth said, sweeping toward the table that was scattered with papers, ink pots, and quills. Violet, Lady Jane Seymour, and Lady Catherine stepped back with curtsies, watching with wide eyes as the queen studied their notes.

Kate glimpsed Lady Catherine's glance back at Senor Gomez, who gave her a strained smile.

"What is the subject of the masque?" Elizabeth asked.

"'Tis the tale of Diana the huntress goddess and Niobe," Kate said.

Elizabeth's smile turned catlike, her dark eyes shining. "Very good. One goddess teaches another her true place in the hierarchy of the gods."

Kate felt a tiny touch of cold disquiet in her stomach. "The theme is meant to be of two goddesses living in amity in their two kingdoms, Your Grace."

Elizabeth looked startled to be contradicted, even mildly so. Kate quickly curtsied.

"If one ruler is in the wrong, as Niobe is, is it not the duty of the wiser goddess to counsel her to correct her course?" Elizabeth said. "I am quite sure our Scots visitors would find such a theme most edifying. As would their queen and her French mother."

The queen reached for a quill and ink pot and quickly marked out a few of the notes Lady Catherine had written, scribbling over them with new ones. "Aye," she whispered as she worked. "Even goddesses must learn well not to o'erstep their own borders."

The queen wrote a few more lines, then stepped back from the table with a satisfied smile. Not even the tiniest splotch of ink marred her pale gown. "Now I must go. I leave you all to your work. It shall be a fine masque, Kate, and everyone will exclaim over the great talent I harbor at my court."

Elizabeth took Robert Dudley's arm and sailed out of the room, the courtiers who had been waiting outside the door falling into a long, sparkling line behind her.

Kate stared down at the altered pages. Elizabeth was surely right; even Mary, Queen of Scots, safe in her luxurious French nest, could not mistake the English queen's meaning. But everyone would think Kate had written the words making one queen dominant over the other—Elizabeth clearly the superior goddess in all eyes.

"The joys of patronage, eh, Kate?" Rob murmured in her ear.

She had to laugh, even as she worried. If the Scots and the French thought *she* was the one who interpreted the masque thus, as a rebuke to France and Scotland, and if Elizabeth denied the message in one of her labyrinthine conversations . . .

She shivered.

" 'Tis not so very bad," Rob said. "We can fix it so the royal message is more—subtle."

"Oh, Rob," Kate said with another choked laugh. "When were you ever subtle?"

He pressed his hand over his heart. "Ah, Kate, you do wound me. I thought you had a higher opinion of my acting skills."

Kate gave in to her laughter. "I am very glad to see you again, truly. Shall we walk outside for a little while? There is so much we need to talk about. . . ."

Snow was drifting in small, fine white strands as Kate met Rob by the garden door, but it didn't seem to deter them or the queen's other courtiers from making their escapes from the stuffy corridors of the palace into the cold, clear air. She glimpsed Lord Hertford and his sister, Lady Catherine's best friend, Lady Jane, playing at a game of quoits with their friends in the snow, and the Spanish ambassador de Quadra went on his stately evening progress with his servants.

Kate drew the hood of her cloak closer around her cheeks, and smiled as she took in a deep breath. She had much work to do, many Christmas festivities to prepare for, but she had to admit that she, like the noisy quoits players, was glad to be outside for a time.

She glimpsed Rob hurrying toward her down one of the graveled pathways, his violet velvet doublet and emerald green short cloak vivid against the evening grays and browns of the winter garden. He held his plumed cap in one hand, and his golden hair gleamed like a new guinea. Someone called out a joke to him, and he burst out laughing.

Kate touched the tiny lute pendant that was concealed beneath her blue wool bodice. She had always known Rob was handsome, of course; they had flirted and laughed many times, and he had helped her out of many puzzles. But now she was struck by the warmth he seemed to trail behind him, spreading its golden glow to everyone in his path.

Could he help her charm some answers out of people now?

"Kate, lovely one," he cried merrily as he saw her standing there. "I'm so happy you could walk with me this evening."

Kate laughed. "I am glad of a moment's respite.

The queen does keep a most merry Christmas."

"As does Lord Hunsdon. There have been new plays at Eastwick every week since November. He also insists on new music for when he comes to court next week."

Kate took Rob's proffered arm and they walked together deeper into the garden. He led her not toward the quoits players and their applauding audience, but into a quieter herbal maze, where the laughter was just a distant murmur. "How is your work with Lord Hunsdon, really?"

"I am most grateful to his lordship for giving us employment," Rob answered carefully. After his uncle, the former leader of the acting troupe, had been killed at Hatfield, Rob had become responsible for them, and without a patron they could have been arrested as vagabonds. Lord Hunsdon, the queen's cousin, was one of the greatest patrons of all. "He knows much about the theater, and is an appreciative audience. He also wants to help the queen in any way he can. I like to be a part of that, as you know."

Kate nodded. "I do know, and you have come far in your work. I wish you only the finest things in life, Rob. Tell me—what sort of plays does Lord Hunsdon enjoy the most? Which of your roles is his favorite?"

"I had thought at first it would be plays about great heroics in battle, but it turns out he likes a pastoral romance with plenty of songs the best,"

Rob said with a laugh. "You could help me with that, for I do the battle scenes better. But remember our play of shepherds and shepherdesses at Hatfield?"

"I do indeed. We worked well together then, I think." She glanced over her shoulder to make sure no one could hear their conversation. They were almost alone, the wind being too sharp for most of the courtiers. "You say you would like to serve the queen however you can?"

Rob gave her a sharp glance. "Indeed I would."

"Then perhaps you would help me with something? The queen has asked me to help her watch Lady Catherine Grey," she whispered.

Rob burst out with a surprised laugh. "Lady Catherine!"

Kate nodded wryly. "She is not always easy to find, you know. There are so many people who bear closer watch at court right now. But the queen fears that Lady Catherine, as a possible heir to the throne, might be thinking of contracting a romantic attachment without permission of the council. You know that a party from Scotland is expected any day now?"

He nodded, his laughter fading. "I have heard they come to seek a Protestant queen's assistance to overthrow their Catholic queen regent. Is it known how long they will stay to guarantee their success?"

"I do not know yet. The queen often keeps her

own counsel on such matters, even from ministers like Cecil, much to his chagrin. She won't reveal her plans in the midst of her Christmas revels, at least."

"Lord Hunsdon takes much interest in the work of everyone around him," Rob said, leading her onto the pathway of another twist of herbal shrubs. "He has asked if I would write a tableau of the ancient Scottish kings to perform before the queen when he comes to court. Surely there is a good reason for that."

"Does he wish to influence the queen toward interfering in Scotland, then?" Kate said, her thoughts whirling.

Rob shrugged. "Lord Hunsdon, too, keeps his own counsel. He claims he wants only to entertain his cousin, and my task is to help him with that."

"As mine is to entertain the queen," Kate answered.

Rob stopped walking, and drew her to a halt with him. Kate glanced up at him in the fading light, and saw that he suddenly looked rather older, his merry face turned solemn. "But we both know that is not all there is to our life's work," he said quietly.

Kate bit her lip. "Nay."

"And we wouldn't really have it any other way, would we, my bonny Kate?" He smiled again, the quick glimpse of the shadow-Rob gone.

She shook her head ruefully. "I suppose I would not, not now."

"I am the same. So tell me—how can I help you in your task now?"

"I do not think you should seduce Lady Catherine to find out her secrets," Kate teased him.

"Nay? Ah, Kate, you do wound me again! Flirting with fair maidens is not my only skill, you know."

Kate *did* know that, only too well. "I doubt Lady Catherine would flirt with you in return, anyway. She does seem most intent on Lord Hertford." No matter how unworthy of such devotion the young lord seemed to be.

"It would not be worth the danger. Unless you think she might conspire with some of the queen's enemies to achieve her aims?"

Kate thought of the way Lady Catherine had been seen in conversation with the Spanish—and of the lady's tearstained face when she declared that all she wanted was her love. "I do not think that is her aim, though certainly I have been wrong before. She seems to have far simpler goals now than advancement at court." She caught a glimpse of Lord Hertford in the distance, taking a breath after his game. He talked with Senor Gomez of the Spanish ambassador's party, the two men laughing together over some joke. "But I know there is one place you can go where I cannot."

118

"And where is that?"

"Wherever men go for their pleasures, of course. Men like Senor Gomez and his dour cousin, or even the Scots, who they say relish earthly pleasures despite their Protestant ways. Perhaps you could join them in a card game, invite them to some revel?"

Rob burst into surprised laughter. "Take them to the Cardinal's Hat and ply them with some of Celine's strong wine and painted girls?"

"Perhaps not, though I think Celine would welcome you! Perhaps just a game of cards and some good English rum for the holidays?"

Rob's astonishment faded into an admiring smile. He took her hand and raised it to his lips for a courtly kiss as she laughed.

"My fair Kate," he said, "I would happily do your bidding in everything. But this is one errand I can undertake with particular enthusiasm."

Kate took his arm again as they continued their walk back toward the palace. Night was coming on quickly now. "I thought you might say that. . . ."

Rob watched the upper windows of the long wing of the palace after Kate left him. Sometimes a face would appear behind the small panes of glass, wavy and pale, as indistinct as a ghost. None of them was the face he waited for—none was Kate. Yet still he watched, the icy wind whipping around him, catching at his cloak. He felt very alone, yet also as if he could soar up beyond the spires of the city.

He had almost hoped the months away from Kate, months when he worked for Lord Hunsdon writing plays and performing music, trying to build a new career in the world, would blunt the edges of his feelings for her. He knew he was not as good as she deserved; his life had been too mottled for that, his past always too ready to catch up with him. She deserved security, a calm place in the world. He knew that if he was a truly noble person, the kind of person that he portrayed in plays, he would not write to her any longer. Wouldn't seek her out.

Yet even as he knew that, some force drove him to write those letters to her, to think of her as he worked into the night writing scenes. She inspired those writings, with her shining green eyes, her ready smile. Her kind heart, and fierce loyalty. Kate was all the things that seemed good in the world, things he had seldom seen before, and selfishly he wanted more of them in his life. Wanted to be worthy of her.

In their time apart, he had come to half fear that giving her the lute pendant had been a step too far in her mind. Did she wear it? Did she think of him when it caught the light, and if so did she think well of him or only remember his faults? That she had asked him for his help now made him dare to hope. She worked for the queen herself, and would surely not trust him with something of such importance if she did not think him worthy?

Rob turned away from the bright windows of the palace and made his way across the darkened, snow-dusted garden. He now had a chance to show Kate that he had changed. He could not disappoint her—or himself.

CHAPTER EIGHT

"What then doth make the element so bright? The heavens are come down upon earth to live!"

A dozen of the queen's strongest men carried the Yule log into the great hall. They had indeed found a great one, as long and thick as one of the gilded ceiling beams, Kate thought as she led some of the ladies in the song. Greenery and garlands tied up with red ribbons adorned the great oak log, which would be lowered into the largest of the stone fireplaces, where it would burn until Twelfth Night.

Kate laughed as she watched the log paraded around the hall, its bright streamers waving merrily. Across the room, she glimpsed her father with Master Finsley and the Parks, and her heart warmed to see his laughter.

It had been a most nostalgic Christmas thus far, with her father nearby and memories of the old queen brought forward, both good and bad. It made her remember more of the holiday when *she* was a child, the music, the sweetmeats she had filched from the grown-ups' tables, the rustle of fine silks, and the smell of greenery.

"Who has the embers from last year to set the light?" Rob called out. As one of the queen's pages stepped forward with a torch to set the log alight, another servant handed Rob his staff of bells for his new office. As everyone laughed, he paraded around the hall, shaking them in a merry tune. "As the queen has made me her Lord of Misrule for the night, I command those of you whom the queen calls on to tell your favorite Christmas memory."

Queen Elizabeth settled herself on her cushioned chair by the blazing fire. The spangles embroidered on her gold brocade gown sparkled, and her ladies in their white and silver spread around her like flowers. Mistress Ashley tucked one more pillow behind the royal back before taking her own seat. "And who shall go first, O high Lord of Misrule?"

"Why, Your Grace herself, of course," Rob said with an elaborate bow.

"Oh, aye, lovey," Mistress Ashley urged. "Tell us of your favorite Yule."

Elizabeth stared at the Yule log for a long moment, its flames reflected in her dark eyes. She seemed very far away. "I remember the year I was summoned to court, at Hampton Court, by my father, King Henry, and his new queen Catherine Parr. I had met the queen at their wedding the summer before, and she was most beautiful and kind, but her splendor at Christmas was astounding to me, as I had lived so quietly in the country during my childhood. She wore a gown of white, trimmed with sable and red ribbons, and rubies in her lovely auburn hair. She kissed me most graciously, and danced with me that night. I sat with her in the queen's gallery at church as well, and she taught me to learn from the Scriptures for myself. I did learn much from her that Christmas, and in all the Christmases after." The queen blinked, as if she were dragging herself back from those years past with her step-mother, and she laughed.

"What of you, Robin?" she called to Robert Dudley. She waved at him where he stood by the fire, as sparkling as she was in a doublet of gold and green. "What is your Yule memory, pray tell us?"

Dudley came to kneel by the queen's chair, his hand over his heart in elaborate obeisance. Kate noticed Cecil and Bishop de Quadra exchange rolled eyes. Robert Dudley told an amusing story of a boyhood snowball fight with his many brothers that soon went awry, and had everyone laughing.

Next, the queen called on Kat Ashley, who told of days when the queen was a toddling child and would try to sing the old Yule songs even though she mistook some of the words, and thus made her kingly father roar with laughter. Bishop de Quadra related a Spanish custom of "El Tio," a hollowed-out log filled with sweets that the children would knock about until it broke and spilled out its treasures.

"Fetch a log immediately!" the queen called. "Anything that involves sweetmeats would be most happily included in my own celebrations. And what of you, Monsieur de Castelnau? What are Christmases like in France?"

Monsieur de Castelnau, elegant and smiling as always in his black and red satins, stepped forward with a bow. "We enjoy a traditional spiced claret punch where I grew up, Your Grace, to the north of Paris. And there are many merry songs, and dancing. When your cousin, our Queen Marie, first came to the French court when she was a child, she declared that there was a tradition in *her* homeland where she must make one of her ladies-in-waiting queen for the day. She declared Mademoiselle Beaton would be queen, and dressed her up in her own royal gown, and served her with her own tiny hand. She quite won the hearts of all the French court that day."

"Of course she did," Elizabeth muttered. "Thank you, monsieur, for such a glimpse of our most gracious cousin—and for this glimpse of the Yule customs of other lands. But what of you, cousin Catherine? Perhaps you would care to share a memory."

Lady Catherine Grey, who sat on the other side of the room with Lady Jane and a pack of their ever-present lapdogs, looked startled to be so called upon. "I—my childhood Christmases were most ordinary. My parents enjoyed the hunt during the day, and at night we would dine on their prizes, and play games. I have always enjoyed the dancing. . . ."

"I would wager your sister did not like that part of the holiday so very much," Elizabeth said sharply.

Lady Catherine's eyes widened, and the room turned hushed. "N-nay," Lady Catherine stammered. "Jane did like to read to us from the Scriptures, though, and talked much of the birth of Our Lord. She was greatly learned. But she would sing, too."

"Hmm," the queen murmured. "Well, I do like a Yule dance. Shall we have a candle branle, everyone? My Lord of Misrule, will you lead us?"

It was quite late when Queen Elizabeth called her ladies around her to help her retire. The sky outside was the deepest, most impenetrable shade of purple, almost black, and flickering bonfires dotted the icy river's banks. The queen laughed as she swept along the halls, making everyone else laugh, too, her merriment infectious.

"We should have more dancing before we sleep!" Elizabeth cried as she twirled through her privy chamber. She spun around in a circle, her golden brocade skirts as vivid and alive as those distant fires. "Kate, where is your lute?"

"It is in your bedchamber, Your Grace, where I left it earlier," Kate answered.

"We must have music, and more light, and . . ." Elizabeth pushed open her chamber door, and suddenly froze. Her ladies stumbled around her, their laughter fading into confused murmurs. Kate tried to peer past them, but couldn't see beyond the doorway. The queen was changeable of mood, of course, but not usually quite so quickly. Kate was sure something was very amiss.

"Leave me now," Elizabeth snapped. "I would retire in peace, with only a quiet song to soothe me."

"Lovey, what is wrong?" Mistress Ashley cried in bewilderment. Elizabeth caught her Mistress of the Robe's arm and pulled her into the chamber behind her.

Kate just had an instant to slip inside, acting on instinct, before the door slammed shut. From the room behind her, she could hear the rustle of skirts and whispers from the confused ladies, but the sounds quickly grew fainter, as they melted away to find their own beds. The queen's ladies were accustomed to such changes in mood.

But Kate knew there was usually a very good reason behind Elizabeth's temper, and her glance quickly scanned the bedchamber. A fire crackled in the fireplace, keeping away the cold that seeped past the window. The ladies' cushions and work-boxes were still scattered about, and Kate's own lute sat in its stand by the queen's desk. The bedcovers were turned down, the sheets glowing white in the shadows. The queen's velvet-and-sable robe waited on a chair, warming near the fire.

Then Kate saw it. A square of parchment pinned to the black and gold bed curtains, a pale splash in the darkness.

With a hoarse cry, the queen snatched it down and threw it across the floor, where it fluttered to rest beside one of the fine carpets. Kate knelt down to study it.

It was a drawing, somewhat crude lines from a charcoal pencil but clear enough to decipher. Against the cross-hatching of a background, a girl stood with her arms raised, a look of excitement and alarm on her pointed-chin face. And alarmed she could well be, for a much larger, bulkier, bearded man dressed in an embroidered doublet was slicing her skirt to ribbons with a dagger.

Nearby lurked another lady, swollen with pregnancy beneath her robe, looking on with an expression of fear and—and was it something like resignation?

Beneath it were a few lines of doggerel: *Old Tom is his Name, A bird of Venus, and a Cock of the Game, Who once being in Love with pretty Lady Beth, Did crack her Nut, and thou mayst pick the Kernel. . . .*

Kate glanced up at the queen, who stood in the middle of the chamber, as still as one of the marble statues in the winter garden below. She had gone perfectly white, except for two feverish patches of red on her cheeks, and her hands were held out like those of the girl in the drawing. Mistress Ashley plucked at the queen's golden sleeve, a look of horror on her lined features.

"What does it mean, Your Grace?" Kate asked quietly.

Elizabeth suddenly swooped down with a cry and snatched up the paper from Kate's hand. "It is naught but a ridiculous event that happened when I was a girl, when I lived at Chelsea with my stepmother, Queen Catherine," Elizabeth said, her voice quiet but so taut it sounded like a bowstring about to snap. "Her husband, Sir Thomas Seymour, was a man who knew not the limits of flirtatious behavior. He often tried to come into my bedchamber before I was dressed, until I learned to rise before the dawn. That day he found me fully dressed in the garden—and cut my gown off me, while my stepmother tried to stop him."

"Lovey . . . ," Mistress Ashley said, her voice wavering.

"You remember—I am quite sure, Kat." Elizabeth spun toward Mistress Ashley, suddenly fierce and furious. Mistress Ashley stumbled back a step. "You were there that day, as I recall. You saw what happened, and did nothing to stop it."

"What could I have done?" Mistress Ashley mumbled, her face gone ashen. "I was a mere servant, he the master of the house, a charming gentleman. The Dowager Queen was there, I thought nothing improper could happen. . . ."

"You *thought*," Elizabeth whispered. Her face was very pale, except for bright red spots of fury in her cheeks. "I was just a girl. If my own mother had been there, she would not have stood it for an instant! If my mother had seen . . ."

The queen's long fingers closed around the paper, crumpling it with a sharp crackle. "But I will not worry about something that happened long ago. The question is—who knows about it now? And how could they have gotten in here, in my very bedchamber, to leave this?"

"The guards were in the privy chamber, and they said nothing about anyone being in here," Kate said, thinking quickly about the different ways into the royal bedchamber. They were not many.

"Surely, lovey, you can't think—" Mistress Ashley cried, only to bite her lip.

"Go, Kat, and fetch Cecil," Elizabeth snapped. "And, Kate, bring me the guards who are meant to listen to this room at all times. I want to know what they saw at every minute tonight."

Mistress Ashley rushed away, and Kate rose to rush on her own errand. But her attention was caught by the window, the only window in the chamber. It stood ajar, only the merest sliver, but enough to let in a whisper of chilly wind off the river.

Kate hurried over to study the iron frame of the

clear, precious panes of glass. There were scratches around the latch, and when she pushed it open to peer outside she saw a patch of dark earth cleared of snow in the garden below.

Perhaps someone adept, and not too large, could climb up from the garden terraces.

Someone like an actor? She thought of Rob, so neatly managing the Christmas Yule log scene tonight, his players twirling around in their acrobatic tricks.

"What do you see, Kate?" Elizabeth came to peer over Kate's shoulder at the night beyond her window. She frowned, but her dark eyes shone with her usual razor-sharp attention, not with the haze of remembered scenes.

"None could come in through the front door," Kate said. She studied the wide ledge just outside the window, which was covered with only the lightest layer of snow, whereas the other windows were covered with small drifts.

Elizabeth swept her fingertips over the powdery drift on the ledge, her eyes very far away. "I shall send some of Cecil's men to examine it."

Kate nodded. She thought of a young girl, cowering behind her bed-curtains, afraid her stepfather would come bursting in at any moment. Catherine Parr and Thomas Seymour were both long gone. "Who would wish to remind you of such a painful thing in the past, Your Grace?"

The queen's mouth hardened into a flat red line.

"Who could know what happened that day? There were rumors then, just as there always have been of me, but who would care now? They are dead. I am the queen." She stared down at the crumpled paper in her hand, but she didn't seem to see it. She was gone again, into the past. The past that was always there, just beyond their fingertips. "I confess the past has haunted me of late, Kate. At night, when I try to sleep, I see people who are long gone now, remember mistakes that I made when I was too young to know how to guard myself. Those mistakes should be dead and buried with them, but they are not. Why is that?"

Kate remembered her father saying much the same thing, that the past had seemed so close to him lately. She thought of Queen Catherine's music in his shaking hand. The pregnant woman looking on with horror in that terrible drawing. "The past is still a part of us, Your Grace. For good or ill, it makes us who we are now. Surely the past has only strengthened you."

The bedchamber door opened, and Cecil appeared, with Mistress Ashley scurrying behind him. He wore his dark brown fur-edged bed robe, his nightcap still on his head, and his eyes were bright with worry.

"Your Grace," he said quickly. "What is this about midnight threats?"

Kate curtsied, and went to question the guards as Elizabeth told her chief secretary what had happened. The guards had seen nothing untoward all evening. Everyone had been in the great hall to see the Yule log brought in. Only a few servants had passed by on their errands, and none had even stopped, let alone tried to get into the royal bedchamber. The guards had heard nothing at all from inside; perhaps they'd heard a dog barking outside.

Kate examined the empty privy chamber and the corridor, and even went outside to the cold garden, but could find nothing else to show her how anyone got inside to leave the drawing. At last, achingly weary, she made her way up the stairs and along the corridors toward her own small room. One of the other doors opened before she could reach its shelter, and Hester Park peeked out.

Her round, rosy face was framed by the frill of her cap, but she frowned. "Is aught amiss, Kate?"

Kate remembered that once Mistress Park, too, had worked at the court of Queen Catherine, and she wondered if the woman remembered the scandal of Tom Seymour. She wondered if she should ask her about it, about her memories of that time, but something held her back. Something vague and insistent, yet hazy, about the past, something that lingered at the back of her mind amid childish memories. "Nothing at all, Mistress Park. The queen sometimes has trouble sleeping and likes a song at night."

Mistress Park nodded. "Aye, I think she was like that even as a girl. The nights can surely be long in winter, even in a palace. Don't you think so, my dear?"

"Aye," Kate said softly. "I do think so indeed."

CHAPTER NINE

A cold wind swept around the royal party as they emerged from the palace gate and arrayed themselves around the water steps along the Thames, waiting for the Scots' barge to appear. Despite the cold day and the heavy, leaden skies that threatened more snow, crowds waited to cheer their queen along the riverbanks and walkways.

Elizabeth waved at them, smiling, the dark circles under her eyes from the sleepless night covered in powder, concealed by her sparkling gown. Everyone else around her, including Cecil and Dudley, who studied each other warily, seemed to want only to get inside away from the cold.

Or away from the complications that the Protestant Scots lords brought with them.

Kate stood near the back of the company, behind the queen's attending ladies, to keep an eye on the proceedings. She watched as at last the barge surged into view along the frost-choked river, docking at the queen's steps.

A clutch of men clambered onto land, their plain dark cloaks solemn next to the bright silks of the English courtiers, and of the queen herself, who stepped forward to greet them with an outstretched hand. "Welcome to our court!"

The man at their head, an older, portly gentleman with gray liberally streaking his pale red beard, swept into a bow. "Your Grace does us much honor in receiving us. I am Lord Halton, and these are my secretaries, Reverend Donnelton and Lord Macintosh."

"Secretaries, aye? This court does seem rich in them these days," Elizabeth said, but she received the men graciously with offers of her hand and smiles. The reverend had a dour, pinched, lemon-like face, but Lord Macintosh was handsome and young, with dark hair and an elaborately curling beard, bright yellow feathers in his fashionable hat. Elizabeth smiled at him a bit longer than the others. "You are all most welcome. You have come at a very merry time for my court, as we celebrate the Christmas season. I hope you shall all dance with us."

"I fear my dancing days are quite behind me, Your Grace," Lord Halton said. "But we are happy to be here. Shall we have a meeting with your privy council soon?"

"*I* do care for dancing, Your Grace," Lord Macintosh interjected quickly.

Elizabeth took them all in with a sweeping glance and a gesture of her peacock feather fan, as if she waved Lord Halton's serious and pressing question aside. The emeralds set in the ivory handle sparkled, as bright and vivid as her blue-and-silver-satin gown, her stiffened ruff of

136

silver lace, and the strands of sapphires and pearls threaded through the elaborate braids of her bright hair. She looked like a peacock herself, all bright plumage and sparkling smiles, not at all like the frightened, furious woman who had crumpled the threatening drawing in her hand only the night before.

The queen was surely a greater actor than any that Rob Cartman employed in his troupe.

"How very kind you are, Lord Halton, and you, Lord Macintosh, to leave your home and travel so far to relieve our gray winter with your company!" Elizabeth said merrily, as if the Scots' visit was only to dance at parties, and not a petition to help fund their Protestant rebellion against the government of Mary, Queen of Scots.

She held out her hand, sparkling with more sapphires and emeralds, for the handsome Lord Macintosh to kiss, then laced her fingers around his arm. Macintosh looked dazzled, as everyone did when they first met the queen; Robert Dudley scowled darkly. "We do have a great many Yuletide festivities planned for your visit."

"We do thank Your Grace most heartily for your welcome," Lord Macintosh answered, his Scots burr as hearty and bracing as a sharp green whiff of thistle on a cold breeze. Several of the queen's ladies were already smiling at him from behind their own feathered fans. "Our two nations on one island are surely united, as ever, in the warmest bonds of friendship."

Kate thought Marie of Guise might not think so, especially after word of their masque traveled back to Edinburgh. And she was sure that Monsieur de Castelnau, who watched the scene from the back of the crowd with a small smile on his face, would have a messenger galloping to Paris within the hour.

After a few more pleasantries as the cold river wind swept around them, catching at the visitors' plaid cloaks, Elizabeth tightened her clasp on Macintosh's arm and led them all back into the palace. "There will be a feast tonight, Lord Macintosh, with all our English Yuletide favorites, followed by a masque that my own musicians have composed, just for you and your party. I hope you will enjoy it. . . ."

Kate looked around for Rob, reminded that they still had work to do in putting the finishing touches on the stage. She didn't see him anywhere, and hoped he was not off flirting with one of the ladies.

For the sake of finishing their work, of course.

"May I escort you, Senorita Haywood?" a quiet voice asked at her shoulder, startling her from her search. She spun around to find Senor Vasquez, his arm in a dark blue velvet sleeve held out to her. He looked reluctant, solemn, and Kate was surprised. He didn't seem to enjoy being around people as his friend Senor Gomez did. Yet still he offered his arm to her, frowning as she just looked at him.

"Thank you, Senor Vasquez," she said, and placed her hand lightly on his midnight blue sleeve. Under her touch, his arm was more solidly muscled than she would have expected from a secretary, and it twitched as if he wasn't sure how to stay still for the courtly contact. She wondered why he had asked her to walk with him, then. Perhaps because no one else was nearby? His left hand opened and closed, and she noticed it seemed stronger than his right, larger, as if he was used to using his left hand more in exercise. He glanced around nervously at everyone they passed, and gave a visible start at the sound of the Scottish accents.

But she had little time to ponder the oddities of the Spaniard. The narrow corridor opened to the chamber set up for the queen's Scottish feast. Kate hadn't seen it before it was decorated, as she had been leading the masque rehearsal in an adjoining room, and it was dazzling how much had been achieved by the queen's efficient servants in a short time. It seemed the queen was indeed intent on impressing—but was it for Lord Macintosh and his Scots, or for someone else? A secret message?

The dark-paneled walls were covered with dark blue cloths woven with English roses and

Scottish thistles, all red and purple and green, shimmering with silver thread, while the floors were covered with priceless rugs over the lavender rushes. Tiered buffets displayed a vast amount of gold plate and silver salt cellars, as if every sparkling serving piece had been polished up to add to the richness.

The queen's courtiers also contributed to the bright dazzlement. Bishop de Quadra and his Spaniards were somber, as usual, all black and deep green, especially against the shimmering white and gold of the Swedes. Monsieur Castelnau and the French had vanished. Elizabeth's ladies were like a bouquet of purple and gold and pale green. The whole scene was like a shifting scene of stained glass.

At the end of the room rose an arch painted with a hunting scene, horses and their riders arrayed in vividly depicted velvets and feathers, hawks swirling overhead and a pack of hands running ahead. The queen was at their head, her painted red hair even brighter than in real life. Yet in the sky above the riders rose a plume of smoke, as if there was a battle in the distance, a reminder of all that was at stake in these meetings.

The courtly richness was also very much on display at the long tables that ran along either side of the room, spread with snowy-white damask cloths, and gold velvet cushions on the benches, even at the lower end of the room where Kate sat.

The dais where the queen sat with the Scots leaders was draped with gold satin, the table covered in violet figured silk.

"Shall you sit here, Senorita Haywood?" Senor Vasquez asked, stopping next to a table near the center of the room, Kate's accustomed place when she ate with the court. She wondered how he knew that.

"Thank you," she said, sliding onto the bench. The chamber was filling up now with the courtiers, and she had no time to ask him all she wanted to know. Instead, she studied the table before her. Each place was set with its own small loaf of fine white manchet bread wrapped in a cloth embroidered with an *E* surrounded with roses, along with a silver goblet filled with rich red wine. Servants appeared bearing gold platters of venison, capons, partridges stuffed with spices, eels in lemons, and game pie with fragrant, rare Spanish oranges. Bowls of herb salads dressed in wine and ginger-pickled vegetables followed.

Violet sat down next to Kate, moving carefully with her swollen belly under her loose velvet gown, and to Kate's surprise Senor Vasquez stayed with them, sitting at Kate's other side. His kinsman Senor Gomez joined them as well, his light chatter about the banquet arrangements and the fashions around them covering Senor Vasquez's silence. There was music from a gallery hidden behind the tapestries, and Kate listened to the tune carefully as she nibbled at a bit of gingerbread covered in gold leaf.

"So, Senorita Haywood, there is to be a masquerade later, is there not?" Senor Gomez asked. "Are you to play a part?"

"I am only to help with the music tonight," she answered. "I fear I am no actor."

"Are you not?" he said. "But I would have thought you would have graced the royal stage."

Kate laughed. "Nay, not me. I would forget my lines with so many people watching me."

"And so many trying to guess the meanings behind every word?" Senor Vasquez suddenly said, with a scowl.

"I—nay, of course not," Kate managed to answer. "Her Grace wishes only to entertain her guests."

"And she does so with surpassingly fine style," Senor Gomez said soothingly. He shot an unreadable glance at his kinsman, who snorted and turned away.

"I have had roles in masquerades before. It is such great fun," Violet said. "But alas, the only part I could play now is surely a barge on the river!"

"You would grace any scene, Lady Violet," Senor Gomez said with a laugh. "There are so very many lovely ladies at the English court. It has been a remarkable surprise. I am glad to hear they can all be seen in such masques, I look forward to seeing it. Who takes the lead part in this one?"

"It is Kate who has organized them all, as she does so well," Violet said. "I believe Mary Radcliffe has taken a large role in this one. It is usually Lady Catherine Grey, who is so gifted at theatricals, but she is in mourning now, of course."

"Such a pity," Senor Gomez murmured. "Her rare beauty is spoken of even in Spain. But tell me more—what is usually the subject of such masques? At home, we see them only on feast days. . . ."

Kate peered between two draperies of silver silk, meant to be the clouds of the goddess's celestial realm, her fingers automatically moving over her lute strings to play the dance of Leto's hand-maidens. The scene on the stage was just as it should be, the ladies in their white gowns moving through their steps as the pages moved the clouds overhead with their levers.

Lady Catherine Grey joined the other ladies through the dance with smooth, gliding steps, small gestures that told them where to fall into line so that everything appeared uniform and perfect, a swirl of white. She was a good dancer, when she concentrated on her role—and with Lord Hertford in the audience, Lady Catherine was sure to be at her best. Queen Elizabeth had asked Kate to watch Lady Catherine, and she knew Lady Catherine had thrown caution to the winds before, but today she seemed to be on good behavior. Kate couldn't help but feel sorry for the lady, always being watched, always being judged.

The song changed as the goddess Niobe made her entrance from a staircase hidden among the satin clouds, and Rob took over the tune from the other side of the stage. Like Kate, he performed the music rather than taking a part at the front of the stage, which surely disappointed the ladies. Kate rested her lute across her knees, and watched him. He looked absorbed in the music, guiding the tune of the singers with nods, lost in the world they created. Kate wished she could do the same, but she couldn't afford to lose herself in the music that night. There was too much to watch.

She glimpsed her father sitting with Master Finsley and the Parks, and her heart warmed to see him smiling as he watched the lavish masque. He had not seen such splendor since their days at Queen Catherine's court, and she had worried it would tire him, but he laughed with Mistress Park, nodding when she pointed out something on the stage.

The queen sat on a raised dais with her Scots guests, her high-backed chair between Lord Halton and Lord Macintosh. She leaned toward Lord Halton and whispered something in his ear, making him smile. Yet the French ambassador, sitting just on the other side of Lord Halton, did not seem amused by the two goddesses and their battle for supremacy. Monsieur de Castelnau was too sophisticated to show any reaction, but he did not smile, as he usually did, and when Kate looked for him again a few minutes later he and his men were gone.

She looked for the Spanish, and found Senor Gomez and his fidgety cousin with the bishop on the other side of the queen's dais. Senor Vasquez still seemed distracted by something, tapping his hand on the edge of his stool, his gaze darting around the room, and Kate wondered what it was that made him look like that. What did he watch for there? Senor Gomez touched his sleeve, as if to distract him, and Kate noticed that Senor Vasquez automatically reached for the jewel-hilted dagger at his belt, again with his left hand. He nodded to his kinsman, and went very still as the masque moved into song.

Lady Jane Seymour, Lady Catherine's best friend, sat with some of her crowd at the back of the room, and like Senor Vasquez she seemed much too distracted to pay attention to the masquerade. She looked around, fed morsels to her lapdog, and laughed, but all the time she had to fight to keep a smile on her face. And Lord Hertford was nowhere to be seen.

It was a most interesting crowd indeed.

CHAPTER TEN

St. Stephen's Day, December 26

"Make way for the queen! Make way for the queen!"

The guards at the head of the royal procession called out as they slowly made their way past the sparkling palaces of the Strand, through Cheapside, and toward London Bridge. Eventually they would arrive at Greenwich Great Park for the royal St. Stephen's Day foxhunt, but Queen Elizabeth seemed in no hurry at all. From atop her prancing white horse, she waved and smiled at the crowds as they cheered for her and tossed bouquets of winter greenery and herbs. The bitterly cold wind was forgotten in the excitement of seeing the queen. Even the court, after dancing all night at the Christmas Day banquet the night before, seemed enlivened by the happy clamor.

Kate studied the scene from atop her own horse, her hands gripping the reins as tightly as she could. She had grown up at court and in towns, and was always suspicious of horses. She had traveled these same dirty, crowded streets, beneath the almost touching eaves of houses that blocked the light with their tiles and thatching, the smoke from their chimneys, so many times, going on errands to shops or searching out villains for the queen.

But as usual when Elizabeth went abroad, the city was transformed. The cobbles were scrubbed clean, covered by a new layer of straw and frost that had fallen in the night to make the city shimmer. Wreaths of Christmas greenery were draped from windows, where even more people crowded for a glimpse of the queen.

And Elizabeth rewarded them. Dressed in a riding costume of white and gold velvet, with a tall-crowned, plumed hat on her red hair, she waved and laughed.

"Good people, pray, do not remove your hats!" she called. "It is much too cold."

But of course they did remove their hats, flourishing them in the air as she passed by, with Robert Dudley riding to one side and Lord Macintosh to the other. A long line of her courtiers snaked after her, a glittering train of red and green and gold.

Kate remembered Elizabeth's entrance to London for her coronation almost a year ago, on just such a cold day. The pageants and plays, the yards and yards of scarlet velvet and cloth of gold, the fountains running with wine, the ecstatic jubilation after all the gray years with King Edward and Queen Mary. The brilliant hope centered around the red-haired daughter of Anne Boleyn.

None of that had faded in the last year. The crowds jostled in the icy cold, far from their firesides, just to wave at Queen Elizabeth. That was one of the reasons why Kate was proud to serve her. With Elizabeth, there was hope for the country. Without her, England would be an uncertain and bleak place.

It was work she was proud to do, and hoped to continue long into the future.

As they turned into Cheapside, the path took them past the tall, quiet, prosperous-looking house of the attorney Master Hardy, Anthony Elias's employer. Kate tried not to look, tried not to imagine that Anthony might be at the window with Mistress Derwood, but she couldn't help but take a peek. The shutters were drawn over the house, not even a servant looking out for a glimpse of the queen, as if the household was away. Kate sighed, half relieved, half disappointed.

She shook her head to clear it, taking in a deep breath of the cold air. It smelled of woodsmoke from dozens of chimneys, spiced cider from the vendor's cart near the walkway, fresh greenery, and the distant, sour tang that always hung over the city. She couldn't think about Anthony now, with her energetic horse frisking about and crowds pressing close on all sides. She had to keep her place in the procession, where she could keep watch on the queen, and not fall behind.

On the vast edifice of London Bridge, lined with

looming, half-timbered structures of houses and shops that rose against the sky, Elizabeth stopped to listen to a children's chorus sing a Yuletide song for their queen. They stood on a dais, rows of tiny figures in white robes, silhouetted against the river as Elizabeth leaned closer to listen.

"Blessed be that maid Marie, born was He of her body! Very God ere time began, born in the time of Son of Man." Their sweet, high voices rang out in the cold air, like glass bells soaring over the earth. Their round little faces, scrubbed clean for this important moment, shone with nervousness, joy, terror, and giddy pleasure.

Kate smiled to see them, for she knew something of what they felt. When she was their age, her father had handed her a lute, specially made for her small hands, and bade her play for Queen Catherine Parr, who had smiled down at her indulgently. In that moment had been born her love of music, of sharing the joy of it with other people. She suddenly wondered if one day she might have a child to teach music to as well, just like those cherubs in their white draperies.

She glanced downriver, toward the chimneys and high walls of Whitehall, and thought of her father there, sitting around the fire with his old friends. How had he felt to see her play for a queen when she was a child? Protective, proud—afraid?

She turned back and found Rob watching her

from his horse a few riders down in the procession. He was frowning, as if deep in thought, and then suddenly it turned to a smile when their eyes met. It felt like a touch of golden sun in that gray day, and she couldn't help but smile back—even as she hoped he did not know what she was thinking about.

She faced ahead again as the children's song ended, and a little girl with bright red curls stepped forward to shyly hand a bouquet of green herbs to the queen. Lord Macintosh leaned down to take the bouquet and hand it to Elizabeth, who smiled at the girl and murmured a few words that made the child giggle.

In the midst of the lovely scene, Kate's gaze caught on the heads displayed on pikes high over the entrance to the bridge, a gruesome contrast to the sweet music and joyful cheers. Those empty, dark eye sockets declared silently that all was not entirely merry in the queen's realm, even at Christmas. Everyone had their secrets, and some led to pikes on the bridge. Kate thought of the drawing left on the queen's bed, of Queen Catherine's music pressed into Matthew Haywood's hands and hidden all these years.

They moved forward again, the long train of horses snaking over the bridge and out of London proper. As they skirted past the twisting lanes of Southwark, Kate glimpsed a tall woman with improbably red hair and a bright green gown standing on the riverbank with a group of other ladies in vivid gowns, and she recognized Mistress Celine from the Cardinal's Hat brothel. Kate happily waved at them before they were lost to sight in the crowds.

The narrow streets flowed off into snow-dusted fields and hedgerows, with the stone chimneys of farmhouses and fine manors in the distance. The tightly packed procession, so carefully lined up at Whitehall, fanned out as couples and groups found each other for laughing conversations and quick whispers. Kate saw Lady Catherine Grey whispering with Lord Hertford and his sister, though the queen seemed to take no notice as she laughed with Lord Macintosh.

Rob drew his horse alongside hers, and Kate smiled at him. His hunting clothes were more somber than his usual garb, dark red velvet and black leather, but they fit him just as well as his courtly doublets and hose. Yet his eyes seemed to have sleepless dark shadows under them.

"How do you fare today, Rob?" she said, and he cringed at her hearty tone. He had stayed up later than the whole court after the dancing, vanishing somewhere with his new Spanish "friends." Kate thought it best not to inquire too closely yet.

He managed to rally and gave her a smile. "Better now that I see you, bonny Kate. There is much I need to tell you. Your Spanish acquaintances are an interesting lot."

Kate's curiosity was piqued, but there was no time at that moment for him to tell her more. The gates of Greenwich Palace stood open for them as they turned down a wide graveled lane. In the distance, the palace's redbrick towers loomed against the pearl gray sky. But they turned away from the castle itself, which would be closed and shuttered until the queen's next residence there in the spring, and rode toward the wide meadows and woods of the Great Park. The winding, sloping fields, so vividly green in the summer, were brown and gray now, streaked with veins of snow. The bare trees stood like black skeletons, frosted with sparkling diamond ice. It would surely be the last hunt for a while.

But Kate found she didn't mind the bleak landscape at all. The rush of cold, fresh wind against her cheeks, the crisp country smells, and the open space felt wondrous after long days indoors. It felt free, and made a new song start in her mind.

"Are you thinking of music, Kate?" Rob asked as they all came to halt outside the gamekeeper's cottage. The Greenwich stewards had to give their formal greeting to the queen before the St. Stephen's Day fox and the pack of hounds were released.

Kate laughed. "However did you know? The wind sounds like a madrigal. Just listen!"

The fox streaked away across the gray field in a

russet blur, and the hounds let out great howls. Elizabeth and Dudley spurred their horses in pursuit, and everyone else galloped behind them. The court became a bright stream of velvets and plumes, darting over the fields and between the trees. The horses' hooves were like thunder over the frozen ground, and they tossed their glossy manes, as if they were as thrilled as their riders to be set free into the world.

Even Kate, the least enthusiastic rider, had to laugh as she let her horse have its head. The wind caught at her cap and tugged strands of her dark hair from its net. The drawing in the queen's bedchamber, Queen Catherine's music, the Spanish and the Scots—they seemed to vanish with the earth that flew away beneath her.

"I'll race you!" she shouted to Rob, though she was quite sure she could never best him in a ride. He laughed, too, the warm, golden sound carried away on the wind. Their horses neck and neck, they followed the queen to leap over a shallow ravine and skitter around a sharp corner into the Greenwich woods.

The hounds howled in the distance, and the riders turned to follow the beckoning sound. Kate swung her horse around, with Rob close behind her. They galloped deeper into the woods, leaping lightly over fallen logs and ditches, veering between the stark branches of the winter trees. Other riders brushed past, and behind one of the trees Kate caught a glimpse of blue wool trimmed with white fir, golden hair—Lady Catherine, her horse standing still, drawn close to Lord Hertford's as the two of them talked.

Then they, too, were gone, left behind in a flash of movement.

Suddenly a scream pierced the air, long and high, higher than the wind and the pounding of hooves. Kate almost tumbled from her horse at the shock of the sound. Her heart pounded, but it also felt as if an icy calm lowered over her, and she saw the woods around them sharper, brighter. That strange calm had come upon her before, in moments of danger.

Another cry rang out, echoing from somewhere in the woods around them, followed by a man's shout. The other riders nearby pulled up their mounts as they looked around in confusion. Kate's horse laid back its ears, and she tightened her hold on the reins as she feared it might bolt.

Rob leaned over, even as he drew in his own horse, and grasped her reins to help her slow down and regain her balance in the saddle. He held her protectively close, his lean, athletic body taut as he raised his head to listen carefully.

Kate, too, held her breath as she listened. She tried to decipher where the cries came from, but in the woods sound seemed both very distant and impossibly close.

The men around them drew their daggers and short swords, staying close to the ladies. Kate was glad of the weight of her own blade at her belt, its weight greater than a mere eating knife would be but still light enough to fit her palm. The lessons in using a dagger she had learned from one of Cecil's guards reassured her.

"What could it be?" she asked Rob quietly. In her mind, she saw again that drawing left in the queen's chamber.

"Stay close to me, Kate," Rob answered, his actor's gaze, trained to miss nothing, sweeping over the confused courtiers around them.

Kate hoped the queen was already sheltered and safe inside Greenwich Palace. Elizabeth had been close to Robert Dudley at the start of the hunt, and surely he would not let the merest hint of harm touch her. Would he?

But what if it was the queen who had screamed?

Kate shook her head, enveloped in a haze of confusion. Everything felt most unreal, as if she were caught in a bad dream, or a masque gone horribly awry. The woods, so full of freedom and adventure only a moment ago, were suddenly dark and menacing.

Kate's throat felt dry, aching so she could barely swallow, and she nodded. Rob set out on the nearest pathway back to the palace, and Kate spurred her horse to follow him, listening to the distant clamor. The wind tore at her hat, sweeping through the thick velvet of her jacket, and she shivered.

They emerged from the shelter of the woods to find a cluster of courtiers gathered near a low stone wall by a stand of old oak trees. At first glance, it could have been the capture of the hunted fox, but Kate could see the pale fear on the ladies' faces—and the fury on the men's, the flash of gray sunlight on their swords. Their horses snorted and tossed their heads restlessly.

Rob grasped Kate's horse's bridle again, holding her close as they edged cautiously nearer. They came to a halt just beyond the tangled edge of the crowd.

For a moment, Kate could see nothing—the knot of frightened people and horses was too close. But then it parted, and she glimpsed Elizabeth and Dudley, their horses drawn up beneath one of the bare winter trees. Dudley held his dagger aloft, unsheathed, and was shouting something in furious tones, but Queen Elizabeth just stared straight ahead as if frozen, her face stark white.

Kate followed her stare—and a cry escaped before she could catch it. Hanging from one of the branches was a poppet, with bright red silk yarn hair crowned with an elaborate gold wire diadem, and wearing a fine white satin gown streaked with what looked like blood. In the crook of one arm, the doll held a baby, also with red hair.

Pinned to the bodice was a piece of parchment, written in stark black letters, the same as on the drawing that was found in the queen's chamber—*The Lady Beth.*

Dudley rose up in his stirrups, slashing out with his dagger to cut the horrible thing down. It tumbled to the frosty ground, landing in a red-and-white jumble. The hounds crept closer to it, baying and snuffling, but even they wouldn't touch it. Surely it reeked of evil, of some traitorous intent.

More guards in the queen's livery came galloping over the crest of the hill from Greenwich. As they surrounded Elizabeth in an impenetrable wall, she rode away, leaving one of the men to scoop up the poppet and wrap it in a rag.

Kate glimpsed Senor Vasquez at the edge of the crowd, his face ashen beneath his beard. To her surprise, Lord Macintosh of the Scots delegation was beside him, and leaned toward him to say something. Senor Vasquez scowled.

Catherine Grey edged her horse close to Kate's. "Kate, are you ill?" she cried. "Your cheeks are so pale."

And Lady Catherine's were too pink. Because of Lord Hertford? Or something worse?

Kate shook her head. "I just fell behind in the hunt, and then caught up to find—this." She gestured to the ground where the crumpled doll had fallen.

Lady Catherine shuddered. "My cousin does have many enemies indeed. It's easy to forget how many still hate the Tudors on a fine day like this. One sees a tiny glimpse of freedom, and then . . ."

Lady Catherine bit her lip, and Kate wondered what freedom she sought. She shivered, and realized the wind had turned even colder. She had forgotten what dangers were out there for a moment, and she should not have.

Rob seemed to see her shiver, and he reached out to cover her gloved hand with his for a moment.

Lord Hertford drew near to them, his gaze never leaving Lady Catherine's face. "Come, ladies, let me see you to Greenwich Palace," he said. "The queen has been taken to her privy chamber, and the steward is preparing a fire in one of the rooms for her ladies until you can be taken back to Whitehall."

"You do seem rather knowledgeable about our change in arrangements," Lady Catherine said tartly, not looking at him. Had they had some quarrel? But she followed him toward the waiting palace, the other ladies hurrying after them. Kate glanced back to see Rob riding off with the guards, and she followed the ladies into the palace.

"I am no shivering coward!" Queen Elizabeth shouted. "I will not let some ridiculous mischief ruin my Christmas."

As her ladies looked on, Elizabeth slammed her fist down on the table that had been hastily prepared for her in the Greenwich sitting room. A pitcher of wine crashed over, spilling a horrible, bloodlike splash of dark red onto the bare floorboards. The ladies cried out, and a maidservant scrambled to mop it up.

Cecil leaned on his walking stick, a look of long-suffering patience on his prematurely lined face. He knew to let Elizabeth burn out her temper.

Kate hoped she could be as patient as he was. He would surely prevail upon the queen to have more care now, even if he couldn't persuade her to his argument of curtailing the elaborate Christmas festivities to see to her safety. At least until the threatening villain, who seemed capable of creeping into the queen's own palaces—even into her chambers—was caught.

Which Elizabeth had said would surely not be long, since Robert Dudley and his men were tearing the Greenwich fields up even at that very moment. Dudley had organized the hunt himself; he would let no one ruin it.

"Your Grace," Cecil said softly, "none could ever accuse you of being a shivering coward. But it is not wise to go among crowds when there is some plot at work so close to you."

"Plot!" Elizabeth scoffed. "It was hardly a plot, I am sure. Just a bit of holiday mischief, perhaps directed at Robin and his carefully planned hunt. He could certainly stand to be taken down a peg or two."

"I cannot disagree with Your Grace about that," Cecil said wryly. His antipathy toward the flamboyant and obviously ambitious Dudley had long been well known, and anything that removed him from the queen's close favor for even a short time would be welcome to Cecil. "Yet we cannot be sure this was merely a prank. The fact that they have managed to infiltrate the gates of one of the royal palaces is most alarming. With the Spanish, and the French with the Queen of Scots all so close . . ."

"Do not speak to me yet again of the Queen of Scots! I am sick of her name. She is all anyone thinks of. Can I not enjoy my Christmas at least without her interfering?"

"I fear we cannot stop her *interfering*," Cecil said. "She is a constant threat. And surely she knows you have received the Scots rebels by now."

Elizabeth shot a glance toward her ladies, who were listening most avidly. "We will speak of this later, Cecil. In the meantime, we must bide our time until Robin tells us it is safe to ride back to Whitehall. Ladies, shall we play a hand of primero? And Kate, mayhap you will fetch more wine?"

"Of course, Your Grace," Kate said quickly. As she hurried out the door, she saw Lady Catherine sit down with the queen, shuffling the cards between her pale hands.

She didn't know Greenwich very well, though its halls and chambers were not as labyrinthine as those of Whitehall, and most of the rooms were empty of furniture until the queen's next official visit. It took her a while to find the kitchens and send a servant with more wine and refreshments to the queen. On her own way back to the sitting room, she found a small table by one of the doors to the garden, its cloth blown about by a breeze from the half-open portal.

She rushed to close and lock it, remembering Cecil's concern that whoever the note-leaving culprit was, he had found a way to creep into the queen's own palaces and chambers. Before she swung the window shut, she glimpsed Sir Robert Dudley and a few of his men on horseback, outlined at the crest of a hill against the gray sky. Sir Robert gestured angrily, his men nodding, before he spurred his horse forward. It seemed they had not yet found whoever left the note.

As she turned away, she saw there was a small basket on the table, halfway covered by the cloth. Inside, she caught a glimpse of a silvery shimmer, a flash of red, and she shivered when she realized it was the poppet that had been hanging from the tree. It seemed someone had left it there, half-forgotten, as if no one wanted to be near it for very long.

She didn't quite want to look, but she knew she should study it, to see if there were any clues left there as to its maker. She tiptoed closer and edged the cloth away. It was not quite as hideous as she remembered, rendered more harmless left there in a jumble than it was hanging from a tree. It was small, the face carved crudely of wood and painted with features, but the little silk gown with its lace trim was quite fine. The wig, almost the exact shade of Elizabeth's red-gold, seemed to be of real hair. But it was the small crown that was most interesting.

It was made of silver wire wrapped in cloth-of-silver ribbon, as so many of the headdresses were for the queen's masques and plays. The design was intricate, of Tudor roses and various fruits and nuts, trimmed with red ribbon and glass beads, with a band of lustrous sable fur at its base. The silver seemed slightly tarnished, but it was obviously an expensive piece.

Who could have found such a thing?

Kate reached out and lightly touched it. It wobbled and toppled from the doll's head, making her jump back a bit. Perhaps the thing was just as sinister in the deceptive safety of the palace as it was in the tree.

She turned and rushed away toward the queen's sitting room, feeling colder than she ever had before.

CHAPTER ELEVEN

St. John the Evangelist Day, December 27

Kate drew the heavy folds of her fur-trimmed wool cloak closer around her as she hurried through the Whitehall gardens toward the building where the Office of the Revels had stored their costumes for the masque. The wind that swirled in off the river was biting, and she was glad she had the excuse of an errand to keep her from going ice-skating with Lady Catherine and her friends again.

But the errand wasn't a pleasant one. Tucked in the purse tied to her sash was the tiny crown from the horrid hanging effigy. It was a fine piece, much like a headdress the queen actually owned. It couldn't have been made at just any gold-smith's; it had to come from someone who specialized in making such headpieces, a tiring-maker who catered to the court and the theatrical troupes.

Surely someone who worked for the Master of the Revels would know which jeweler in the city worked in such a style, and they in turn might remember who had ordered such a thing. It was a small matter, but the only clue Kate could yet think of that might tell them who had had the doll made. The queen had so many enemies—the Spanish, the French, who wanted to see their Queen Mary on the English throne, disappointed suitors, jealous rivals. But this one was getting much too frighteningly close.

The Office of the Revels was very busy organizing all the queen's Yule events, with pages and servants rushing back and forth carrying gilded props and bolts of glimmering silks. Someone was decorating a large backdrop with a snow scene and a clear blue sky, and the smell of the paint was heavy in the chilly air.

Kate managed to catch a harried-looking man in a rumpled brown wool doublet as he ran past. "I beg your pardon, sir," she said quickly, for she knew very well how annoying it was to be interrupted in the midst of a creative flurry. "But I have come on an errand for the queen. Where might I find Sir Thomas Benger?"

The page became a little more helpful at the mention of the queen, and led her to a small chamber at the back of the office where Sir Thomas was inspecting some of the props for an upcoming masque.

Kate had known him at Hatfield, where he helped Princess Elizabeth keep up a semblance of a royal court in her small household, and he had just become her Master of the Revels, an expensive honor to his purse it was rumored he was halfhearted about at best. But his eye was sharp as he studied the array of helmets and false swords before him.

"Ah, Mistress Haywood! A most welcome distraction," he declared. "Come in, come in. Does the queen require us to examine another new play?"

"Not at all, Sir Thomas. I hope I bring you very little extra work, for I know well how busy this time of year can be," Kate answered. "I have a question of my own for you."

"I will be happy to help if I can."

Kate unwrapped the little crown and held it out to him. "Would you happen to have an idea of who made this? I know you use many different seamstresses and artisans, but it seems rather distinctive."

"Indeed. A very pretty piece, though quite miniature. It must be a prop for a play, though such a shame no one could see the intricate work close up from a stage." He balanced the crown on his palm to study it closely. If he had heard of what happened on the queen's hunt, the poppet with its tiny crown, he gave no sign. "I do think the threadwork on the wires is rather distinctive. Master Orrens, perhaps."

"Master Orrens?"

"He works on Monkwell Street, came from France many years ago, I think. He sometimes makes headdresses for courtly masquerades, though I seem to remember he worked more for King Henry's court. Do you have a new commission for him?"

"Mayhap, if he is really who I seek," Kate said. "His work is quite lovely."

Sir Thomas reached for a scrap of paper and his quill. "I will give you his direction. Tell him if he is still working, we would like to have him make some new costumes for the court. Mayhap for the summer progresses."

"I will tell him. Thank you." She just hoped he truly was the man she sought, the one who could tell her more about the crown and where it came from.

Kate made her way back to the waterside gallery. She didn't see Lady Catherine and her friends there, so they were probably still on the river—or in secret romantic meetings. Robert Dudley and his followers were also absent, which meant the queen was still playing primero with him in her privy chamber, as she was when Kate had left. Kate paused to glance out the window at the garden below, and she glimpsed her father walking there with his stick, leaning on Hester Park's arm as Master Park pointed out a sight in the distance, and they all laughed. Kate smiled to see her father enjoying himself again.

She caught a glimpse of a silver flash against the dark brown of the winter hedges, and turned to see Rob Cartman walking with a lady on each of his arms. One of the ladies was giggling as Rob smiled down at her, and he suddenly twirled them both in a wide circle as if they were dancing in the winter wind.

Kate jerked her head around to turn her attention to the gallery again. Surely what Rob Cartman chose to do with his time was not her concern! She had better business to attend to.

But as she turned away, she saw something at the edge of the walled garden that made her pause. Lord Macintosh, of the Scots Protestant lords, and Senor Vasquez were standing by the stone wall, talking together closely. Their faces were dark, intent, and Senor Vasquez was scowling.

They seemed most unlikely friends. Curious, Kate made her way to the staircase at the end of the gallery that led down into the gardens. It was crowded with courtiers passing the long hours whispering, laughing, and playing cards, and no one paid her any attention. She drew up the hood of her cloak and stayed behind the tall hedge so they wouldn't see her.

". . . only a ruddy Spaniard would trust someone like that," Lord Macintosh was saying. He tried to laugh derisively, but Kate could hear the barely leashed anger underneath. "Smugglers will only see to their own ends. If one thing goes wrong . . ."

"So pay them enough and they will do your bidding, *sí*?" Senor Vasquez said with a snort.

Kate remembered his glowers at the banquet, his dour attitude in such contrast to that of his friend

Senor Gomez. She peeked carefully around the edge of the hedge, but she could see little other than the two men standing close together, watching to make sure they were not overheard. What were a Scotsman and a Spaniard doing together worrying about smugglers, of all things? Making some coin on the side while they were in England?

"There is no one else?" Lord Macintosh said.

Senor Vasquez laughed, a bitter sound. "Do you think one of the queen's captains would do it, and not go scurrying off to milord Cecil with word of it? We may be on an island, but even you must know it is no simple matter to find the right kind of ship for our purpose. These arrangements were made long ago, and must be carried out at exactly the right moment. Why else would I come now to this barbaric land?"

Lord Macintosh was silent for a long moment, and Kate carefully edged forward again to study their faces. Macintosh was much larger than Vasquez, and the Spaniard huddled against the cold, but it seemed he was the leader in whatever scheme the two of them were arranging. She hardly dared breathe as she watched them. Even in a court full of whispered secrets, she was astonished at them.

Finally, after a long, tense moment, Lord Macintosh nodded. "I am new to Whitehall, and have only just received word of what must be done. I shall think carefully of what you have said."

"Do not take too long about it. Time grows short."

Macintosh scowled. "The lady does not seem enthusiastic. In fact, she has said nothing at all to me."

Senor Vasquez shrugged. "How can she? She is carefully watched. But she, too, will follow the arrangements. The good of three nations depends on it now. . . ."

"Speaking of being watched . . ." Lord Macintosh glanced over his shoulder, and Kate ducked back around her corner. "I must go now. I will speak to you again soon, senor, but not here."

"And what I was promised?"

"You shall have it," Macintosh said, a sneer in his voice.

When Kate peeked out again, the two men were gone. She almost wondered if she had imagined the whole thing—it seemed so very ludicrous. What were a Spaniard and a Scotsman, a *Protestant* Scotsman, doing conspiring together? She couldn't fathom how their interests could possibly align.

Of course, she thought, it could have something to do with King Philip of Spain wanting to keep Mary, Queen of Scots, off the English throne. He had no love of the Valois family, despite his new wife, or for France to take over England—it was said he even preferred a heretic queen to that prospect. Yet would he go so far as to enlist the Scottish Congregation lords to his aid?

And who was *she*, whose consent involved boats and smugglers? Kate's head whirled with wild thoughts, with fears for Elizabeth's safety. The threatening notes, the hanged effigy, the strange music, all the new foreign lords crowding the palace corridors—how could they be connected?

Kate shook her head as she suddenly remembered what her errand in the gallery was in the first place, to fetch her lute and some of the music from the chamber where they had worked on the masque. She hurried down the corridor, intent on retrieving them and then finding Cecil to tell him what she had heard.

Her thoughts were spinning as she climbed the stairs back into the warmth of the palace and turned down the corridor. She felt the need to write down all she knew thus far, which was precious little indeed. She needed to see the connections, like the bars of a song.

She turned into the chamber, and saw that it was not quite empty. A tall, lean man in a black-and-dark-tawny–velvet doublet was bent over the table of music. For an instant, she was afraid that it was Senor Gomez, and that he had some part in whatever scheme his friend was concocting.

But then he straightened, and she saw it was not Senor Gomez at all. It was her father's friend

Master Finsley, and in a beam of light from the narrow windows she didn't know how she could have mistaken him for the younger Spaniard. She had a sudden memory of him from when she was a child, his hair dark, his smile wide as he talked to his sister. He had been a handsome man then, and was still. She wondered why he had never married, what he had been doing since his days at Queen Catherine's court.

"Mistress Haywood—Kate," he said with a little bow and a smile. "I was sent to fetch something for Mistress Park, and couldn't help but look at these. Are they all your own work?"

"Aye, most of it," Kate answered. She went to his side to glance over the pages scattered over the table, all the odds and ends she had drawn together to help make the new masque. "This song was my father's, but we haven't yet used it this Yule season."

Master Finsley studied the music carefully. "Matthew and I have played many of his old pieces together over the last few weeks, but I cannot remember this one."

"It is not so very old. He wrote it when we lived at Hatfield. The queen's Christmases then, when she was a princess, were much quieter, and we didn't have a chance to play this one. It could be used for dancing." She remembered the secret manuscript her father had shown her, the one Queen Catherine Parr gave him.

She studied Master Finsley carefully, but she could see only kindness in his smile. He, too, had served Queen Catherine and her Protestant court. He must have seen a great deal in those days.

"You have much of your father's talent," he said. "And your mother's, too. I hope Queen Elizabeth treasures that talent. It is a rare thing."

"Her Grace has been very kind to me, and to my father," Kate answered. "I am glad you came to visit him. I know he thinks much about the past lately."

"We had some fine times together, your father and the Parks and I, to be sure," Master Finsley said with a laugh. "And I fear we had some dark ones, as well. I am glad to see that promise you showed as a child has come to fruition."

"I remember your sister from when I was a child, Master Finsley. She was very kind to me. Any seam I can sew now, which I fear is not so great, is thanks to her. She was most patient with my fumbling about with needle and thread."

He smiled sadly. "Allison was a kindhearted woman indeed. It's been lonely without her."

"You never married, Master Finsley?"

"I never met a lady as lovely as your mother," he said with a smile. "Allison kept house for me, and I had my work for Queen Catherine. It was a most satisfactory life. But I am surprised *you* have not married yet, my dear."

Kate laughed. "I, too, have satisfactory work,

Master Finsley. It would be difficult to give it up."

"Very true. I am sure the queen has much use for your talent." He studied the pages of music again. "Do you perchance have any more of your father's work? I would love to look at it."

"I have some," Kate said carefully, thinking of the hidden pages. "Perhaps we could all meet after the queen's feast and play some music in my father's room? I would so enjoy hearing more about your time together in Queen Catherine's day."

"I would enjoy that as well."

Kate gathered up her music and made her way up the stairs toward the quiet corridor where her chamber waited. There was much to be finished before the evening's revels, and she had to send her message to Cecil. But there was a most unexpected sight waiting for her outside her door. Lady Catherine Grey sat on the floor in a puddle of black satin skirts and the black fur tippet she had worn for skating, sobbing into her hands.

At the sight of Kate, she scrambled to her feet.

"Lady Catherine, are you ill?" Kate cried as she ran to the sobbing girl's side. Kate glanced quickly around to see if anyone else was there, if anyone had seen the queen's cousin in such an unhappy state. But it seemed Lady Catherine was alone, and few people ventured very often to such a quiet part of the palace.

"Oh, Mistress Haywood, I am so sorry to

im-impose on you in such a manner," Lady Catherine said with a sniffle. "I just could not bear it. I couldn't be stared at a moment longer, and I remembered you had a room here. . . ."

Kate nodded, thinking of how Lady Catherine's life was the opposite to her own. Kate did the watching, but everyone was always watching Lady Catherine, wondering what she was going to do next, what she was thinking of her treatment as the queen's cousin, if she wanted to be the heir. It must be maddening. "You are not imposing on me, Lady Catherine. I am happy to help, if I can. Here, let's go inside where you can sit quietly. No one will stare at you there."

Kate opened the door and quickly ushered Lady Catherine inside. The lady's pretty heart-shaped face was splotched and reddened from crying, and it seemed she had no handkerchief. Kate found one of her own in the clothes chest, and pressed it into Lady Catherine's hand before she went to stir the warm embers of the fire back to life. She let Lady Catherine sit down on the stool near the hearth and compose herself a bit before glancing back to smile at her.

"I fear I have no wine to offer," Kate said.

"You are so very kind, Mistress Haywood," Lady Catherine said, wiping her eyes. "No one else here at court is like you. No one I have ever known, really."

"You have many friends, Lady Catherine."

Lady Catherine bit her lip and stared down at the handkerchief balled up in her hand. "I do know many people, of course. Everyone wants to find favor with a Tudor, even one as *out* of favor as I am. My mother loved parties, loved people and laughter around her, and I inherited the same from her. I could never do without company. But—friends? I am not so sure, of late."

Kate sat back on her heels to study her visitor more closely. The Lady Catherine of only a few months ago had been so confidently sure of her position, of her place at the center of her group of friends, but now she had changed. Was it just her mother's recent death—or something more?

When Queen Elizabeth asked Kate to keep watch on Lady Catherine, Kate had never expected the task to come easily. For Lady Catherine Grey to so eagerly reveal the vulnerability beneath her Tudor glitter. It made Kate feel a sharp, guilty pang to think of using the lady's sorrow, even to help the queen in these dangerous games of royal heirs and plots.

But Lady Catherine had been a courtier since birth. Her mother, King Henry's own niece, had been so adept at such games that she managed to save herself and her two remaining daughters, to find favor at court, even after her husband's execution for treason. Lady Frances Grey had steered her family through the perils of four monarchs, with her charm and beauty always intact. What if Lady Catherine took after her mother in political adeptness as well as her love of parties? What if this, too, was some elaborate masquerade?

Kate took in every detail of Lady Catherine's appearance. Her fine satin gown, the fur at her throat, the pearl-edged cap on her disarranged golden curls, her wide blue eyes still shining with tears. The faraway look in them, the way her hands trembled. Kate, too, had learned many things in the past year at the queen's court, and from working on endless masquerades. She could see only real confusion and sadness on the lady's face—and a tinge of desperation.

And desperate people did such wild things. Lady Catherine had been friends with the last Spanish ambassador, the Count de Feria, and the count's English wife, Jane Dormer. She had been convinced they could help her in her quest to marry Lord Hertford. Was she *still* friends with the Spanish? With anyone who might help her in her romantic quest?

"Should I send for one of Mistress Ashley's herbal possets?" Kate asked.

"Nay!" Lady Catherine cried. "Not Mistress Ashley. She is one of the people I want to hide from the most. She is always watching me so carefully, always frowning as if she heartily disapproves of me."

"She is only being protective of the queen.

People say she was like a mother to Her Grace when the queen was a child."

Lady Catherine frowned. "I mean the queen no harm! She is my own cousin. Why can't Mistress Ashley, everyone, see that? I would never want what she has. A throne means danger. Trouble. That is all. I saw what it did to my parents, to my poor sister Jane. Why would I want that?"

Yet Lady Catherine had acted in the past like she was affronted that the queen would not name her heir, not give her what was her due as a Tudor. "What would you want instead, Lady Catherine?"

"What every lady wants. Love. A home. Children. That is not so very much to ask, is it?"

Kate shook her head. They seemed small things; yet they were things she herself dared not think about. How much harder it must be for Lady Catherine. "Nay. Not so much."

"My cousin thinks that because her heart is ice, so must be those of all her ladies. It is most unfair."

It was certainly true that the queen seemed to think little of the prospect of marriage, even though she must one day choose among her many suitors and give England an heir. Kate could not blame the queen if she was afraid. Marriage for the royal family had not been a safe, easy thing for many years. All the queen's stepmothers, her poor, doomed mother, Queen Mary, and her pathetic love for King Philip, it was enough to frighten even someone as stouthearted as Elizabeth. But not enough to frighten Catherine Grey, it seemed.

"If you could be someone else," Kate said, "would you?"

Lady Catherine looked utterly baffled, as if the possibility of being anyone, anything, besides Lady Catherine Grey was beyond her scope of thought. Yet Kate had seen her perform in masques, seen how adept she was at changing personas like a cloak.

"I think . . . ," Lady Catherine murmured uncertainly. Then she shook her head, and something hardened in her tearful blue eyes. "I want to be myself, but without this infernal Tudor blood. It has caused me and my family naught but trouble."

Kate nodded. She could not argue against that statement. Royal blood seemed to have brought little good to Lady Catherine, despite her beauty and vivacity, her fine clothes. It had killed her father and sister, and made her little more than a pawn to move about at someone else's will.

Kate had sometimes felt wistful that she and her father were their only small family, no siblings or cousins to grow up with her, her mother long lost. With the revelation that Eleanor Haywood had been the illegitimate half sister of Anne

Boleyn, Kate gained something of a new family. But it was a shadow family, a family that only she could really know about, not one such as Lady Catherine's—for good or ill.

In that instant, she completely understood Lady Catherine's desire to create a new family, a home and shelter free from the sorrows and mistakes of the past. Surely it would be wonderful to feel no longer alone against the cold world. But it would be a difficult thing, well nigh impossible, for a royal woman like Lady Catherine to create such a haven.

Impossible for a woman like Kate as well. There would always be secrets lurking in the corners of even the coziest of homes. What man would understand that, would help her?

She resisted the urge to snatch back her handkerchief and burst into tears herself. Instead, she smiled at Lady Catherine and picked up her lute. She ran her fingertips over the small initials *EH* etched into the neck. *Eleanor Haywood.* That always helped settle her mind. She still had to take the small false crown to Cecil and try to find out what Macintosh and Vasquez were plotting, but just for a moment she could sit by her fire with her mother's lute.

"Shall I play us a merry song?" she said, making herself smile cheerfully. It wasn't just Lady Catherine who had learned about courtly masquerades. "'Tis only the gray coldness that casts us into such melancholy, I am sure. Yet it's Christmas, which is meant to be the happiest time of year."

Lady Catherine laughed. "Oh, yes, please! I would love a song. I do so enjoy your music, Mistress Haywood. You have been too kind to me today. I know I should not take up your time thus, but your chamber is so peaceful and warm. I share a room with Juno—Lady Jane Seymour. She is my dearest friend, and we have such fun, but . . ." Her voice trailed away.

"But sometimes it is very hard work just to keep smiling."

Lady Catherine looked startled. "Exactly so. But a song can always make me smile. What will you play? Something of your own?"

Kate quickly glanced through a stack of music on her table. It was just as she had left it, neatly stacked and held down by a small silver box that held her few pieces of jewelry—the garnet earrings her father had given her, a rope of pearls from the queen, Rob's enameled lute.

And yet the papers did not seem quite the same. Surely that was not the order of the songs?

"Is something amiss, Mistress Haywood?" Lady Catherine asked.

Kate pushed the papers back into a stack and made herself smile. "Not at all. My father brought me some of his own compositions, pieces he wrote when I was a child and he served Queen

Catherine Parr. He also brought me some other songs from that time, and I believe there was one written by Lady Frances Brandon."

"My mother?" Lady Catherine said, her voice brighter. "You have a song of my mother's?"

"It was signed by her. Would it make you sad to hear it?"

"I should love it very much. My mother did take such joy in music, and she often talked to us of her time with Queen Catherine. I remember little about it, I was so small, but Mother said Queen Catherine was a woman of much culture and learning."

Kate found the song among her father's pieces, and showed it to Lady Catherine.

"Aye, that is my mother's hand. How very astonishing, Mistress Haywood! It's like she is suddenly here in this room with us. I am sure she led me here to you today." Lady Catherine bit her lip as she studied the spill of ink notes on the yellowing paper. "I do wish . . ."

"Wish what, Lady Catherine?"

"Her writing makes me remember. She had meant to send a letter to Queen Elizabeth requesting permission for me to marry. She was so sure if she could remind the queen of our family ties in the past, she would not refuse. But Mother died before she could finish the message. And none can replace her voice."

Kate swallowed hard, sad for her own mother,

for all that might have been. "But she can be here with us for a moment. Here, I shall play, if you would like to sing this part here . . ."

And for just a little while, the world was lost in music.

CHAPTER TWELVE

Holy Innocents Day, December 28

"*Non, non*! I say it again—down on three, up on four, then *passe* and jump. Is not so hard! Again, again."

Kate had to duck her head to keep from laughing as Monsieur Dumas, the tiny bandy-legged French dancing master, lost his temper yet again at the courtiers trying to perform his complicated version of a galliard.

It was a quiet hour in the palace. The queen had been closeted with her privy council since morning, and Robert Dudley had led some of the court to a hunt. Kate was happy to play familiar dance tunes for an hour's dance practice, to forget about everything else that was happening outside this warm chamber, heavy with fragrant green wreaths for the season.

She watched the dancers as her fingers moved over the strings. She had played this tune so often she had no need to look at the music, though the dance was a new version from France, which the queen wanted to watch at that night's feast. The dancers kept missing their footing in the complex series of jumps and tumbling down amid a tangle of embroidered skirts. When they laughed and pushed each other down again, Monsieur Dumas became even angrier.

"*Non, non!*" he shouted again. "Thees will never be done in time. *Imbeciles.*"

Kate bit her lip to hide her own giggles. She glimpsed Lady Catherine Grey whispering with Lady Jane Seymour across the room. Lady Catherine seemed to have regained her spirits after her tears of the evening before, and Kate wondered again at the Tudor changeability. Anger, tears, remorse, laughter, all in the course of minutes. Just like Queen Elizabeth at times.

It was said the queen also had a sizable share of temper from her Boleyn blood. Boleyns were legendary for their energetic tantrums, though Kate was glad she seemed to have inherited her father's steadier emotions rather than those of her mother's Boleyn relatives.

Most of the time.

Just beyond Lady Catherine, Kate saw Monsieur Castelnau, the French ambassador. Despite leaving Elizabeth's masque of warring queens, he had said nothing else about the play's message for Queen Mary, and was smiling today, as he always did. But then, he had a long diplomatic career behind him, years in Paris, Vienna, Rome, making sure his thoughts and those of his French masters were never really known. He would give little away, no matter how Queen Elizabeth provoked him.

"Now, *mesdames*, one more time," Monsieur Dumas shouted. "This time with a bit of grace, I beg you. Just because you are English does not mean you can be like the sheeps gamboling in the fields, *oui*?"

Lady Catherine led her friends back into line, and Kate played the first few notes of the song.

Suddenly, the chamber door burst open, banging against the paneled wall like a violent burst of fireworks in the sky. The dancers fell out of step all over again, and Kate jumped up from her stool. She spun around to see Sebastian Gomez standing there.

Lady Jane Seymour shrieked, making the others cry out and run, as if they would flee from what they knew not, and Kate could see why they were terrified. Senor Gomez, usually so handsome, smiling, and charming, his rich Spanish clothes impeccable, looked like a figure newly escaped from the lower depths of the Tower.

His dark hair stood up on one side, and his skin was grayish, pale and clammy. His purple velvet doublet was partially unfastened, and the white shirt beneath was stained bright red. More of the horrible scarlet stickiness covered his hands, and streaked across one of his cheeks. Yet it did not seem to be his own blood, for she could see no wounds.

He said nothing for one long moment, just stood frozen in the doorway as the ladies' shrieks spiraled louder and louder. Several of the queen's guards appeared behind him in a clatter of swords, but even they came to a bewildered halt at the strange sight.

Kate's heart pounded so loudly she could hear it in her ears, drowning out the screams. Time itself seemed to slow to a crawl around her, and everything but Senor Gomez was hazy. Like a terrible dream, catching her in its sticky net—but this one couldn't be banished by waking. It was all too real. And she had seen things like this before.

Someone was dead.

She carefully laid her lute aside and moved slowly toward Senor Gomez. His frozen stillness broke, and he looked at her with desperation in his eyes. He held out his hands, and Kate saw they were shaking beneath the streaks of blood.

"El está muerto," he gasped.

"He?" Kate asked gently, making herself move slowly, deliberately, to stay calm. When she had faced such terrible situations in the past, at Westminster Abbey and Nonsuch Palace, she had discovered that flying into a panic only made matters worse. So she remained calm, no matter how much she longed to scream and run away.

Something terrible had obviously just happened, in the queen's own palace. Running away to hide was clearly not a good idea.

She quickly glanced back, and caught Lady

Catherine's eye. Lady Catherine did not seem to be as panicked as her friends, and she quickly nodded. She gathered Lady Jane and the others, and quieted their shrieks.

Kate turned back to Senor Gomez. "Who is dead, senor? Was there a duel?"

He shook his head, and something inside him seemed to snap with the movement. His face crumpled. "Come with me, senorita. I think you are the only one who can help keep everyone calm in this moment."

He spun around and ran, so fast that Kate could barely keep up with him. The guards followed her, staying close, and behind them was the French ambassador.

It was a cold day, but very still with little wind. Kate could feel the iciness down to her bones, but she pushed it away and kept moving forward. Senor Gomez led them to one of the spiral-shaped herbal beds, brown and crackling-dry with the winter. In its center, sprawled faceup, was Senor Vasquez.

Or at least Kate thought it must be Senor Vasquez, because of his clothing—a midnight blue satin doublet she remembered him wearing at the queen's banquet—and his dark hair. His throat had been cut, and dark blood splashed his lower face and his chest, matted in his hair and beard. His eyes were open and glassy, staring sightlessly up at the gray sky. Senor

Gomez knelt beside him with a choked sob.

Kate swallowed a cold, sickening wave of nausea, and made herself tiptoe closer. She quickly scanned the herbal bed around him, the raked gravel path that showed no footsteps, the way a few of the dry branches were snapped. Though it was near midday, the gardens were empty, since the queen had not yet taken her daily walk and everyone else was tucked up near a fireside or practicing their dancing. She would ask later if any servant or stray courtier had seen anything, but she doubted they had.

"Did you find him thus, Senor Gomez?" she said gently.

He nodded, still staring at his dead friend. "He said he had an errand today for Bishop de Quadra, but we were to meet later at the tennis court for a game. I was late this morning, and as I was making my way there, I—I found him thus."

"And there was no one else nearby at all?" Kate asked.

Senor Gomez shook his head. "I saw no one at all."

Kate leaned down to carefully examine Senor Vasquez's body, knowing that these early moments were vital and she would not have another chance. She bit back the sick feeling, and made herself treat the scene as if it was a masque.

The smell, a coppery tang, was somewhat disguised by the cold. The blood was still a bright red, not much matted, which meant the wound should be fairly fresh. Had he met someone here in the garden, as he had with Lord Macintosh?

Senor Vasquez clutched a dagger in his hand, his fingers curled around the hilt like a claw. The blood was clotting on the blade. It appeared to be a scene of suicide, Senor Vasquez coming to the garden to kneel on the gravel path and slit his own throat. It was not impossible; Kate remembered his melancholy demeanor, his strange words, not to mention his mysterious plotting.

Yet something was not right about such a sinful scenario. It nagged at the back of Kate's mind as she scanned the gruesome scene again, trying to see what was amiss. Then she realized what it was. The dagger was in Senor Vasquez's *right* hand, and the deepest cut was on the left side, growing thinner as it moved to the right. Yet when she had sat beside him at the queen's banquet, he had kept nudging her as he cut his meat with his *left* hand.

Even Kate knew if he cut his own throat he would use his dominant hand, and the wound would slash toward the other direction.

"What is the meaning of this?" someone demanded furiously. The gaping crowd parted to let Bishop de Quadra through. His aristocratic face looked dark and thunderous, his hands curled into fists against his rich black velvet robes. That expression changed at the sight that greeted him, falling into shocked dismay. He made the sign of the cross.

Kate stood up and slipped away through the people who were still gathering in the garden, many of them. She didn't want to be noticed any more than she already had been.

She saw that Senor Gomez had also vanished.

As she hurried back toward the palace, she saw Robert Dudley and his guards rush out, still dressed for the hunt. She glimpsed Cecil's bearded face at one of the windows. If the privy council had heard word of what happened, that meant the queen would know as well.

Kate had to go to her right away.

"Whatever drove that poor man to commit such a sin is terribly sad," the queen said, anger tightly leashed in her voice. "But why did he have to do it in *my* garden? And in the midst of our Yule season?"

Elizabeth stood by the window in her bed-chamber, the glass open to let the chilliness inside, fighting against the warmth of the fire. Her ladies sat on their stools and cushions, sewing, playing cards, whispering, pretending not to stare fearfully at the queen.

"I do not think Senor Vasquez killed himself, Your Grace," Kate said quietly.

Elizabeth spun around to face Kate, her dark eyes burning in her white face. "What do you mean?"

Kate quickly explained what she had seen in the

garden—the dagger in the wrong hand, the way the blood had fallen.

"So he was meeting someone in the garden, someone who murdered him?" Elizabeth muttered. "The Spanish can be irksome, I admit, and everyone can be short-tempered when closed in here together by the cold weather. But why him in particular?"

"His friend Senor Gomez did say he wondered if Senor Vasquez had a—a romantic attachment of some sort," Kate said. "He said he once glimpsed Senor Vasquez with a red-haired lady, but that he denied any romance. He was very devout, which seems to be another reason why he would not kill himself, I think."

"A red-haired lady?" Elizabeth said sharply. "You *do* keep your ears open, Kate. Very clever. But he did not know who this lady was? If this was a mere personal disagreement, we could avoid much trouble, I think."

Kate shook her head. "Senor Vasquez did not really seem the flirtatious sort, Your Grace, though he did seem to have a secret."

"And what was that?"

Kate told the queen of her encounter with Senor Vasquez and Lord Macintosh in the garden, what she had overheard between the two unlikely conspirators. "I wonder if the red-haired lady could be the *she* Lord Macintosh said seemed reluctant."

"Lord Macintosh was keeping secrets with a *Spaniard?*" Elizabeth hissed. "What could they have in common? And both of them dare come here, demanding *my* help for their wretched causes. . . ."

"The Bishop de Quadra begs an audience with you, Your Grace," a page boy announced from across the room.

Elizabeth tapped her coronation ring on the windowsill, her lips pursed. "Z'wounds, but I suppose I must see the man now. We will speak more of this later, Kate. In the meantime . . ." She paused, her dark eyes glittering with a hard, diamond light, glancing in the direction of her whispering ladies clustered on the other side of the room.

"Your Grace?"

"When the Spanish are here, perhaps you could take a glance at Senor Vasquez's belongings before they are packed away? If he is indeed involved in some conspiracy, with the Scots or anyone else, mayhap he was foolish enough to leave some letters lying about. Or something to lead us to this red-haired lady."

Kate only had time to nod before the queen gestured for de Quadra to be admitted. The bishop always seemed to be dressed for mourning in his black cassocks, but today there was fury as well as sorrow on his heavy-jowled face.

"Your Grace," he said, his accent heavier than

usual, "thank you for seeing me on such a sorrowful day."

"Indeed, Bishop," Elizabeth answered. "Trust my word, we shall find out what happened. The happy relationship between England and my brother's kingdom cannot be marred. . . ."

Kate slipped out of the room and made her way up the nearest staircase, down the twisting corridors to the wing where the Spanish embassy was housed, safely distant from the French. When Elizabeth first took the throne and the Count de Feria was King Philip's ambassador, they had stayed at Durham House on the Strand, once the home of Duke of Northumberland—and the site of Lady Jane Grey's lavish wedding to Guildford Dudley, as well as her sister Lady Catherine's union to the heir of the Earl of Pembroke, whom Lady Catherine did not seem to greatly miss. But Elizabeth had soon realized it was wiser to keep the Spanish closer and under her observation.

Not that close watch had stopped what happened to the unfortunate Senor Vasquez.

Vasquez had shared a small chamber with Senor Gomez beyond the bishop's lavish reception rooms, where King Philip's portrait watched over the scarlet velvets and carved chairs and tables of his embassy. She had not been sure how to get past the watchful Spanish servants, but even they seemed to be in hiding after what had happened.

The king's painted eyes watched over an empty room. But she knew she had to be quick.

The small room was filled with the two narrow beds, their dark green wool curtains drawn back, two desks, two stools, and a few carved clothes chests. The desks were covered with piles of documents, no doubt secretarial work for the bishop, along with inkpots and books.

Kate scanned the titles stamped on the leather covers. Theological works, mostly, in Spanish and a few in Latin. The papers, too, were in Spanish, and her small knowledge of the language was enough to see they would tell her little of Senor Vasquez's personal business.

She knelt down beside the chest carved with the initials *JldeV*. One of Cecil's agents had taught her once how to pick locks, and she used one of her ivory hairpins to make quick work of the padlock. She had to push away a prickling feeling of guilt at so invading a dead man's privacy, but she hoped he might forgive her if it helped her find who had killed him.

She pushed aside the dark-colored doublets, the shirts and hose, but she could find no sign of any secret romances or political plots.

There were more books at the bottom, poetry, it seemed, and one with rather shocking engravings of bare-breasted women. She gave a sniff at the sight of them, and riffled the cheap, thin pages to be sure nothing was hidden between them. She felt around the edges of the chest to see if there was a false bottom or hidden drawers, yet to her disappointment there was naught to be found.

She sat back on her heels to study the small room, and saw Senor Gomez's vihuela propped beside the fireplace. A thick stack of musical manuscripts sat next to it.

A few of them were marked with Senor Vasquez's initials, the same ones carved on the chest, and she studied them. Just madrigals, mostly, and some music for church services. But one, near the bottom of the pile, was very strange. It was laid out like a song, but the notes were not like any she had ever seen. Tiny squiggles and curves, some of them in different colors of ink. It reminded her of the Plato she had been studying at Cecil's behest, the method of using music as a code. It also made her think of something else, something just beyond the edge of her memory. . . .

Kate heard a muffled laugh from the next room, a burst of words in Spanish. She quickly tucked the strange music under her wide velvet over-sleeve and made her way out of the chamber, after making sure everything was left in order behind her. She kept to the edges of the reception room, scurrying out before the two maidservants could see her.

She hurried to her father's room, passing courtiers who whispered together in doorways, their faces pale and shocked as word passed of what had happened in the garden.

Matthew was sitting by his fire, his gouty leg propped on a cushioned stool, a book open before him. A pitcher of wine and a bowl of the queen's favorite candied suckets sat on a table nearby. It was a most cozy scene.

"Kate, my dearest," he called when he saw her, "you are just in time. Gerald and the Parks are just on their way to join me for some wine."

"I am glad I got here before them, then," she said, going to sit on the stool beside his chair. "You have heard of the poor Spaniard in the garden?"

Matthew frowned. "Indeed, the maid told me when she brought the wine. Dreadful matter. The Spanish and their strange ways. After the days of Queen Mary . . ."

Kate swallowed hard and nodded. She remembered the dark days at the close of Queen Mary's reign, when her father had been tossed into a damp, dank gaol and she had feared for his very life. The days when everyone feared that Queen Mary's Spanish husband had brought the ways of his country to England. Those days could never come again. The only way to keep them at bay, to keep England safe, was to make sure Elizabeth stayed securely on the throne. "I fear Queen Elizabeth thinks there is something even more sinister to the matter."

His frown deepened. "What do you mean?"

She quickly took the music from her sleeve and laid it out for him to see. She told him of Senor Vasquez and his possible murder, as briefly as she could, and she said nothing of how she had actually come to have the music in her possession. Her father did not need to know *everything* she did at court.

"What do you think of this?" she asked.

Her father's eyes brightened as she examined the music. "This makes no sense, even as some strange Spanish church music. What is it?"

"I am not sure yet. I have had some lessons on the vihuela of late, but I don't think these notes would work even on that."

"Quite right, quite right." He looked up at her for a long moment, his eyes searching, full of worry, but he said nothing. "Can you leave it with me for a while, my dear? I will take a closer look, compare it to some other works."

"Of course."

"Perhaps we could show it to Gerald and the Parks also?"

She could see how that might be of benefit, as Master Finsley and the Parks had long experience with all sorts of music and with courtly life as well. But something held her back, told her that the fewer people who knew of this paper right now the better. "Not as yet, I think."

He nodded, and as a knock sounded at the

door he tucked the document away behind his chair cushion. Mistress Park hurried in, with her husband on one arm and Master Finsley on the other.

"Oh, Kate, my dear girl!" Hester Park cried as she kissed Kate's cheek and settled herself in the cushioned chair across the fire from Matthew's. Master Finsley and Master Park took the stools, and Kate saw that Master Finsley carried his lute. "How happy I am to see you today. When we heard of the poor young man in the garden—saints preserve us. What a terrible thing to happen during the queen's Yule."

Kate studied Mistress Park's bright eyes, her reddened cheeks. It seemed she had missed something of court intrigue in her retirement. "It is a terrible thing. You must be sorry you have left your comfortable cottage to return to court."

Mistress Park shook her head and reached for the fruit suckets. Kate poured out wine for everyone. "Oh, my dear, we were here during Queen Cat Howard's time, so long ago! We have seen such matters, and worse, before. The poor young queen dragged off to the Tower, screaming. So many arrests and rumors. One man was even poisoned at a banquet, right in front of us! Do you remember that, Edward? I think he was Italian, from the court of Florence. . . ."

Her husband chuckled, almost as if poisonings and beheadings had taken on some glow of nostalgia. "Indeed I do, Hester. Everyone then was sure it must have been the anchovies. Such a vile thing to eat, even in Lent. But it turned out to be his wife who did it, was it not?"

"So it was." Hester clucked. "Shocking. Perhaps it was the same with this young man. Do they say he had a lover, Kate?"

"Hester," Matthew said reprovingly, "Kate is much too occupied with her work, not to mention too young, to concern herself with such matters."

If he only knew . . . Kate thought wryly. In her year at court, she had seen many flirtations and romantic plottings, not to mention stranglings and poisonings and thefts.

Hester laughed. "Fie, Matthew! I was much younger than her when I married Edward and came to court, and you and Eleanor were just as young. Kate must listen to gossip, as everyone does who wants to survive at court."

"I have heard nothing like that about Senor Vasquez," Kate said quickly. "Only that he maybe was seen strolling with a lady by the river."

"The man *was* Spanish, Hester," Master Finsley said. "They use up all the heat of their blood in prayers, surely, and not for romances."

Hester sighed. "So sad for them. I heard this Senor Vasquez was quite handsome, if rather dour. In Queen Catherine Parr's time, Senor Mendoza was still the Spanish ambassador after so many years. He was completely gray and could scarce walk with the gout. I thought him so ancient then." She wistfully patted at the silvery curls peeking from under her cap.

"But Queen Catherine's court was scarcely dull," Master Finsley said.

"Not at all," Hester agreed. " 'Tis why we are not so easily shocked now, Kate my dear! Even a lady as great and virtuous as Queen Catherine was ever followed by gossip."

Kate thought of Queen Elizabeth and the drawing left in her room, and the rumors about Elizabeth, Queen Catherine, and Thomas Seymour that still persisted. "Such as when King Henry thought to accuse Queen Catherine of treason?"

Hester's eyes widened with surprise as she looked at Kate. "Do you remember those days, my dear? You would have been the merest child."

Kate shook her head. "I must have heard Queen Elizabeth speak of it."

"Queen Catherine was like a mother to her," Edward said. "It would have been a great tragedy if her enemies had succeeded in their plots to overthrow Queen Catherine, as Queen Anne was."

"A tragedy for us who served her, as well," Hester said. "Though we lost Queen Catherine soon enough, when she died in childbed only a few years later."

"Though 'twas a blessing for her she never saw the trouble her scoundrel of a husband Tom Seymour got himself into," Edward said.

Hester clucked again, and popped another cherry sucket into her mouth.

"Does Queen Elizabeth often speak of her step-mother, Kate?" Gerald Finsley asked quietly.

Kate turned to look at him. He watched her steadily with his faded pale eyes. "She does remember Queen Catherine with great fondness," she said carefully. She did not speak of the sorrow Elizabeth had shown over her step-mother and what happened with Tom Seymour.

"Queen Elizabeth owes much to that lady," Hester said. "Queen Catherine sheltered her from a great deal. Such as . . ."

"Surely Queen Elizabeth brought much joy to Queen Catherine as well," Matthew interrupted sternly. "Queen Catherine longed for children, and Queen Elizabeth was like a daughter to her, no matter what foul gossip persists. But we have not come together to remember such a dark past today! We have little time together, my friends. Let us play some music. Gerald, I see you have brought your lute. Shall we play something for Christmas?"

"Aye, Matthew, a fine idea," Master Finsley said, reaching for his instrument. "Kate, will you sing?"

Kate nodded, and settled in for an hour of her favorite thing—music with friends.

As Kate tried to make her way back to her chamber later, she found her path blocked by a crowd that grew thicker and thicker, pressing her in with fur sleeves and embroidered trains. The heavy, humid scent of French perfumes and burning oils from the braziers in the corner, the high laughter and nervous chatter, closed around her in the shadows created by torchlight and tapestries.

After what had happened in the garden, the crowd and its constant surging movement was almost too much. Kate found herself glad that so much of the time she could hide above everyone's heads in the musicians' gallery—though the queen did seem to have required her presence at the courtly balls and banquets more and more of late.

Kate suddenly froze in the midst of the crowd, and it felt as if she was caught in a dream moment. Everyone's movements seemed to slow down to a brightly colored blur, their laughter like the indistinct hum of summer insects. Their splendor was too much of a contrast to the silent body in the garden.

Kate knew she had to find out what was happening, to protect the queen, but could she do it? The vast palace and everything in it seemed so overwhelming.

A sudden jostling push sent her stumbling out of the tight knot of the crowd to the front of the corridor, and the dream snapped back into sharp-edged reality. Just like the musical code in

Plato—when things were looked at just a bit differently, a whole new pattern was revealed.

"Pardon, mistress," the man who jostled her said.

As Kate gave him a small curtsy in reply, she noticed that the wave of people had drawn back a bit to make room for a group of men hurrying along the corridor. Unlike the peacock vividness of most of the courtiers, they were clad in somber, sensible blacks and dark browns, albeit of fine velvet and trimmed with fur. Their arms were filled with papers and books, their voices low and intent. They had some errand.

And Kate quickly saw why. They were Sir William Cecil's secretaries, and the work of the queen's chief secretary never ended. She glimpsed Cecil himself in their midst, nodding at something one of his men was whispering. Sir William was not an old man at all, yet he always looked beyond his years. But his eyes were always bright and alert, always watching.

"Ah, Mistress Haywood," Cecil called as he drew near, and caught sight of her hovering at the edge of the crowd. The people near her looked at her with surprise, as if they had not seen her there before. "Well met, I think. Come, walk with me for a moment."

Kate nodded and fell into step beside him.

"What think you of this unfortunate Spanish business?" he said.

"I—I hardly know what to think, Sir William."

"You knew the Vasquez fellow?"

"A bit. I talked to him at a banquet, and his cousin has helped me with some music. He thought Senor Vasquez might have some secret romance, but I know of nothing specific. He seemed rather an unusual man, with few courtly skills, but I have heard of nothing that could have led to—this." She glanced back to see if anyone was close enough to overhear her before she went up on tiptoe to whisper in Cecil's ear. "I did overhear something most odd, though." She told him of the strange conversation between Lord Macintosh and Senor Vasquez.

Cecil merely nodded, his expression never changing, as if such conspiracies were part of his everyday life. As indeed they were. "He was secretary to Bishop de Quadra, of course. The bishop is most angry, and relations with Spain are so delicate as it is. We have so many other things to worry about at the moment, this cannot be allowed to interfere. I am sure the bishop will merely say he cannot know everything his secretaries are up to here at court."

Kate nodded, thinking of the Scots and the French, of the queen's many suitors who pressed around her. "What has the queen told you? I know she was to meet with you after she saw the bishop, Sir William."

"She has, rather reluctantly, agreed to stay in

her chamber under guard for the moment," Cecil said with a flicker of a frown. Kate could well imagine the "reluctant" part; the queen did so hate to be confined in any way. "But she will not stay there long. Not while there are Christmas festivities to be had. To quiet the bishop for the moment, I am on my way to speak to Lord Macintosh of the Scots delegation. He was known to have quarreled with Gomez."

Kate nodded, and remembered what she had overheard between the Spanish secretary and the Scotsman. Though she still did not understand it at all, she quickly told Cecil about their conversation. "Could he truly have done this?"

Cecil shrugged, but Kate could see the wary, speculative gleam in his eyes. "Ah, Mistress Haywood, I know you have seen what men are capable of when their passionate anger is roused, or their fortunes are at stake. It is a sad fact that far too many do not pause to consider the consequences."

Kate had indeed seen such things often at court, where feelings and ambitions ran so high. "But Lord Macintosh came here for a much higher purpose than to quarrel with one Spaniard, surely."

Cecil suddenly touched her sleeve and she felt the tension in his hand. "This Scots project is of utmost importance to the safety of Queen Elizabeth. She may have dismissed such knowledge in favor of Christmas frivolity with that blasted Dudley, but I must make sure she remembers it. Mary of Scots and her French mother threaten the English throne."

Kate swallowed hard. "But surely Lord Macintosh must be just as passionate about his course. If he seeks Scottish independence from France . . ."

Cecil gave her a crooked smile. "My dear Mistress Haywood, your youth and dedication do serve the queen well, and I think you are a great asset to her. Yet surely you know by now that some men do not let their best interests rule their emotions as they should."

"I have seen that, Sir William."

He gave her a wry smile. "But you would wish it otherwise?"

Kate nodded, even though she felt rather naive in the face of all his knowledge. She *did* wish to think the best of people, even when she was faced with the facts of their greediness, their lust. She needed to know that there was a more noble purpose to their work here at court. "Of course I would wish it otherwise. But I know it cannot always be so. Human nature will not allow it."

Cecil nodded. "Will you come with me to speak with Lord Macintosh now, Mistress Haywood? You were of much help last summer at Nonsuch when I had to question young Master Green."

Kate thought of the days when Violet's now-husband was locked in a village gaol, his quarrel with another young man misunderstood—as perhaps was the case now. "I would be happy to help, if I can. I am learning to be a good listener."

"Indeed you are. It comes from the musical training, no doubt." He shook his head, his shovel-shaped beard trembling. "I never had the patience for such myself."

Kate remembered how Cecil sat at his desk for hour upon hour, reading stacks of letters with their tiny, cramped, often coded writing by candlelight, never tiring, seldom giving in to his wife's entreaties to rest. Only Queen Elizabeth could match him for energy, though hers was of the restless, dancing, never-still type. "I do not think impatience is a fault you can claim, Sir William."

He laughed. It was a sound heard so seldom in the palace corridors that Kate almost stopped in her tracks in surprise, and his secretaries looked at him with wide eyes. "I would never finish my tasks if that was so. And how are you coming with the Plato manuscripts I sent you, Mistress Haywood?"

"I find them most interesting. The idea of using musical cadences for messages must be very useful."

"Good, good. I think that once we understand the Platonic idea, it should be simple enough to come up with our very own English code, don't you?"

Before Kate could answer, they reached the wing of the palace where the Scots were assigned their rooms, far from the Spanish. It was quieter there, the gallery facing away from the river. A guard in Cecil's livery waited outside one of the closed doors, but other than that it was perfectly silent in the corridor, the hum of lively conversation and games, the gossip of murders, far away.

"Is Lord Macintosh not under heavier guard?" Kate whispered, thinking of the Scotsman's burly shoulders.

"He has nowhere to go," Cecil answered. "Besides, he claims steadfastly he knew little of Senor Gomez's doings, though they were acquainted, and he was not in the garden today at all. In fact, he says he has an alibi, though he will not yet say what it is."

"Do you believe him?"

"What you overheard certainly makes me wonder, Mistress Haywood—though I do not believe anyone, as a matter of principle. Let us just ask him, shall we?" Sir William nodded at the guard, who quickly swung the door open. Cecil gestured to most of his men to wait in the corridor, taking only Kate and two others with him.

It was a small room, much like Kate's own at the other end of the palace, with a narrow window at one side and a fireplace at the other, and furnished with a narrow bed, a desk, a traveling trunk. Lord Macintosh paced from one end to the other, needing only a few steps to do so. She remembered him at the banquet, dancing, laughing with the other Scotsmen—and she also remembered him arguing with Senor Gomez.

At Cecil's appearance, Macintosh went very still and swung around to face them like a wild animal in the menagerie.

"Well, Lord Macintosh," Sir William said without letting Macintosh speak first. His voice was most affable, as if he merely greeted the man on a stroll in the gallery. "We hear you knew poor Senor Gomez rather better than might be expected, aye?" He lowered himself carefully into the room's one chair, wincing at his rheumatism, and Kate had to resist the urge to help him, as she did her father. She stayed near the door, trying to be unobtrusive.

Lord Macintosh ran his hand through his reddish hair, leaving it standing on end. "I knew him, aye, but everyone at a royal court knows everyone else," he said, his Scots brogue thick. "It is our duty."

"But surely your quarrel here is with France? What was your business with Senor Gomez?"

Macintosh studied Cecil carefully, and something in Sir William's steady gaze and unwavering little smile seemed to convince the Scotsman that dissembling would not work. He did not seem good at it anyway; he struck Kate as more a battlefield sort than a courtier. "When we arrived here, Senor Vasquez did approach me that evening. I confess I had drunk too much of your queen's good wine, and he offered to help me to find my chamber. He seemed a quiet sort of man, and his cousin was most friendly too, so I agreed. On the way, he said they had heard my fortune was not so great . . ."

"And is it not?" Cecil asked.

Macintosh scowled. "Nay, not now, not after the French took over so much in my homeland. Senor Vasquez told me his master wished to offer me a bargain in exchange for my help, for aid against our common enemy France. 'Tis true I have no liking for Spaniards, but better them than the French. I saw no harm in talking to him. Until I found out he thinks your English throne would be better occupied by another. Not Queen Mary, but I still told him nay."

Kate studied Macintosh carefully, wondering if the man could truly be as dim-minded as he sounded now, and if so why had he been chosen by the Scots as part of their vital delegation? She glanced at one of Cecil's secretaries, whose raised brows seemed to say the same thing.

"Why did you not go to Queen Elizabeth immediately?" Cecil said, his voice still calm and quiet. "Her Grace is most gracious and generous to those who are loyal to her, and she values honesty above all."

Macintosh frowned, seeming confused by Cecil's very calmness. "I—well, I thought to learn more to bring Her Grace more information."

"Indeed? Most clever of you. What did you learn?"

"Naught, for there was no time. Vasquez claimed they had proof Queen Elizabeth was not the rightful queen, and that we should be negotiating with another power, but he died before he brought it to me."

"Aye, a most convenient demise. If you were angry with him that he would not give you such information immediately, or that he did not pay you whatever amount you agreed on for your help . . ."

"Nay!" Macintosh shouted, his tone growing more desperate. "I am no traitor, not to Scotland. I knew Vasquez was wrong, and aye, I was angry that he tried to draw me into Spanish schemes, but I could not have killed him. I promise you that, Sir William, and I will gladly go to my knees before the queen and beg her pardon."

"Why don't you just first tell us what you know. There will be time for begging the queen later. And you can start by telling us where you were earlier today, when you claim you could not have been in the garden."

Macintosh glanced at Kate. "I was with a lady."

"Of course," Cecil answered. "And does the lady have a name?"

Macintosh looked again at Kate, and she just smiled at him.

"Ah, I see, a gentleman who will not speak of such things before a lady," Cecil said. "You can tell us her name once Mistress Haywood has left us, but in the meantime she is assisting me. Tell me what Senor Vasquez offered for your help in this scheme. I assume it was a plan to replace Queen Elizabeth and then negotiate with whoever this new monarch was to be to oust the French army?"

Put in such plain terms, it sounded like treason of the highest sort, and Macintosh knew it. He collapsed at the edge of the narrow bed, his hands over his face. "I never would have let it go further! Gomez and his master are treacherous, as all the Spanish are, and I should never have taken any coin from them at all. I thought the small amount they gave me could hurt no one, that I could find out more. . . ."

"But you discovered you do not have the makings of an intelligencer," Cecil said dismissively. "Once we have settled this matter, you can return to Scotland and fight on the battlefield, then. Just tell us what you know, and if you have any ideas of who could have killed Senor Vasquez. It sounds as if he must have made many people angry."

"Indeed I am sure he did," Macintosh said eagerly. "I cannot have been the only one he approached."

Cecil nodded. He gestured to Kate, who leaned down to hear his whisper. "We will find out about this supposed rendezvous, Mistress Haywood, if you could perhaps take a small look at the Spanish chambers tomorrow afternoon? They will be quiet then. I will speak to you later. I would like to hear your thoughts about the players in this little scene."

Kate nodded and hurried from the room. At the door, she glanced back to see Lord Macintosh watching her. Something about his frown, his puzzled expression, unsettled her, and she happily left the quiet wing of the palace for the crowded corridors that had seemed too noisy earlier. Now, they seemed an escape.

CHAPTER THIRTEEN

Later that night

"They say Senor Vasquez was in love with a merchant's daughter, who was betrothed to her father's elderly business partner, and the father found them together and had Senor Vasquez murdered!" Violet Green whispered, her eyes wide and bright with romantic tears. "Is that not tragically sad? The poor man seemed so very dour, so—so Spanish. Could he really have had such romance in him?"

"Oh, Vi," Kate whispered back. They sat in a corner of the queen's presence chamber, embroidering as they watched Elizabeth receive yet more Christmas gifts from her many suitors' ambassadors. It was a scene of great splendor, Elizabeth in a gown of forest green velvet embroidered with rubies and pearls that was as rich as the red-and-gold canopy of state over her head. The array of gifts on the long table before her sparkled as the ambassadors read out odes to her great beauty and virtue. But it was also a very long scene, and looked as if it would go on even longer, which made for some dull moments. No wonder such poetical fancies were flying about.

Kate herself had considered just such a thing,

as her fingers automatically and none too skillfully plied her needle. But Senor Vasquez's romance seemed unlikely.

"That is certainly a most . . . specific tale," she whispered to Violet. "Where did you hear it?"

"From Lady Southerland," Violet answered, turning the blackwork cuffs of the tiny smock she was making for her baby. "And she said she heard it from Lady Hunsdon herself. Is it not a sad one?"

"Sad—and probably not true," Kate said.

Violet gave a sad frown. "Nay, perhaps not. But what then did happen, do you suppose?"

As the Swedes moved forward with gifts from King Erik, Bishop de Quadra stepped to the side of the crowded chamber, near to Monsieur de Castelnau and the French. The two men bowed to each other with ostentatious politeness.

Kate pretended to have her head bent over the embroidery, but she saw when Senor Gomez slipped away from the rest of his group.

She murmured an excuse to Violet and laid aside her embroidery to follow him. It was most unusual for anyone to leave a royal audience, but Senor Gomez did look rather pale, the lines of strain on his face making him look older than the handsome, charming man who had taught her a song on the vihuela.

She found him at the far end of the waterside gallery. The space was almost deserted, as everyone was gathered where the queen was, but his dark clothes made him blend into the late-afternoon shadows as he stared out the window at the river.

She was struck by how very much he looked like Senor Vasquez. Up close, the two men were rather different, Senor Vasquez's features being sharper, leaner, but from such a distance they were both tall and fashionably slim, dark-haired, bearded, with Spanish-cut clothes. Was it possible someone had mistaken Senor Vasquez for his friend in the garden? He was the one who played the vihuela, even though the strange music had borne Senor Vasquez's initials.

Was Senor Gomez involved in the scheme with the Scots as well? Or was it something else altogether, something she had yet to piece together? Something commonplace, like the romance Violet spoke of? Jealousy, greed? A religious mania?

She moved slowly toward Senor Gomez, her silk skirt with its quilted underkirtle rustling in the silence. He glanced up, and gave an automatic-looking smile. Yet his eyes were still shadowed.

"Senorita Haywood," he said.

"Senor Gomez," she answered. "I wanted to tell you how truly sorry I am for the loss of your friend. I know how bleak it can feel to have those we care for suddenly snatched away."

His smile turned sad, more true. "We should

be accustomed to such things, should we not? Plagues, battles . . ."

"Childbed fever," Kate murmured, thinking of her own mother, of Queen Catherine Parr.

"We can all be carried away in an instant."

"Yet the way Senor Vasquez was taken was . . . different."

His jaw tightened under his close-cropped beard. "Jeronimo feared God, as a good Catholic should. He would not do such a thing, such a vile sin."

Kate thought of the dagger in the wrong hand. "You think he was murdered?"

If he was shocked by the word, he did not show it. "All I know is this, senorita: He would not have done that to himself."

"You said once he might have a ladylove. Could she know about his death?"

Senor Gomez laughed roughly. "He claimed he knew no such lady, so I could not say. I do hope he took some comfort in such a way before he was taken from the world, but he was so very austere."

"Did he take any comfort in music, as you do?"

"He did play the lute, as any gentleman should, but I do not think he loved it as you and I do."

Kate nodded, wondering again who the strange music actually belonged to. "So he did not write songs himself?"

"Not that I know, senorita. Why do you ask?"

Kate shrugged. "I am always curious about people and their music, I fear. I only wanted to tell you how sorry I am, senor."

"You are kind, Senorita Haywood. In Spain, they say the English are rough and barbaric. I am happy to say I have not found it so at all."

Kate gave a quiet laugh. "We hear that the Spanish are dour and shun all merriment. I have not always found that to be so, either."

She left Senor Gomez alone with his grief as she made her way back down the gallery. Her conversation with him had only left her with more questions.

Before she could return to the presence chamber, she caught a glimpse of a glossy black satin gown swirling around a corner as a lady ran away from the queen's audience. Curious, Kate hurried to follow, and was surprised to see it was Lady Catherine Grey fleeing the crowd. Lady Catherine glanced back once, but she didn't seem to see Kate. She disappeared through a doorway, and by the time Kate could catch up she had vanished.

Rob appeared suddenly, stopping to watch the gathering, unaware that Kate was so close. Kate studied him closely. He smiled with his usual flirtatious expression, but his eyes were solemn. She did need help, and Rob, despite his mysterious ways, had proven himself trustworthy in the past.

"Can I show you something, Rob?" she asked quietly. "I would greatly like your advice on a matter I think might be of some importance."

Rob pushed himself away from the wall, suddenly entirely serious. "Of course I will help, if I can. Are you in some danger, Kate? As you were with that sad business of Nell?" Kate swallowed hard at the reminder of Nell, the pretty, red-haired Southwark goose who had been killed during the queen's coronation—and had once been Rob's mistress. "I do not think it is like that. I'm not sure yet what is happening. It is like a song where all the notes are jumbled."

He frowned in puzzlement. "What do you mean?"

"Come with me. I will show you." Kate took Rob's hand to lead him from the corridor. She glanced back over her shoulder, but Lady Catherine hadn't reappeared. Kate would just have to deal with her later.

She took Rob up to her father's chamber, where she had left the strange Spanish music for Matthew to look at. She knew the room would be empty, for her father and his friends had borrowed one of the queen's litters to go buy some paper and ink. She quickly sorted through the sheaves of her father's new music tucked into his portable desk until she found it.

She held it out to Rob. "What do you make of this?"

Rob frowned at the closely written characters. He carried it to the small window and held it up to the light to better read it. "I do not understand this at all. It's like no music I have ever seen, even ancient church music."

"I know. See this character here, and this one? Then they're repeated." Kate stood at his shoulder and pointed out some of the parts that had puzzled her the most.

He turned it to look at it from another angle. "Where did you get this?"

Kate hesitated. She did trust Rob, aye—but how *much* did she trust him?

He looked down at her, his gaze steady. "Kate. You *are* in danger, aren't you?"

"Worse. I fear the queen might be."

He glanced back at the paper. "Does this code belong to Her Grace?"

"It is a code, then?"

"It must be. Lord Hunsdon is cousin to the queen, a man with many alliances and enemies. He knows how to use the talents of his retainers. I have carried a few messages for him since he engaged my actors."

Kate smiled. Surely if Lord Hunsdon trusted Rob fully, she could as well? But she worried about what those "messages" might be. Rob had too much of a propensity for trouble already. But actors, like musicians, could go places no one else could, practically unnoticed, and they had a high rate of literacy and sharp memories. "Have you seen this code before?"

"I am not sure. Mayhap something very like. It is not English, is it?"

"I think it must belong to a Spaniard. Look how the letters are formed." He looked at her again, his eyes narrowed. "Was this in the possession of the man who slit his own throat in the garden?"

Kate swallowed hard. "I am not sure yet. Maybe it was his."

"And this is some scheme that endangers the queen?"

"How could it not be? I am not at all sure he killed himself. Mayhap something—or someone— is in the castle. And if that is the case, the queen could be in danger."

Rob studied the document for a moment more before he folded it and tucked it away in his elaborately slashed and puffed sleeve. "Come with me, Kate."

Puzzled but intrigued, Kate followed him out of the room and up yet another flight of stairs and down a crooked corridor to one of the newer wings of the palace. There seemed to be innumerable chambers there, wedged in wherever there was a bit of space, to house some of the hundreds of people who clustered around the queen.

Rob led her into a long narrow chamber lined with beds and clothes chests, each closed off from the others by screens and curtains. It reminded Kate of the dormitories that accommodated the young maids of honor, rows of ladies watched over by the Mistress of the Maids. But not always so strict that there was no time for midnight feasts and practical jokes. Kate had lodged with them enough at the beginning of the queen's reign to know that though it could certainly be merry, it was also exhausting.

And distracting—there was no quiet time for writing music, or privacy for carrying out the queen's more secret errands. She was most grateful to have her own chamber now, no matter how tiny, or how much jealousy it attracted from those who did not merit court lodgings.

But Rob didn't seem to mind his accommodations at all. The room was quiet at that hour, with everyone else off seeking card games or playing tennis at the indoor courts. He led her to a space at the very end of the row, which she would have known right away was his. His bright green short cloak was tossed on top of the iron-bound chest, and the bedcovers were rumpled. A lute sat in its stand next to a folding traveling stool.

"It's not much, I know," he said with a laugh. "But it is home for now."

He pushed the cloak aside and opened the plain wood clothes chest to take out a small stack of books, which he handed to Kate.

She studied the simple leather covers, with no lettering or embellishment. "What are these?"

"I told you Lord Hunsdon has many interests, many ways of helping his cousin the queen. He gave me these to study." Rob opened the top volume and riffled through the densely written parchment pages. Kate glimpsed lines and drawings, circles bisected and layered with symbols, sketches of strange trees and flowers. It didn't look like any book of sonnets or prayers she had ever seen.

In fact, it rather reminded her of Dr. Dee's alchemical volumes from Nonsuch.

Rob seemed to find what he was looking for. He turned the book around to show the page to Kate. "Do you think this looks somewhat like your strange music?"

Kate peered closer. For an instant, she was sure it looked like nothing at all. A circle, much like Dee's horoscopes, was divided into four smaller circles that were then divided into several segments, each drawn with letters and numbers, and odd symbols, including some musical notes. But as she studied the drawing, suddenly the lines seemed to click together in her mind.

"I see!" she cried. "If the circles are turned this way and lined up, one can tell where to substitute a letter for a musical note." She told him of her recent studies of Plato, and he nodded.

"Or, if it is turned this way, there is something

completely different," Rob said. "One needs the key to break the code, which would be most useful here."

"Does Lord Hunsdon send many letters thus?" Kate asked.

Rob shrugged. His expression was that careless one, a half smile that she had come to distrust. It usually meant he was up to some trouble. "He merely said that an actor, a man who must write quickly and be always studying human nature, might find these books interesting. I am sure men like Cecil and Dudley have similar volumes."

Kate was sure they did. She turned the volume upside down to look at the circles from a new angle. "These *are* most interesting. But could this really be the key to the Spanish music?"

"Perhaps not *the* key, but surely something like it, with these symbols here." He pointed out something that looked a bit like a treble clef. Opposite it was the letter *T* and the number four. "It might give us a place to untangle it."

Kate nodded. "Where did these books come from? They look rather old."

"Lord Hunsdon did not say, but I suspect a monastery. There is a watermark on the endpapers of some of them. The monks of old used to be fascinated with cryptography, I think. But look at this." From the back of one of the other books, he withdrew a loose sheet of parchment.

It seemed to be a sonnet, but not a very good one. The rhymes were strained at best, the images overwrought—a tale of a "silver goddess" who would soon descend from the clouds to save England and bring her into the ways of the light.

"I hope *you* did not write this," she said wryly.

Rob laughed. "If I had, I would not admit it. Nay, it came with this volume as a sort of key. When Lord Hunsdon was living in exile on the Continent, he searched out and compiled many things like this."

Kate quickly compared the letters of the terrible poem to the circles, and began to see other words in their place.

An image flashed through her mind, of Queen Catherine Parr's *Lamentation of a Sinner* in its awkward musical setting. The queen had not been a woman known for her awkwardness in anything; quite the opposite. But Queen Catherine had also had to find a way to keep secrets from a most dangerous husband, the king. Perhaps in music, right in plain sight?

"Rob," she said, excited to have a possible clue to lead them out of confusion. "You are quite splendid!" Impulsively, she went up on tiptoe and kissed his cheek.

He gave her a quizzical glance, suddenly looking rather young and vulnerable. He quickly covered that small glimpse with a smile. "I see

I must find strange books to give you more often. Shall we meet later to look more at your music?"

"Of course, I—" From the corridor beyond the large chamber, there were suddenly the sounds of running feet and a slamming door, reminding Kate that they were never alone at Whitehall, even in their quietest moments.

"Of course," she said. "But it must be someplace where we cannot be found out. . . ."

Lady Catherine Grey slipped into her tiny chamber and pulled the door shut behind herself, closing herself into blessed, dark silence. Lady Jane Seymour, who shared the space, was attending on the queen, as was everyone else, and surely no one would think to come looking for her for a few moments at least.

Catherine sank to the floor amid puffs of her black and white skirts, and buried her face in her hands. She longed for the comfort of one of her little dogs close to her, or the squawks of her parrot, but she dared not go yet to her own chamber. Her maidservant would be there, and would fuss if she saw that Catherine had been crying.

The queen's servants would be there, too, under the guise of laying the fire or delivering wine. But Catherine knew why they were really there. To watch her, and report her every movement, her every word, back to her cousin. Everyone was always, always watching.

Her head was pounding, one of the sick headaches that had plagued her on and off since childhood, gathering in painful streaks behind her eyes. She dragged the pearl-edged headdress from her hair and threw it across the room.

How had everything that seemed so bright and promising only months ago gone so horribly wrong? That summer at Hanworth, the Seymour country estate, was so golden. Long days rowing on the lake, having picnics under the trees, playing at primero, laughing with Jane and her family. And at night . . .

Ah, at night her sweet Ned would kiss her under the moonlight, and whisper that he was hers entirely, that their hearts would always be as one. She had dared to imagine life would always be that way, light and bright and perfect.

Now Ned just put her off. *"Nay, my sweet, your stepfather advises we should wait and gather the support of the privy council before we approach the queen,"* he would say when she pressed him. *"I say he is right. We can be together as we dreamed, but it must be in the right way, a way that preserves your royal rights."*

Her royal rights! As if she cared about that. She had cared once, very much. But she saw what "royal right" did to her sister Jane, to her father, and she wanted none of it. She had seen a better

227

way of life, and she didn't want it to end on the block.

And what did her stepfather know! Adrian Stokes had once been her mother's Master of Horse, as Dudley was to the queen. A man Frances Grey married for the protection of his lowly name, when to be an heir to the Tudor throne was a great peril. And married for love. Aye, even Catherine could admit her mother and Adrian had been much in love. What did he know of maneuvering around the royal court? Her mother would have known, none better, but Frances was gone, and Catherine felt so alone.

With Ned, she had not felt alone. She had felt that the two of them could face anything at all together, and their love would triumph. But now she felt him pulling further away from her, drawn into a world that didn't include her. They even whispered that the queen would soon send him on a mission to France, and he seemed to relish the prospect.

She had tried to fix things herself, and now she feared she had failed at that as well. It had seemed like such a fine idea, to use the schemes of others as they had thought to use her as a mere pawn. By the time they realized they had under-estimated her, it would be too late, and she would have what she wanted. So she had allowed the Spanish to think she agreed with their conspiracies, planning to use it for her own ends.

Yet it was all slipping through her fingers, faster and faster, like a silken scarf, and she feared she might end up like Senor Vasquez. She had made a great mistake, and now she was truly alone. Only the musician, Mistress Haywood, seemed to look at her with any kindness now. In her green eyes, Catherine saw some of her sister Jane, a sort of—seeingness. But without Jane's core of cold steel.

Yet even musicians couldn't be trusted now. For was not Mistress Haywood employed by the queen? And the queen was Catherine's greatest enemy.

"Oh, Mother," she whispered. "What have I done?"

CHAPTER FOURTEEN

The Feast of St. Thomas, December 29

Master Orrens, tiremaker, Monkwell Street, Cripplegate, near St. Olave's Church and the Talbot tavern, just down from the Barbers' Hall.

Kate glanced down at the scrap of paper in her gloved hand, given to her by the clerk in the Office of Revels, and then up at the street around her. She saw the tower of St. Olave's not far away, old, square, solid stone, darkened with decades of city smoke and soot, rising above a crowded churchyard. She had to be near the place.

The crowd, hurrying on their own errands, jostled past her, and she stepped back into a quiet doorway to get her bearings. It was a typical street, narrow and close-packed with houses, but respectable-looking, as befitted the domain of a merchant who sometimes provided services to the royal court. The shops on the lower stories displayed wares such as fine leather-bound books, silk ribbons, and beautifully wrought brooches and rings. A tiremaker, a man who made finely wrought headdresses for the ladies of the court and for theatrical masquerades, would fit in well there. The cobbles of the street were fairly clean, and no laundry linen flapped from the upper windows.

Kate was tempted by the smells of candied almonds, cinnamon, and sugar drifting over from a nearby comfits shop on the cold wind. It had started to snow, great, fat, wet, white flakes falling from the slate gray sky, and even her fine new red cloak and fur-edged cap wouldn't keep out the cold. But there was no time to tarry. She had to be back at Whitehall in time to play for that night's Christmas mummers' mask and the dancing after.

She glanced down the street again, and saw one of the painted signs swinging in the wind. The colors of it had faded, but she could clearly see the image of a wirework crown, edged with something that made it shimmer in the gray daylight.

"Kate!" she heard a man call out, and she spun around, so startled by the sound that she almost tripped on the cobblestones.

It was Anthony Elias, stepping out of one of the shops across the lane. He waved and gave her a tentative smile, which widened when she waved back.

Kate wished her heart hadn't beat just a tiny bit faster at the sight of him after so long. He was as handsome as ever, with his glossy dark hair brushed back under his cap, his eyes as green as a spring day in winter. He wore dark, somber colors, as befit an apprentice lawyer, but in finely woven, well-cut wools and a touch of velvet. A parcel was tucked under his arm.

"Kate," he said as he hurried to her side,

231

dodging dogs and children as he crossed the lane. "You are looking very well."

"And you, Anthony," she answered honestly. He *did* look well—so handsome, as he always had, ever since they first became friends at Hatfield. But something felt different now, some sort of distance.

"I am surprised to see you away from Whitehall," he said. "It must be busy at this time of year."

Kate laughed. "So it is. Queen Elizabeth loves any excuse for a revel, and Yule is her favorite time of year. I am just here to perform a quick errand for her. As you must be, for Master Hardy." She nodded toward the parcel.

"Aye. The Hardys are preparing to go to the country for Twelfth Night, to visit Mistress Hardy's family, and I am to go with them. But business must always come with us."

Kate thought of the young lady she had seen with Anthony on the day she went ice-skating. Mistress Hardy's niece—pretty, sweet, well-born, suitable to make a prosperous lawyer's wife. "I am sure Mistress Hardy's pretty niece goes with you?"

"It is her parents we visit." A faint blush touched his cheeks. He hesitated, as if he wished to say something, but then merely glanced away. "You are on errand for Her Grace, you say?"

"To a tiremaker just along the way," she said carefully. Even though Anthony had helped her before, she wasn't sure how much to tell him now.

"The queen orders new headdresses?"

Kate laughed. "You have become more conversant on ladies' fashion, I see. Though she certainly never says no to new garments, this time she merely had a question for Master Orrens. She had ordered his wares before."

"Let me escort you, then."

"I should not take up your time, Anthony."

He smiled gently. "I have the whole afternoon for you, Kate."

Kate considered this. It would be nice not to go alone to a strange shop—and to have a few more minutes with her friend. Perhaps he would see something there she missed. "Then I happily accept your escort. It should not take long."

They made their way along Monkwell Street, talking of cases Master Hardy was letting Anthony take responsibility for, gossip tidbits from court. Master Orrens's shop, though, appeared to be closed. The window of the lower floor, which should have been open to display his fine wares, was shuttered, and no light shone from the upper windows, either. Yet the doorstep was swept clean.

Kate knocked at the door, and after several long moments there was a shuffling sound, and a scrape as the portal slid open. A maidservant peeked out timidly, her young face freckled under her cap.

"I would like to see Master Orrens, if you please," Kate said.

The maid's eyes shifted between Kate and Anthony. "He isn't here now, miss."

"Do you know when he will return? I was sent here by Queen Elizabeth herself to inquire about a headdress he once made her."

The maid's mouth gaped from shock. "The queen! He's been gone for days, miss. I don't know when he'll be back, or where he's gone. He said he was going to order supplies, but it's never taken so long before. The cook thinks he has gone back to France, mayhap."

Kate looked up at Anthony, who gave her a questioning frown. "May we just come in and look around, then?" Kate asked. "The queen is most eager to order more of Master Orrens's work, and I am sure that when he returns he would not be happy to find he had lost the royal patronage."

"Oh, no, miss! If the queen herself—I should not like to lose my place here, it's the best I've had."

"I shall be most careful, I promise you," Kate said earnestly, and at last the maid stepped back to let her enter. Anthony stayed close beside her as the maid led them along a narrow, dark corridor, past the closed door of the shop itself, into what seemed to be an office. It was a small room, stuffy with the window shut and the fire banked, with a table piled up with papers and a couple of stools. Shelves rose along one wall, filled with ledgers.

"What is your name?" Kate asked the maid.

"Mary, miss."

"Do you know anything about how Master Orrens organizes his records in here?"

"Not much, miss." Some of Mary's uncertainty had faded into curiosity. "I think he writes about materials that have been ordered and arrived here, and the sales go in those books."

"I see. Well, I do not want to keep you from your work. Master Elias and I will just look around."

Mary nodded, but Kate noticed she hovered in the doorway, her eyes bright as she waited to see what would happen next.

For the moment, that would be nothing. Kate pursed her lips as she studied the dusty piles of papers and ledger books. She wasn't sure where to start looking.

"What are you searching for exactly, Kate?" Anthony asked quietly.

"Someone once ordered a crown that is in the style of Master Orrens, and the queen would like to know who that was," she answered. "The Office of the Revels gave me his name."

Anthony gave a rueful laugh. "Rather like the proverbial needle in a haystack."

Kate laughed, too, and felt her enthusiasm for the hunt rising in her mind. She did rather like a challenge. "We have found other documents with far less clues, I think."

"Beg pardon, miss," Mary the maid said. "I don't read very much, but I know Master Orrens keeps records of his materials here. If you know what the crown is made from, perhaps it would be easier to trace the sale in those ledgers?" She pulled out a box overflowing with what seemed to be order sheets.

"Very clever, Mary," Kate said, and the maid giggled. "I know the crown was silver wire wrapped with gold thread, and the base was of sable and red ribbons, which cannot be very common. But I don't know when it was made."

"I know these go back to the 1540s, when Master Orrens came here from Lille. He said his wife kept the records then, until she died of the sweating sickness."

"Here, Kate, you look through this half, I will do the other," Anthony said, dividing up the documents.

Kate glanced through them—gold from Seville, silver wire from Amsterdam, silks from Antwerp, pearls and glass beads, furs. Master Orrens's art was not a cheap one. "Do you help make the headdresses, Mary?"

"Oh, nay, miss. I just clean and tend the fires, do a bit of cooking. Master Orrens keeps his workshop in Chelsea now. They're only brought here to the shop when they're done."

"Chelsea?" Kate asked. She wondered if the workshop was near the palace where Queen Elizabeth had lived for a time with Queen Catherine Parr after King Henry died.

"Master Orrens says there is more space to be had cheaper there. I think when he first came to London so long ago, the workshop was in the garden at the back. He's made pieces for the royal court since King Henry's time, or so he says."

"Indeed?" A man like that could be very useful, with information going back so far—if he could be found.

"Could this be what you're seeking, Kate?" Anthony asked. He showed her a crumbling document stamped from Antwerp, with the year 1547 at the top. "It is surely something of an unfashionable piece by now."

"The queen can be most thrifty when it suits her," Kate said as she scanned the neat columns. "She would not waste such a quantity of silver and gold wires, I am sure."

The list also included a fine pelt of sable from Muscovy, which had made the base of the crown as it sat on the poppet's head. There was also scarlet silk, and red glass beads.

"Are all the final sales in the ledgers?" she asked Mary.

"I don't know, miss. But surely the old ledgers would be back here." The maid dug to the back of a series of shelves and pulled out some heavy, dusty old books.

As Kate glanced through them, she saw that luckily Master Orrens was more organized than his desk made it seem. The ledgers were mostly in order of year, and he was careful in marking who ordered what, and the money they owed for it. It seemed that when a young Master Orrens first came to London, his business was made successful by the extravagant Queen Catherine Howard, who had surely patronized every seamstress and goldsmith in London. She and her ladies had ordered several pieces.

After that, Master Orrens's court orders tapered away sharply, though he still did some work there.

At last, she found what she sought. Master Orrens had made for Queen Catherine Parr one small crown of gold and silver, with red beads and a sable base—meant for a christening gift. It was delivered to the queen shortly before King Henry died. Kate remembered tales of how the queen had loved children, had longed to have one of her own, but there were no children with the king, and the baby daughter she had with Tom Seymour had died soon after birth. It seemed a sad gift, so elaborate and careful, for a baby not her own. Or perhaps it *had* been for her own child? The longed-for infant?

Kate's thoughts were racing. Where had the crown been all that time? Could it really be the same as the one that appeared on the head of the poppet? What did it mean? And where was the maker now?

Startled by what she had found, Kate carefully put the ledgers back where they had found them. "Thank you, Mary. The queen will be most grateful. I should like to speak to Master Orrens as soon as he returns, if you would be kin enough to send me word. Or if he has indeed returned to France for some reason, as your cook suggested, I would like to know that. My name is Mistress Haywood, and I am at Whitehall until the court moves to Richmond in the new year."

"Oh, yes, miss, of course. I'm ever so happy to help the queen. I saw her pass by in her coronation procession. All gold and white—like an angel." Mary frowned, her eyes bright as if she would start crying. "Is Master Orrens in some trouble?"

Kate wasn't sure what to tell her. It was strange the man would vanish now. "I am sure he is not, Mary."

Anthony walked with her back to Monkwell Street, and they made their way through the lanes back to the river, until the stone walls of Whitehall came into view. They walked quietly, as Kate went over all the questions that finding the source of the crown had answered—and created.

"*You* are not in trouble, are you, Kate?" Anthony asked solemnly.

She gave him a quick smile. A horse galloped

past, bound so fast for the palace that it scattered cursing pedestrians in its trail. "No more than anyone else in London, I am sure."

"Kate . . ." He paused, and shook his head. He looked as if he wanted to say something, but he just smiled ruefully. "I hope you always know I am your friend, and you can call on me whenever you need help."

"I do know that, Anthony, and I cherish your friendship," she answered, and found contentment in her own words. "I hope you enjoy your time in the country with the Hardys."

"And I hope you stay safe with your courtly Christmas. I know how you love the work." He took her hand and kissed it before he turned and made his way back along the street. His tall figure was soon swallowed in the crowd.

Kate watched until she couldn't see him any longer. But she couldn't stand there for long. The wind was growing even colder as evening moved in, and she had to return the crown to a safe-keeping spot. She hurried up the stone steps and through the Holbein Gate that led across the street into the palace itself—only to find Rob standing in the doorway.

It looked as if he had been waiting there, for he leaned against the whitewashed wall, his arms crossed over his chest. He smiled and looked deceptively lazy. But she recognized the catlike gleam in his bright blue eyes.

"Out for a stroll with your lawyer friend, Kate?" he said with a laugh. "Nice for some people to have a long pause from working."

Kate laughed. "Because I see you are practically a slave to duty, Rob Cartman! Have you been lazing here for long, watching all the pretty ladies go by?"

"If you must know, I have been looking for you. The queen wishes to have the new Venetian branle for the dancing tonight, and we have not yet practiced the music. But Violet Green said you left the palace hours ago."

He had been looking for her? Really? Kate felt a bit nonplussed, and yet strangely pleased, by the thought. "You are quite right, Rob. I should not neglect my first task here at court, to entertain the queen. Let me fetch my lute, and I shall meet you in the musicians' gallery."

He caught her hand as she walked past, and Kate looked up at him in surprise. His smile turned rueful. "I was worried."

"Worried? For me?"

"After what happened at the hunt, and with Senor Vasquez—of course I was worried. Were you really out for a romantic walk?"

Kate was tempted for a moment to say she was, partly because she truly didn't want anyone to worry, and partly because, silly as it was, she rather liked it that Rob could be jealous of *her*. But she knew she couldn't. She had already brought him into the sad matter of Senor Vasquez's death by showing him the music.

She shook her head, and stepped closer to speak quietly to him. "I took the poppet's crown to a tiremaker in Cripplegate to see what they could tell me about it."

He frowned. "Did they know anything?"

"I did discover something interesting—and strange." She glanced around at all the people hurrying past. "I will tell you of it in the musicians' gallery, before the others arrive. Have you deciphered anything in the music?"

"I have some ideas, but nothing certain yet. You do get into more complicated conundrums than any play, Kate."

"Nay, my life is much duller than a play! Especially *your* plays," Kate said, thinking of some scenes she had seen Rob play out on the stage, of the deaths of kings and tragic romances.

"'Dull' is the last thing I would call you," he said with a smile. To her surprise, he reached out and softly brushed his hand over her cheek before he stepped away.

Kate was so flustered she hardly dared look at him. Better to go back to what she knew. "I—I shall see you in a little time in the gallery, Rob."

She hurried up to her room, sweeping off her damp cloak to let it dry over her stool. She quickly took off her pattens and changed into her fine Spanish leather court shoes. She peeked into the small looking glass that hung near the fireplace, trying to tidy her hair. Not that she cared how she looked when she met with Rob—certainly not.

Kate laughed at herself, and turned away to find the music she needed to rehearse. As she picked it up, she noticed that the stacks of papers and books on her desk were not quite as straight as she had left them.

"Surely not," she whispered. Perhaps one of the maids had come to tidy, though they seldom ventured so far into the depths of the palace, unless it was to clean out the grate. She shuffled through the music, which she had left in the order of the Christmas festival where it must be played, and found her suspicions all too correct. The pages were out of order.

Someone had been searching through her papers.

Kate hurried up the steep spiral staircase toward the musicians' gallery, her lute in her hands, her heart still pounding with the disquieting thought that someone had been in her chamber. The great hall far below was bustling like a beehive, servants setting up the long table and benches for that night's banquet.

But the gallery itself was quiet, deep in shadows. Music stands and stools clustered in an empty huddle near the railing, and Kate knew that very soon the space would fill with the noise of lutes and tambors. For now, she was alone there—except for Rob at the far end of the long, narrow gallery.

He did not see her yet, and she paused to study him in that rare unwary moment. He leaned against the railing, watching the scene below. He, too, was half covered in shadows, his golden hair glowing in contrast. He frowned, and Kate wondered what was making his thoughts so serious now.

She had known Rob for over a year, and had seen so much with him—the murder of his uncle at Hatfield, the death of his mistress at the Cardinal's Hat, his time in prison. He had helped her with so very much as well.

So often he exasperated her, made her laugh even against her will when she wanted to be stern, made her see the world in a slightly different light—or he surprised her when he understood so well how *she* saw it. And sometimes she was even startled anew by how handsome he really was.

And how many personas he had, just like characters he portrayed so adeptly on the stage.

He turned and smiled at her, and that moment of seriousness was gone. "Fairest Kate, here you are at last."

Kate shook off her confused emotions toward him, and the disquiet that had been tugging at her mind since she thought her papers had been searched through. "I still get lost here at

Whitehall, I fear," she said with a laugh. She didn't want to tell him her suspicions, not yet. "Shall we practice the new music for tonight? There isn't much time before the banquet."

"Of course, though I suspect you know it perfectly already, as you always do." Rob fetched his own lute, and they sat down together on two stools near the wall, far from the sight of anyone in the hall below.

As they tuned their instruments, she whispered, "What did you discover on your night with the Spanish, then?"

Rob's expression, his half smile, didn't waver. He bent his head over the lute and whispered back, "That the Spanish, for all their vaunted devoutness, can drink as much strong ale as any Englishman. Senor Gomez seemed eager to forget what happened to his kinsman for a time, which I understand. The tavern made its share of coin that night."

"A tavern owned by friends of yours, I'm sure."

"Perhaps. I am lucky to have friends in many places, Kate, as do you."

Kate thought of some of the unlikely friends she had made in the course of her work for the queen, from Cecil to Mistress Celine, the bawdy house owner. "And your tavern-owner friends did not water down the Spaniards' drink, I suppose."

"Indeed not. They were very generous. But it

seems even the strongest ale cannot quite loosen tongues enough."

"They did not say what they are really doing here in England for de Quadra and King Philip?"

"Not precisely. Senor Gomez did mutter darkly about the 'perfidy of English ladies,' before he tried to teach the whole great room a bawdy Spanish song."

Kate had to laugh at the image. "Are there bawdy Spanish songs?"

"There are bawdy songs in every language. But in between choruses, Gomez did say that if he returned to Spain empty-handed he would not have his promised reward, and he seemed to grow rather angry about that. I think he was worried about more than what happened to his kinsman."

"Promised reward?" Kate said. What could it be? Marriage to some fine lady? A fortune? Or a bishopric, as he was said to be devout. "For what?"

Rob shrugged. "He would not say, or rather he would not say anything I could understand. I thought actors were cryptic creatures, but they have nothing on the Spanish. He seemed rather fearful that his errand was impossible. I can't help but think it is Senor Gomez who was the better actor of the two."

"Hmm." Kate played the first chords of the song the queen had requested for her banquet. It was not much to go on, aside from what she already knew—de Quadra's men could not be merely "secretaries." Yet there were spies everywhere at court, and they seldom behaved as strangely as Senor Gomez and his late cousin.

"Shall I go out with Senor Gomez again?" Rob asked. "Maybe a trip to the Cardinal's Hat would loosen his tongue a bit more. Celine's girls would be happy to tell you anything they hear."

Kate kicked out at him with her slipper. It was a soft satin creation, and muffled by her heavy skirts, but he still yowled and winced dramatically. "I think it would be *you* who lost your wits there. But, aye—if you can talk to them again, you should. You can better ferret out secrets from men like that than I could."

"Oh, I don't know, Kate," he answered quietly. "I think that you could discover any secret at all from a man, just by one glance from your green eyes."

Flustered, Kate tightened her fingers on her lute strings. "Such fustian. You are not on stage now, Master Cartman. Now, shall we play the rest of the song?"

CHAPTER FIFTEEN

Bringing in the Boar Day, December 30

"The boar's head in hand bear I, bedecked with bays and rosemary! I pray you all now, be merry, be merry, be merry. . . ."

The company in the queen's great hall applauded as the servants carried in the roasted boar, borne aloft on a silver platter. It was a large boar, indeed, caught before the royal hunt at Greenwich went so awry, adorned with garlands of herbs and candied fruits, a whole apple propped in its mouth. It was paraded around the hall before being presented to the queen, led by Rob in a fine bright green doublet and feathered cap as he conducted everyone in the song.

Kate clapped along with everyone else, watching the crowd as more delicacies were carried in. She could read no ill intentions in anyone's smiles. All seemed merry indeed. What lurked behind those smiles? Who had been searching through her chamber?

More servants hurried around the room with platters of the finest of the queen's Yule dishes, roasted deer and capon, meat pies and stews, fish dishes that were doubly precious with the river so cold, as well as the queen's beloved sweets. The last dish brought in was an elaborate subtlety made to look like Whitehall itself, the almond paste formed into bricks and bridges, blue candied sheets for windows.

Kate laughed along with everyone else as jesters from Rob's company of players tumbled and gamboled between the long tables. It was another lavish Christmas display for the queen, with everyone happily flushed with the fine wine that was a gift from the French ambassador, with flirtation and the reckless joy of the holiday. All set up to show that nothing was amiss in Elizabeth's glittering world.

But surely everyone knew all was not well. Underneath all the noisy merriment there was a sword's edge of dark tension, desperation, always hovering just beneath the jeweled surface. Sir Robert Dudley's guards, garbed in his livery, clustered around the queen along with her own servants. She would come to no harm that night. But there was always that shining, sharp blade under everything at court, waiting for those who were not wary to fall down onto it and destroy themselves.

He was going to be so angry.

Mary pulled the hood of her cloak closer around her face and hurried down the torchlit street. The passing crowds jostled her, and she drew away with a surprised hiss. There were people everywhere; rushing past, laughing together on the corners, leaning out of windows to call down to one another. In the flickering light, they barely looked like people at all, but more like figures in a nightmare.

She had only wanted to be free of that stuffy little room for a while, to breathe some fresh air, see people other than the harried landlady. She'd waited her whole life to see London! Read about it, its grand mansions and vast bridges, the fashions and shops. And once she was there all she saw was the innyard from her small window.

So, what happened when she gathered her courage and crept out the kitchen door just to go for a little stroll? She got lost.

"Fool, fool," she muttered. Why had she once thought this was such a fine idea? She would surely be lost in this endless maze of stone and wood forever, or if she did find her way back to the inn, he would find out what she had done and would be very angry.

He had been furious that she had even ventured out of her chamber the day the people from the royal court came to the inn's great room, with their furs and their ice skates. This was far more serious.

Mary bit back a sob as she remembered that day, how intriguing it had been. Surely that dark-haired lady in the red cloak would never make such a mess out of just going for a walk! She had looked so calm, so confident. Surely she knew just how to move around London.

"Cor, look what's wandered our way! A soft little partridge," a man's slurred voice called. He stumbled out of the shadows, a shambling, terrifying giant, and his great paw snatched at the edge of her cloak.

Panic flooded over her, flames against the cold night. "Leave me alone!" Mary cried. She tried to run, but her fine-soled boots slid on the cobbles, and he managed to grab a handful of her hood.

He reeled her in so close she could smell the stale reek of old onions and beer on his hot breath. Mercifully, he was too ale-shot to hold on to her, and she managed to jerk away.

"Don't be that way, you trull!" he shouted.

"Leave her alone," one of his friends said with a laugh. "There are plenty more Winchester geese to be had."

Mary kept running, dodging around corners, sliding on patches of frost, not seeing at all where she was going. At last, she tumbled out of the entrance to a narrow alleyway and found herself facing the river.

A pain stabbed at her side, and she had to stop to catch her breath. She studied the dark expanse of water in front of her, the boats bearing their passengers sliding past, the moonlight shimmering on the waves. Surely if she just followed the riverbank, she could find the innyard again. But which direction?

She glanced to her right, and was startled to see the long expanse of smooth stone wall that marked the edge of the queen's palace at Whitehall.

Fascinated, Mary studied the steps that led from the river to a carved gate, now closed. High above, soft golden light spilled from the windows of a gallery, drawing her closer. She thought she could hear the faint strains of music, some lively dance, and laughter. She imagined the scene that surely waited just beyond those walls. The bright silken gowns and flashing jewels, the handsome young men twirling their ladies around in a volta.

That was the London she had read about in her books, the London she had once imagined she would be a part of herself. Surely just behind those windows there was no loneliness, no uncertainty. She drifted closer, unnoticed in her dark cloak, and dared to lay her hand on one of the cold stones.

A burst of laughter, the splashing sound of a boat drawing up to the water steps, startled her, and she fell back a step. She pressed herself deeper into the shadows, and watched as two men leaped out of the boat to help their ladies disembark.

Mary stared at them, so fascinated that she

forgot her fear. They looked like a dream, all velvet and furs and elegance, like princes and their fair princesses in poems.

One of the ladies clung to her swain's slashed-satin sleeve, laughing up at him as he stared down at her with wonder in his eyes, as if he could not believe the glory of what had landed beside him. It made Mary's sadness prick even sharper. She would surely never have that.

The lady caught sight of Mary lurking there, and her eyes widened. Mary tried to draw back, to run away again, but the lady hurried toward her. She was small, slender as a forest fairy, and just as quick. She held her hand, gloved in pale embroidered kid, out to Mary.

"Please," the lady called. "Do I not know you? Where have I seen you before?"

"I—I did not mean to . . . ," Mary stammered.

"I know! It was the Rose and Crown. Are you lost?"

Mary shook her head, frozen.

"Ned," the lady said. "Won't you escort her back to the inn? It is obvious she is lost and frightened, the poor thing."

The man, no doubt Ned, tall and broad-shouldered, with dark curls under his velvet cap, held on to the lady's arm. "What if she came here to find us?" he whispered, though Mary could hear him. "To tell someone we were there together that day?"

"Don't be silly! Lots of people were there that day."

But Mary had seen the look on Ned's face, dark and suspicious, and it reawakened her fear. She spun around and fled again, even as the lady called after her. She ran and ran, past buildings and carts, until at last she recognized the yard of the Rose and Crown, with the landlady, Mistress Fawlkes, lounging in the doorway to gossip with the brewer. "Here! Where have you been, mistress?" she shouted as Mary dashed past her.

She didn't stop until she was in her own chamber. She slammed the bar into place on the door, and dove under the bedclothes still fully clothed. It hardly mattered what anyone, even *he,* would do to her now. She was safe.

And she would never go out alone in the city again.

CHAPTER SIXTEEN

New Year's Eve

It was cold but still on the river so early in the morning, little wind stirring at the waves. But the sky was a flat slate gray, paler gray clouds lowering over the spires, bridges, and smoking chimneys of London. Kate eyed them suspiciously, willing the snow not to fall until her errand was finished. She shivered and pulled the edges of her fur-edged cloak closer, wiggling her numb toes in her boots.

It wasn't just the cold that made her nervous, though. It was being in a boat on the Thames. Usually she tried to use the vessels only for short journeys across the river, or when she had to provide music for the queen's barges. Longer voyages like this one reminded her too much of that terrible night after the queen's coronation, when she was kidnapped by a villain and almost drowned in the cold waves at high tide.

Now, the waves lapping against the wooden edge of the boat, the shriek of gulls overhead competing with the tolling of church bells, brought the fear of those moments close to her.

Especially since there was someone who seemed to seek harm to the queen all over again.

Rob seemed to sense her apprehension, for he slid closer to her on the narrow plank seat and gave her a wide, charming smile. She had encountered him as she tried to slip out of the palace, and he insisted on going with her. Though at first she protested, instinctively secretive about the queen's business, now she was glad of his warm presence beside her.

"I have been thinking of your strange music, Kate," he said, as lightly as if he remarked on the weather.

Kate nodded, letting her ideas about the music distract her even more from her memories. "Have you deciphered it?"

"Not as of yet, I confess. I wrote it down as soon as I returned to my lodgings. . . ."

"You remembered it all for hours?"

His eyes widened in surprise. "Of course. An actor must remember things as soon as he sees it. You surely do the same."

Kate considered that. "I suppose I do, though I must play a song two or three times before I recall it perfectly."

"Well, you were quite right about that particular piece—it is like no form of music I could find, even in a book I have of Arabic forms. It must be a coded message, and one with a great many numbers. Dates, mayhap, of something meant to occur?"

Kate was fascinated. Along with lock picking,

Cecil's man had shown her a bit about deciphering some simpler codes. It *was* very much like fitting musical notes together. "Something that has already happened?"

"I could not say yet. Does it have something to do with our journey to Chelsea today?"

"I'm not sure. I do not know exactly what I'm looking for there, or how it will fit with the music at all. But I think there might be a clue there to the doll that was left for the queen at Greenwich." And the other notes as well.

They passed under a narrow footbridge, and the flying contents of a slop bucket barely missed their boat. Rob drew her closer, and she was glad of his warmth against the chilly day.

"How so?" he asked.

"The tiremaker who probably made the little crown has done much work in the past for the royal court, and his records seem to indicate this particular piece was made for Queen Catherine Parr for a christening gift. But I know not for who it was made, or where it has been these ten years. Was it merely the nearest thing a villain had to a royal queen—or does it have some significance in itself?"

"Why Chelsea?"

"It was something my father's friend Mistress Park said, when she was reminiscing about her time in Queen Catherine's household. She said Queen Catherine was a great lady, and all her servants were most devoted to her—and that she always took care of them, even when they could no longer work. Since I cannot go all the way to Sudeley, where Queen Catherine died, I thought I would see if there were any pensioners left at Chelsea who remember the Dowager Queen. Queen Elizabeth still owns the house, and when I told her my idea, she gave me a letter today telling the servants that they are safe to speak freely to me. And perhaps I can find the tire-maker while I am there, though his maid did not know where he has gone."

"Do *you* remember when you lived at Chelsea, Kate?"

Kate studied the scenery sliding past as she tried to remember her childhood. The thick press of buildings had grown thinner, giving way to the water steps and fine gates of great houses. The sweet-sick smell of the river had turned to fresh greenery. *Did* she remember when she lived in one of those very houses, and her father worked for Queen Catherine in those brief days before she married Thomas Seymour? Or did she just imagine the gardens, the elegant rooms, the high flutter of feminine laughter and rustle of silk skirts?

"I am not sure. I was so small then, and I seldom saw Queen Catherine or Princess Elizabeth myself. I was only allowed to the great hall for a look at grand parties, and there were few of those. Queen Catherine preferred her studies, and a quiet, discreet life, which is how she married again with so few privy to it," Kate said. "I was mostly looked after by Allison Finsley, who was Master Gerald's sister, while my father worked. She was very kind. Queen Catherine, too, was very nice to me whenever she saw me. She was beautiful, and always dressed so elegantly, and smelled of roses. She would ask about my musical studies. . . ."

Kate frowned as an old memory of Queen Catherine flashed through her mind, a heart-shaped pale face with a sharp nose, a sweet smile. Surely she had just seen such a face, not in the haze of childhood memory but sometime recently? The image of Queen Catherine, dead for ten years, was suddenly so clear.

Of course. The girl at the Rose and Crown.

"Who was she?" Kate whispered.

"Who was who?"

She turned to Rob, and found he watched her with avid curiosity. "I am not sure yet."

She had no time to say more, for the boat was bumping into the foot of the water steps at Chelsea. Rob leaped out, and reached back to help her.

They made their way through the large gardens, which rolled in elegant fields and flower beds down to the river. It had been winter when she and her father arrived there soon after King

Henry's death in 1547, when Queen Catherine moved to her dower house with Princess Elizabeth.

The house, just as elegant as the gardens, all graceful redbrick walls and pale stone trim, appeared to be shuttered, but Kate glimpsed silvery smoke rising from some of the chimneys, and she and Rob made their way to a door tucked to one side.

Her knock was answered by a tall, thin older gentleman in fine but plain dark clothes. He eyed them suspiciously.

"Aye?" he said suspiciously.

"I am Mistress Haywood, and this is Master Cartman," Kate said, in the firm, confident voice she had learned at court. Few wanted to think a mere female musician could have any authority at all, but Kate had found that pretending as if she did often went a long way. "We have come on an errand from Queen Elizabeth at Whitehall."

She handed him the queen's note, and his glower was wiped away. "Certainly, certainly! Anything we can do to assist Her Grace. Please, mistress, come in from the cold and tell me what we can do for the queen. I am Master Stanley, steward here."

Rob took her arm, and they exchanged a wary glance. But Kate was glad of the cheerful fire in the small sitting room Master Stanley led them into, and the cushioned stool he offered. The room was a pretty one, with painted cloths holding back the drafts and enameled candlesticks lining the carved mantel. It made her think again of her childhood, of the way every room near Queen Catherine Parr seemed graceful and comfortable.

She seated herself on the stool, and Rob stood behind her. "Queen Elizabeth wishes to find some of the loyal servants of her stepmother and make certain they are looked after," Kate told Master Stanley. "Are there many still living here?"

"Very few, Mistress Haywood," Master Stanley answered. "When Queen Catherine left for Sudeley, she took most with her and provided pensions for those too elderly to move. There is a gardener, and the queen's old Strewing Herb Mistress. And there is Mistress Bouchard."

"Mistress Bouchard?"

"She was a nursemaid in the household of the Dowager Queen, who came here to live in one of the cottages after the queen died."

"A nursemaid?" Kate thought of the little crown, the christening gift. "For Queen Catherine's daughter who died?"

"Aye, poor little mite. Would you care to speak to Mistress Bouchard? She cannot always remember things now, but she loves to talk about the Dowager Queen."

Kate nodded, though she found herself rather reluctant to leave the warm fire to chase yet more things she didn't understand. But perhaps a former nursemaid would know about the christening gift. She and Rob followed Master Stanley back out the door and across the garden to a cluster of cottages. One was very small, a cozy, plastered one-room dwelling that in summer would surely be covered in climbing roses.

Master Stanley knocked loudly and called out, "Mistress Bouchard? Queen Elizabeth has sent these people to speak with you!"

"What?" a querulous voice called.

Master Stanley let them in, and Kate and Rob walked through the doorway to find an old woman swathed in shawls beside the fire, staring up at them curiously.

Mistress Bouchard was obviously quite elderly, with her heavily lined, apple-cheeked face, and the snow-white curls escaping from beneath her embroidered cap, but her faded blue eyes were bright with curiosity as she peered up at her new guests.

"Who did you say you were?" Mistress Bouchard asked.

"I told you, Mistress Bouchard—they are from the queen," Master Stanley said loudly.

She waved her twisted hands, encased in knitted mitts, at him. "Surely they can speak for themselves, Master Stanley? You should return to your business at the house."

Master Stanley departed with a huff, and

Mistress Bouchard sat back with a satisfied smile. "Now we can talk. Come closer, both of you. It is seldom I have new guests, especially handsome young men." She gave Rob a twinkling smile, and gestured for him to sit beside her. "Which queen are you from? It seems there are so many these days."

"We are from Queen Elizabeth," Rob said. "She is in residence at Whitehall now."

"Is she?" Mistress Bouchard said. "Well, I hope she has learned a touch of prudence in her age. When she was a girl . . ."

"You remember her when she was a girl?" Kate said, thinking of the notes Queen Elizabeth had received, the distance in her eyes when she spoke of Tom Seymour, the man of much charm and little sense.

Mistress Bouchard turned her sharp gaze from Rob to Kate. "Aye, for a time. I once looked after Queen Catherine's stepdaughter—her first step-daughter, Meg Latimer. Now *there* was a good girl, quiet and biddable. God always takes the good ones young, bless her. When Queen Catherine was at last expecting her own child, she sent for me again. I did not expect such a to-do as I found when I arrived, not in the house-hold of a godly lady like Queen Catherine."

"What did you find?" Kate asked.

Mistress Bouchard's eyes narrowed. "Now, what did you say Queen Elizabeth wants with me? I am just an old lady, sitting by my fire. I know nothing now."

Kate and Rob exchanged a long glance, and Kate gave him a little nod. He leaned closer to Mistress Bouchard with a serious expression on his handsome face.

"Her Grace has many enemies, we fear, and they would even use things that happened in the far past to harm her—or harm England itself," he said quietly. "The Queen of Scotland, for one . . ."

"Oh, nay, we would never want a French lady ruling here," Mistress Bouchard said decisively. "But I am not sure I can be of help. I remember few of the household then, and I only stayed after Queen Catherine died until the Duchess of Suffolk came to take the poor baby away. . . ." Mistress Bouchard's eyes widened.

"You remember something, mistress?" Rob said.

"Mayhap, mayhap," the old lady muttered. "Bring me that box over there, young man, and we will see."

Rob fetched the box she indicated from a small table beneath the window. It was a pretty item of chased silver, inlaid with the initials *CPtQ*—Catherine Parr the Queen, as Kate remembered the Dowager Queen always signed herself. Mistress Bouchard took it carefully between her shaky hands.

"Queen Catherine gave this to me for safe-keeping," she said. "And once she was gone—I knew that scoundrel of a husband couldn't be trusted with anything the queen held dear." She raised the lid, and Kate peered into the velvet-lined recesses.

She drew back with a gasp when eyes blinked back at her. Then she had to laugh, for it was not a person there, but a doll. Small but perfectly formed of wax, with a tiny, heart-shaped face framed by dark red hair and dressed in a blue satin gown in the style of Kate's childhood, with a low, square neckline and draped sleeves trimmed with fine sable.

"When the queen ordered this made, it had a small crown. To match the gown, you see." Mistress Bouchard gently touched a fingertip to the fur trim of the little garment. "But it vanished long ago."

"The tiremaker's records said it was part of a christening gift," Kate said. "Could the doll have been the gift? Do you know who it was meant for, Mistress Bouchard? Could it be meant to represent Queen Elizabeth?"

Mistress Bouchard frowned. "Nay, not that minx. I think Queen Catherine ordered it for the christening of her own babe, once she knew she was with child after so long. She prayed for a princess of her own. Or, preferably, a prince."

Kate tried to remember all she had seen at the

tiremaker's shop, all Queen Elizabeth had told her about Catherine Parr and Thomas Seymour. "Yet the crown was made in 1546, surely long before Queen Catherine was pregnant in 1548."

"When Queen Catherine was married to Thomas Seymour. And Thomas Seymour's child would not be a princess," Rob pointed out.

Mistress Bouchard gave a helpless shrug. "All I know, my dears, is that Queen Catherine asked me to keep this safe, so I have. I only wish I could have kept her own baby, her wee Lady Mary, safe, too. Such a pretty babe, red hair and a little rosebud mouth, just like her mother." She closed the box with a snap and held it out to Kate. "You take it to Queen Elizabeth now, Mistress Haywood, and tell her to remember all Queen Catherine did to keep *her* safe."

Kate thought of the music Queen Catherine had entrusted to her own father when Catherine's life was in peril, and was sad to realize that a queen could only trust a very few of the people who served her. Could the doll fit with the music? It felt almost as if Queen Catherine was reaching out to help her stepdaughter one more time.

She took the box carefully from Mistress Bouchard's shaking hands. "I will guard it most carefully. I promise."

Mistress Bouchard nodded, and sat back in her chair, as if satisfied that she had kept her long-ago promise.

"What happened to the baby? To little Mary Seymour?" Rob asked.

"I never saw her after Sir Thomas sent her away with the duchess. For all that the duchess was Queen Catherine's great friend, I heard tell she had her own little ones to worry about in those uncertain days and didn't want the bother of another, especially one who had to be kept in state as the daughter of a queen. Then Lady Mary died when she was still just a babe."

"How very sad for Queen Catherine," Kate murmured. To wait so long for a child, only to lose the faith of her husband, her life, and her precious baby.

"Aye. If they had let *me* go with her, along with the others, I would have looked after her better. The poor little child . . ."

Master Orrens's workshop, where the maid had said he worked on his creations before bringing them to his shop, was one of a long row of plain, whitewashed buildings not far from the manor, near the river where deliveries could easily be made. Smoke rose from the chimneys of all the nearest buildings, but none from the low, squat space of the tiremaker.

Kate went up on tiptoe to try and peer through one of the windows, but the glass was too dirty and she could glimpse nothing of the room beyond.

"Shall I boost you up into the window?" Rob asked.

Kate had to laugh at the memory of the last time she had tried to get into a deserted building near Nonsuch Palace, when she had landed with a most ungraceful tumble on the floor. "Nay, I think we can try the door first. Though it does appear no one is here. I wonder where Master Orrens really has gone? Do you think he could have returned to France, as the maidservant suggested?"

Rob shrugged. "If he is a Hugenot, France should surely be the last place where he would want to go. Especially after he has built up a prosperous business here over so many years. Few men would throw away a fine career such as that."

Kate nodded. Few men would. Many spoke often of high moral ideals, but when it came to it their careers, whether courtly or mercantile, would prevail in the end.

The front door suddenly swung open, startling her. She fell back from the window, and turned to see a young man standing in the doorway. He was tall and thin as a wheat sheaf, his dark hair rumpled, an apron covering his plain russet doublet. He held a length of velvet in his hand, which was surely better than a dagger, but Kate could see the flash of fear in his eyes.

"Who are you?" he demanded. "What do you seek here?"

Rob stepped forward, but Kate took his hand to hold him back. "I am sorry, but we mean no harm. I assure you," she said softly. "We are merely looking for Master Orrens."

"He ain't here," the boy said. "What do you want of him?"

"I am Mistress Haywood, musician to the queen. She has seen some of Master Orrens's work from the past, and may wish to commission more for her courtly masquerades."

"Truly?" The boy looked as if he very much wanted to believe her, yet the suspicion was still there. "You aren't the first to come looking for him of late."

"Am I not?" Kate said. "I understood he has not done work for the court for some time now. Has he retired?"

"He went away a few days ago, said he had to go abroad to find some supplies, but we haven't heard from him since. I've been trying to make some hats we could sell in the shop."

"Abroad?" Kate said. "To France, mayhap?"

The boy scowled. "Where would you hear that?"

"From Mary, at Master Orrens's house. She knows not where he went, too, and that was what she imagined might have happened. She said he came from Lille."

The boy's frown flickered just a bit. "You talked to Mary?"

"I did. She was most helpful. Do you know her?"

"She's my sister. If she thought it was well to talk to you . . ." The boy glanced back over his shoulder, before he carefully closed the door and stepped nearer to Kate and Rob. " 'Tis true I know not where he has gone. But I can tell you one thing."

"Anything you could tell us would be most appreciated, especially by the queen," Kate said.

The boy swallowed hard. "A man came to visit Master Orrens a few days ago, said he was looking for something the master made many years ago, a small crown."

Kate thought of the finely wrought silver-and-gold piece that sat upon the poppet's head. "Who was this man?"

The boy shrugged. His expression had gone from one of suspicion to fear. "He wore a long cloak with a hood, and Master Orrens took him to the back room before anyone could see him. And I didn't see him leave, either. But later that afternoon, the master seemed most worried about something. It was after that he decided to leave. I do wonder . . ."

"Aye?" Rob asked gently. "Where do *you* think he has gone?"

"I wondered if it was that crown. Maybe he went to find it?"

Kate wondered if that could be true—surely Master Orrens had made many such objects?

Would he even remember one piece out of so many? Or perhaps the mysterious visitor had threatened him in some way. But it seemed that until he returned from wherever he had gone, she would be able to find out little else.

She gave the boy her name and direction, as she had with her sister, and asked him to send her word if Master Orrens returned. But it felt like searching for a shred of that crown's gold thread among a field of daffodils.

CHAPTER SEVENTEEN

Later that night, Kate laid out the two pieces of music side by side on her desk, along with the coded poem Rob gave her. The ink was rather faded on the old song Queen Catherine had given her father, but she could still clearly read the notes.

Each of these marks stands in for something else—a feeling or an idea, she remembered Allison Finsley telling her, as she guided Kate's childish fingers over a sheet of music. Each of the marks stood in for something else—could that be the key now? What were the odds that two coded pieces of music would fall into Kate's lap at the same time? Kate had to at least find out if there was a connection.

Kate reached for a blank paper and her quill and ink, and started to line up the document from the Spaniards' room with the words of Queen Catherine's poem. It was a very slow process, and her eyes began to water from trying to see a pattern. Nothing seemed to match up, and she began to feel foolish for even entertaining such an idea.

But then the letters she scribbled on her own paper suddenly came into focus and she could pick out a pattern, matching the letters of the poem to some of the strange numbers. She reached for the volume of Plato she had been studying, the guide to musical codes in *The Republic*, and quickly compared them. The letters snapped into place when she looked at them as matching bars of music and letters.

Melville Village, Scotland—February 1559—The Lady Mary—church of St. Saviour—in the church porch . . .

The Lady Mary. Mary Stuart? Surely not. She was queen of two countries, and from what Kate had heard was most careful of her high position. She had also not been in Scotland since she was a toddler. But why was there a coded letter between a Spaniard and possibly a Scotsman, both of whom were from countries stated to be Queen Mary's foe?

Kate closed her eyes with a groan, sure that there was something just beyond her vision, some glimmering speck that would make everything click into place like a song. Who betrayed his country in such an alliance—the Scot or the Spaniard? Or perhaps they both played an elaborate double game, as everyone at court so often did. But whatever the game was, it had cost Senor Vasquez his life.

And where did Queen Catherine Parr's work come into the scheme?

Kate thought of everything she remembered of Queen Catherine. An educated woman of great intellect and conviction in the new faith, a center of learning at her own glittering court—and a woman caught in marriage four times, the last two to King Henry and then to Thomas Seymour. Tom Seymour—who also played a dangerous game with the loneliness of a young princess. A wicked game that threatened Elizabeth still, and thus all of England.

What was it that bound all these people together, the past and the present—Queen Mary, Queen Elizabeth, Queen Catherine? Kingdoms, thrones, families . . .

Children.

It was said Queen Mary of Scots was sure she would be pregnant by her French husband at any time, bringing Scotland and France even closer, giving her even more reason to claim the English throne. Queen Elizabeth had no child, no husband even, and Cecil and the rest of the privy council, not to mention the queen's many suitors, grew more frantic every day to change that. Queen Catherine had longed for a child more than anything.

Yet there had been no child with the king. And when she *did* have her own child, it killed her, as it had Kate's own mother. But Eleanor Haywood had never seemed truly far from Kate's side, had left her an inheritance with her music. Had Queen Catherine tried to do the same? Had she made her baby dolls and crowns?

A little baby with her mother's dark red hair . . .
Mary.

Kate's eyes flew open as she remembered Queen Catherine's face in her own hazy memory. The heart-shaped pale face, soft gray eyes, waves of dark red hair. A kind smile. And the girl on the stairs at the Rose and Crown. She looked much like a very young Queen Catherine, but also somewhat resembled Queen Elizabeth, with the pointed chin, the perfect posture. Pale skin, red hair. And Kate hadn't come across anyone who'd witnessed Queen Catherine's daughter's death. What if Mary hadn't died after all?

Kate scanned the rest of the document, and managed to read a few more words, though she could make little sense of them. Mary could be any lady, of course, there were so many Marys about. Almost as many as there were Catherines. But who would someone like Senor Vasquez care about enough to keep a paper coded by a song of Queen Catherine's composing? Was it used in something else?

"Kate!" someone shouted, and there was a pounding knock at her door. "Kate, you must help us!"

Startled, she leaped up from her table, nearly toppling her inkwell. She quickly folded the music and stuffed it into the purse tied at her belt before she hurried to the door.

It was Violet Green who stood there in the

corridor, her blond curls falling from her cap, her eyes wild. She held tight to the hand of Lady Jane Seymour, who looked as if she longed to just pull free and run away. But Vi's grasp was too strong on the girl's thin wrist.

"Whatever is amiss?" Kate demanded. "What's happened?"

"Oh, Kate, I do not know where else to go," Violet said. "You will surely know what to do— how to tell the queen."

"How to tell the queen what?"

"I was sent to find Lady Catherine Grey and bid her wait on the queen for her walk in the gardens, but all I could find was this minx." Violet shook Lady Jane by the hand, and deftly dodged away when Lady Jane in turn tried to kick her. "She says Lady Catherine has run away!"

"Run away!" Kate cried. She had seen Lady Catherine's unhappiness, of course—everyone did—but she would not have thought her so rash as that.

Lady Jane set her dimpled jaw at a mutinous angle that made her look much like her brother, Lord Hertford, but her pale blue eyes shimmered with tears. "They are in love! It is not right to force them apart, surely."

"They . . ." Kate said. "So Lady Catherine has gone somewhere with your brother?"

"I . . ." Lady Jane bit her lip and glanced away, but her hand had gone limp and resigned in

Violet's grasp. "I do not know for certain. I haven't seen Ned today. She had a note from him, and she just said she had to go to him."

"Where is the meeting place?" Kate said. Perhaps if she could find Lady Catherine before she did something truly foolish, the queen would not even have to know what happened.

Lady Jane shook her head. "Tell us!" Violet cried. "You will see your friend and your brother in the Tower if they are caught."

"Nay!" Lady Jane wailed.

"She is right," Kate said firmly. "We must find Lady Catherine and help her. Please, Lady Jane, tell me where she has gone. If we can bring her back here before the queen realizes what has happened . . ."

Lady Jane broke down in weeping. "She went to the Rose and Crown."

"The inn?" Kate said, remembering the day they had gone ice-skating, the girl on the stairs.

"They have met there before," Lady Jane sobbed. "I don't want them to be found out. They only want some time to be together!"

"They will be together with their heads on a block if they are not more careful," Kate muttered. She reached for her cloak and swirled it over her shoulders, pulling up the hood. "I will go after her."

"Shall we come with you?" Violet asked. Lady Jane just sobbed.

"Nay, we must have a care, Vi," Kate said. "And you should try to make Lady Jane calm herself. She will give it all away."

Violet nodded grimly. "You must have a care as well, Kate. I am sorry to have brought you this trouble. I just don't know who else to turn to . . ."

Kate gave her friend a quick smile. "You did the right thing. I shall be back anon." She wanted to help Lady Catherine, the silly, romantic, strangely sweet lady. But even more so she wanted to know what was happening at the Rose and Crown.

She ran down the stairs toward a door that led onto a kitchen garden and out to the Strand. For a moment, she was tempted to go back and find Rob, to ask him to go with her, but there was no time. He could be anywhere in the vast corridors of the palace, and she had to hurry if she was to help Lady Catherine.

And if she wanted to find the red-haired girl with the face of Catherine Parr.

CHAPTER EIGHTEEN

The common room of the Rose and Crown was crowded, but none of the people gathered there by the large fireplace was Lady Catherine. A maidservant made her way across the room, a tray of pottery goblets held high in her hands, the landlady nowhere in sight. Kate went up on her toes in the doorway, trying to peer around the cloaks and doublets, through the smoke rising against the cold day.

She remembered the narrow back stairs, where she had glimpsed the strange young girl the day of the ice-skating. Surely the chambers were up there. She pushed her way past a clump of men near the back archway, who were laughing and talking loudly together in what sounded like Dutch. One nearly spilled his ale on her, and the other tried to grab her arm.

As Kate pushed him away, she wondered for an instant why she went to so much trouble for Lady Catherine, when the lady clearly cared little for her own interests.

But she knew why—it was for the queen. The scandal of one of her relatives, one of her possible heirs, eloping would be great. And also, strangely, because Kate found she felt sorry for Lady Catherine. For the sad desperation in her eyes.

The maidservant brushed past Kate, a bowl of fragrant stew now in her hands. "Are you lost, mistress?" she asked in a harried, breathless voice.

"I am looking for my friend," Kate answered. "She is a blond lady, probably in a black gown."

The maid's eyes widened. "I—I shouldn't say . . ."

"It is most important that I find her."

"Mistress Fawlkes said the lady is not to be disturbed."

"Mistress Fawlkes?"

"The landlady here. If I angered her again . . ."

"She need not know." Kate tucked a coin into the pocket of the girl's apron, which seemed to help her make up her mind.

"In the chamber at the top of the third flight of stairs," the girl whispered quickly. "Mistress Fawlkes led her there herself. The lady seemed most unhappy."

"And the lady has been here before?"

The maid hesitated before nodding. "I have seen her here, once or twice. She never talks to me, though, only to the mistress. Mistress Fawlkes has many regular guests. She really will be so angry. . . ."

Kate nodded and let the girl go on her way. She hurried up the three flights of stairs. They grew progressively narrower, the wood creaking under her boots, and the noise from the great room faded behind her. She could hear muffled voices from behind some of the doors, and she wondered about the girl with the red hair. Was she behind one of those doors? One of Mistress Fawlkes's "regular guests"?

But she had to fetch Lady Catherine safely back to Whitehall first.

She found the room at the very top of the house, tucked under the whitewashed eaves. It was colder there, a draft seeping from beneath the tiny windows. There was only one door on the landing, slightly ajar, and she heard a muffled sob.

Kate pushed open the door, and found Lady Catherine in the small chamber beyond. It was plain, with one bedstead drawn around with plain green wool hangings, a washstand and two stools, with a narrow window set up high in the wall. Lady Catherine whirled around to face her, and Kate saw that her face was streaked with tears, her blue eyes red-rimmed. Her usually immaculate, stylish garments were a bit dusty, her sable-edged cloak tossed over the stool, her hair falling loose from her jet-edged headdress.

"Oh, Mistress Haywood!" she said with a sniffle. "Praise the saints you are here. Did he send you with another message?"

"He?" Kate said. "I am here because Lady Jane Seymour and Lady Violet Green were worried that you had vanished. Lady Jane said you were here, and I came to make certain you were well. You will be missed soon."

Her tears vanished in a flash of raw, white-hot Tudor anger. She stamped her kid boot on the wooden planks of the floor. "Juno Seymour! She vowed she would not tell a soul, that little traitor. But if he did not send you, then what—" She bit her lip.

"You did come here to meet Lord Hertford," Kate said quietly. It was not a question.

Lady Catherine's jaw tightened, as if in defiance. She held out a torn piece of paper, crumpled in her gloved hand. "He sent this, asking me to meet him here. Mistress Fawlkes told me he would be here, in this chamber, but I have surely been here more than an hour. Ned would never keep me waiting, unless—unless something terrible happened. Do you—do you think he was caught?"

Kate shook her head. If what she had seen thus far of Lord Hertford was true, then surely he ad been *caught* by a tennis game of a hand of primero. But surely even he, handsome and careless, would not forget a meeting with Lady Catherine.

She glanced at the note. It was short, terse, signed with a slashing *H*. It was not love poetry, but mayhap Lady Catherine did not expect such from him. "Are you certain this was from Lord Hertford?"

Lady Catherine looked down at it, her brow creasing. "I—surely it must be. He said he would send me word when it was safe to meet alone, and I . . ."

And Lady Catherine would wait eagerly for that word, and she would not question a place they had met before in secrecy. "We must return to Whitehall now, before you are missed."

Lady Catherine stubbornly shook her head. "He will be here soon, I am sure of it. If you only knew . . ."

There was the sudden sound of footsteps running up the stairs outside the small room, and Lady Catherine spun around with hope lighting her face. "I knew it!" she cried.

Yet it was not Lord Hertford who shoved open the door. It was Senor Gomez, a sword held in his hand. Its blade gleamed in the faint light, just like the smile he flashed at the sight of Lady Catherine. Two men moved in behind him, blocking any exit.

Kate instinctively took a step back, cursing herself for leaving her small dagger strapped to her arm, inaccessible. The face in front of her was not that of the charming man who had chatted with her at the queen's banquet, or the man mourning the death of his friend Senor Vasquez. This man seemed carved of granite, his eyes freezing cold.

She felt Lady Catherine clutch at her arm,

holding her back even more from the hidden dagger.

"It was most obliging of you to meet us so promptly, Lady Catherine," he said with a low, courtly bow. "Senora Fawlkes was kind enough to send us word you were waiting. I did not expect you here as well, Senorita Haywood, but certainly arrangements can be changed. It matters not to me. You have been most trouble-some, especially after I sent my servant to search your room for the documents we need, the documents my cousin went to much trouble to find and copy, and you were too clever in hiding them. You could surely be of use, once you are taught to be on our side."

"What is the meaning of this?" Lady Catherine demanded, some of her natural Grey imperious-ness coming through her trembling fear. If she was anything like her queenly cousin, Kate knew that fury over having her position ignored might soon push away any cool consideration, which would lose them any advantage.

Kate reached up and took Lady Catherine's hand where it held grasped her arm, and gave it a warning squeeze. If they could just get past Senor Gomez and his men, get out of that isolated room and make a run for it—the inn was crowded in its common room. Surely not everyone there could be mixed up with Senor Gomez and Mistress Fawlkes's scheme.

She took a deep breath, and tried to study the men in front of her with a calm, dispassionate eye. Beneath their cloaks, she glimpsed the glint of armor, a match to their swords. There was only the one door, and the impossible window.

"Where is Lord Hertford?" Lady Catherine cried. "I demand you answer me!"

Senor Gomez scowled. "You need have no fear for your Lord Hertford, my lady. He is involved in the most harmless of card games, in the rooms of the Bishop de Quadra. You do not have to think of him any longer. He was never of a status equal to yours. Soon you will not even have to see him any longer."

"Why?" Lady Catherine cried. "What have you done with him? I demand you let me leave this instant!"

"I am afraid that is not possible. Time grows very short. If our voyage is to proceed as we have most carefully planned, we must leave now."

"Where are we going?" Lady Catherine demanded. Her chin was still up, but her voice quavered. Kate held tight to her hand.

A frown flickered over Senor Gomez's handsome face. "Why, to Spain, of course. King Philip will welcome you there, and arrange a marriage for you with a most suitable consort. You will need such a powerful ally when you are made Queen of England."

"Nay!" Lady Catherine screamed. Kate was so shocked by Senor Gomez's words, and by Lady Catherine's sudden outburst, that she was a split second too late to catch her when she broke away.

Lady Catherine flew at Senor Gomez, her elegantly gloved hands shooting out like claws to scratch at his eyes. He instinctively shoved her back, and she stumbled and fell hard onto the floor. A wave of her golden hair tumbled into her eyes, and she pushed it back, leaving a dark smudge of dust on her cheek.

The fiery glow in her eyes warned she would fly at him again, and there was an ominous metallic clank as his guards raised their swords. Kate quickly knelt down beside Lady Catherine and took her arm.

"I will not go to Spain with you, or anywhere else! I told Bishop de Quadra that when he insisted, and I tell you that now," Lady Catherine cried. She choked on a wild sob, which rather ruined the imperious demand. "Take me to Lord Hertford."

"I am weary of this," Senor Gomez said. "I told my cousin such a scheme depended too much on the whims of weak ladies, but there was no choice in the matter. Your little island is perilously devoid of proper male heirs. But this will soon change, with your cooperation." His scowl deepened, and for an instant Kate was reminded of a painting she once saw, in a church before its wall murals were whitewashed over—an image of the devil, dark, angry, implacable. "My cousin died for this scheme, so it *will* go forward."

Kate thought of Senor Vasquez's body in the garden, a seeming suicide except for the dagger in the wrong hand. "Did *you* kill him?"

Senor Gomez's dark gaze flickered to her, narrowed as if he was surprised she was there. "Of course I did not. Jeronimo was growing weak, wanting to involve the help of the Scots, who are as despicable as the French. But I would never have dealt with him in such a way. He knew the importance of our plan, and he would have done his part in the end."

Kate held tightly to Lady Catherine as she sobbed in confusion and panic. Kate's thoughts raced. Senor Vasquez had plotted with the Scots, and it got him killed in the end—but not by Senor Gomez? Who else conspired with the Spanish to see Lady Catherine on the throne— and what had gone wrong, ending with Senor Vasquez with his throat cut?

And who was next?

"It must have been one of Spain's enemies who learned of our plans, and killed Jeronimo," Senor Gomez said. "I will discover who it was, and they will pay most dearly. But for now we must be away from this city of filth and heresy. A ship waits on the coast to see us to Brittany."

"I will not go with you!" Lady Catherine sobbed. She lunged toward Senor Gomez again, but Kate held her back as one of the guards stepped closer with his sword. Kate doubted he would kill Lady Catherine, his golden sheep, but accidents did happen. Kate frantically shook at her sleeve, trying to dislodge the hilt of her small dagger into her hand.

She had rushed into this terrible situation with foolish, headstrong thoughtlessness, and she cursed herself for it.

"I did not intend to take two ladies, but it seems you may be a calming influence, Senorita Haywood. Perhaps you can talk some sense into this silly girl," Senor Gomez said. He gestured to his guards. "Take them both."

The small room burst into violent noise and movement as the guards ran forward, and Kate shot to her feet. Lady Catherine was dragged away from her, bound and gagged with quick, terrible efficiency as she kicked and struggled. Kate tried to free her dagger, but she wasn't fast enough. The other guard, a burly, bearded man twice her size, seized her in a painful grip, and lifted her off the floor.

She managed to scream only once before she, too, was gagged, her hands tied behind her, and a blanket muffled around her. A hard, iron arm around her waist jerked her off her feet and in a disorienting circle.

She twisted and kicked, cold panic rising up in her throat like an engulfing wave. A terrible metallic taste of fear and fury was in her mouth, thick and suffocating.

She twirled around again, and managed to drive her elbow into her captor's midsection, just to the edge of the armored breastplate.

"*Condenado*, but this is a wild one!" he gasped, and Kate felt her feet caught and raised up by someone else. "We should get paid double the coin for having two English minxes on our hands."

"*Mierda*," Senor Gomez growled. "Get them out of here now! There is no more time to waste. We have to get away, while Mistress Fawlkes can hold them off."

Kate felt herself tossed upside down over a hard shoulder, the air knocked from her stomach. She could hear Lady Catherine shrieking wordlessly behind her gag, felt the rush of cold air around her legs, and then she was tossed down onto the hard floor.

Her head landed against something sharp. For an instant, brilliant silver stars burst behind her eyes—and then she fell down into blank, cold darkness.

CHAPTER NINETEEN

"Well done, Master Cartman! I think we should not invite you to play boules with us again. You will defeat us all," Lord Hertford said affably. He and his friends who were gathered on the frosty boules field behind the palace applauded as Rob's red ball knocked into the goal ball, the "mistress," and sent it sliding over the grass. He had taken double points again.

Yet Hertford and his aristocratic young friends did not seem to mind that an actor was besting them at their game. They had been drinking a supply of fine Rhenish wine all afternoon, and their laughter had grown louder, their jokes bawdier. Rob had only feigned partaking of it himself. When he met Lord Hertford in the corridor and was invited to join their game, it had seemed an excellent opportunity to find out more courtly gossip that might help Kate in her task. So far he had only learned which of the ladies Hertford's friends declared they would corner under the kissing bough—and the fact that Lord Hertford hoped to soon form his own company of players, and steal Rob and some of his men away from Lord Hunsdon.

Rob doubted Hertford could even begin to

afford his own troupe, but he had to admit the young earl was good company, full of jokes and eager to be entertained in turn. Even if he was a terrible boules player.

Hertford had just cast his own ball and earned one point, when a lady's cry interrupted them. "Lord Hertford! Oh, thank heavens I have found you."

Rob turned to see Kate's friend Lady Violet Green hurrying toward them. Despite the chilly day, she wore no cloak over her silk gown, and she was holding Hertford's sister, the pale fragile Lady Jane, by the hand. Lady Violet, much like Hertford himself, always seemed to be laughing, and he felt a jolt of alarm at her panicked expression.

Rob was quicker to reach her than Hertford. "What has happened, Lady Violet?"

"Oh, Master Cartman, I am glad to see you are here as well. I fear I may have sent Kate into trouble, and I need help to find her."

"Trouble?" Rob said. He pushed away the cold fear, the urge to grab his sword and set off immediately, to remain calm and question Violet and the sobbing Lady Jane. "Where has she gone?"

Violet glanced at Lord Hertford. "She went to find Lady Catherine, who I think has gone to the Rose and Crown. But that was a few hours ago, and they still have not returned. . . ."

• • •

"Mistress Haywood! Wake up, please, I beg you."

The voice seemed to come from a long distance away, but tinny and strange, as if shouted down a horn. It made Kate's head throb, and she only wanted to get away from it—and from the horrid jostling that made her whole body ache.

"Stop, I am well!" She meant to shout the words, but they came out a hoarse whisper.

"Thank the saints you are alive," the voice said with a sob.

Then Kate remembered. Lady Catherine at the Rose and Crown; Senor Gomez and his men with their shining swords. Ropes and muffling blankets.

She sat up, gasping as pain shot through her shoulders and stars sparkled behind her eyes. She blinked and shook her head hard, forcing herself to push the pain away and examine her surroundings.

For an instant, she thought they were locked in a wooden box, until she realized it was a coach. She had seen the expensive, rare conveyances only a few times, the queen's gilded creation that was a gift from the Swedish king, and Cecil's, which he used when his gout wouldn't let him ride. This was just as luxurious, with scarlet velvet cushions lining the two narrow benches, and a thick carpet laid on the floorboards where Kate now knelt, her hands painfully bound behind her.

But the windows were covered tightly with thick, waxed canvas nailed down.

And no amount of cushions could make a coach comfortable. The jostling, jouncing lurches were bone-rattling. Kate twisted around to face Lady Catherine. Her hair tumbled down her back, her face dusty and streaked with tears.

"They are taking us to Spain," Kate said, trying to shake off the haze that still lingered in her mind. "To make you a queen, with a suitable Spanish consort. Did you know of this scheme?"

"Nay!" Lady Catherine cried. "I never want to be queen. Look what it did to my sister. And Spain—so far from my Ned! I would never—could never . . ."

Kate could see the truth of Lady Catherine's desperate words written on her face. Lady Catherine was spoiled, true, and foolishly romantic, but not so stupid as to conceive such foul treason. She wanted her Ned above all else.

"I thought I could use them to teach my cousin a lesson," Lady Catherine whispered. "That she would see how much power I *could* have, but that I do not really want it, and if she would just give me permission to marry Ned and leave court, all would be well. But I did not understand."

Nay, Kate thought, she obviously did not. "We must get away," she muttered. She had to push her own fear away now, not let it overwhelm her. She made herself study the inside of the torturous coach as if it was one of Rob's stage props. There was little there but painted wood, and the rugs and cushions. The doors seemed fastened securely shut, even as they hurtled forward at a hurling pace.

She noticed the canvas seemed to have been hastily nailed over the windows, and a few of the iron nails protruded, one a bit farther than the others.

Lady Catherine's hands were bound also, but in front of her rather than behind as Kate's were. She had obviously already found a way to release the gags that were tied on them at the inn.

"Here, try to rub the rope on this nail, Lady Catherine," Kate urged. "If we can loosen the bonds . . ."

Lady Catherine quickly nodded, and scrubbed her hands over the protruding nail. She scraped her fine white skin, but she was not deterred. She kept on until the rope frayed enough for her to snap it apart, and then she quickly worked Kate's hands free.

Kate ignored the sting that rushed into her numb fingers, and pulled a corner of the canvas away from the window. She pulled herself up, pushing away the sparks of pain, and peered outside. They had left the spires of London behind. She could see only fields and thic groves of trees, hedges guarding the borders of fine estates, all blanketed in silvery frost.

Surely even the roads, perilous and bone-breakingly jarring already, would soon become impassable by coach. They were already going much too fast for the rutted, muddy conditions. What was Senor Gomez planning?

"What is happening?" Lady Catherine demanded, half-imperious, half-panicked.

"I can't see anything," Kate answered. She pushed herself to the other side of the swaying coach, bumping into the wooden seats until she could free a corner of the canvas over the window.

She caught a glimpse of Senor Gomez riding beside the coach, moving at a quick gallop, his face set grimly under the brim of his cap, his short cloak and boots splashed with mud. He shouted to someone, probably the coachman, but his words were snatched away by the wind.

Kate ducked down before he could see her peering out.

"I'm sure we can't go on much longer," she said. "The roads will become impassable. We must plan what to do when we stop."

Lady Catherine shook her head, fresh tears pouring from her eyes. "I will never go with them! I will die before I leave Ned."

Aye—it *was* rather like one of Rob's plays. "That's all very well, Lady Catherine, but Senor

Gomez and his friends will surely do all they can to get you safely to Spain. Without you, their scheme can never work. Me, on the other hand . . ."

"Nay. I won't allow that," Lady Catherine cried, her face contorted as if with a horrible realization. Kate couldn't help but feel a pang of grudging respect for her. Lady Catherine had been willing to die for herself, but when it came to others she was not so dramatically brave, so uncaring. "What shall we do, then? How can we escape?"

Before Kate could answer, a loud noise exploded over their heads. It cracked and echoed, almost like thunder, but Kate knew what it was—a firearm exploding. The coach, already unsteady, tipped to one side with a horrible, grating noise, a scream from a horse, shouts.

Kate and Lady Catherine were flung to one side, clutching at each other, but there was no time to cry out. The coach crashed into something amid a great cracking, and went horribly still.

Kate found herself sprawled awkwardly on the wooden floor, her head and shoulders braced painfully against the door, Lady Catherine collapsed over her legs. The canvas was ripped free from the door, and she saw the patch of gray sky beyond, fringed by the skeletal brown branches of trees.

"Lady Catherine?" she gasped.

"I am quite well," Lady Catherine said, trying to push herself up. She gasped with pain, and Kate saw that her fine black satin sleeve was torn and stained with blood.

Kate reached out to help her, just as the broken door was torn open and she and Lady Catherine tumbled out to the frozen ground.

For an instant, she was dazed, her aching head spinning. She quickly scrambled to her feet, pulling Lady Catherine with her as she took in the scene in front of them. The horses were leaping and whining in fear, yet seemed unhurt, unlike the man who had driven them. He was slumped in his seat high on the box, perfectly still, blood seeping from a wound on his shoulder.

Senor Gomez was still in the saddle, his head turning frantically as if to glimpse their assailant. His guards seemed just as confused, and Kate thought she should take the chance to flee into the woods with Lady Catherine.

But their escape path was blocked by another man on horseback. He wore a hooded cloak, his face obscured, yet the gun in his outstretched hand was all too visible.

A lady's face peeked over his shoulder from her pillion seat, and Kate saw to her shock it was the girl from the inn. Her dark red hair was tangled, a bruise on her pale cheek, and she looked terrified.

"What is the meaning of this?" Senor Gomez

demanded in furious Spanish. He swung down from his horse, drawing his sword.

The other man nudged the girl down from her perch with a rough arm and then climbed down himself. His hood fell back.

Kate thought she screamed out, but she heard no sound come from her numb throat. For the face revealed was one she would never have expected—it was Gerald Finsley, her father's old friend. The man she had known since she was a child.

Surely, she thought wildly, he had come to rescue them? Somehow he'd known how to follow them.

That hope shattered into a thousand brittle pieces when Senor Gomez smiled and said, "You. Why have you come today? Was our business not concluded to your satisfaction, Senor Finsley? Surely the gold was delivered to you."

"That was not our agreement, and you know that very well," Gerald answered, in a voice Kate had never heard from him before. A deep, bitter, humorless laugh. "You saw what happened when Senor Vasquez tried to cross me, did you not? Did he think I wouldn't know when he tried to double-cross me with the Scots? We had an agreement, and he tried to use that fool Lord Macintosh instead of me."

"*You* killed Jeronimo?" Senor Gomez demanded furiously.

"Of course I did. You do recall our plan—you were to set my wife, the rightful queen, on the throne, and now I see you were intent on the Grey-spawned harlot all along. I will not be used thus, even by King Philip. I have spent years trying to make things right!"

Lady Catherine cried out indignantly at being called a harlot, yet Kate couldn't take her shocked gaze from the lady who cowered like a frightened little bird by the side of the road. She was so slight, shivering in her thin gown, her brilliant hair tangled around her. The rightful queen? Gerald Finsley's wife?

Kate thought of Queen Catherine Parr, of her music, her longing for children. Kate's mind brought her back to her bedroom table, when she compared her father's music from Queen Catherine with the sheet of music she'd found in Vasquez's room. Those dates in the code . . .

Melville Village, Scotland—February 1559— The Lady Mary—church of St. Saviour—in the church porch . . .

Could it be a wedding date? This Mary was barely old enough to wed, but it was possible. A million thoughts raced like lightning in her mind through the taut silence that fell between the two men. The calm before the storm.

Senor Gomez gave a laugh that crackled in that silence like the ice in the river. "When you wrote to my uncle, you assured us your wife was the daughter of King Henry, hidden away by Queen Catherine for her own safety, and that you had proof. The only thing you had to give us was your own marriage lines, and that proves naught but your own greed. She is the child of the traitor Seymour—that is all. My king needs his own legitimate claimant to the throne. Surely even you, a foul murderer, can't be so stupid as to not see that."

The girl collapsed to her knees with a raw sob, her hands over her face, and Kate longed to go to her. She dared not move, though, while Gerald Finsley still held that gun. The heavy firearm trembled, as if he could barely keep its weight balanced, and she knew any sudden movement might set it off.

Kate's own anger and pain at realizing how much she did not know, how blinded she could be by her affectionate memories of her father's friends, would have to wait.

"That was why you brought me to London," the girl said, her words muffled by her hands. "You cannot think—I'm not . . ."

"Hush, you stupid child," Gerald snapped, not even looking at her. "I would make you a *queen*. No more of your foolishness."

"I fear you are the one who has been foolish," Senor Gomez said. "You agreed to help us, we paid you for that help most generously, and you repaid us with lies and murder. You used the money for your own wife's cause. You should consider yourself fortunate you have escaped thus far."

"Fortunate!" Gerald shouted. "I have spent my life working for this moment, and your treachery . . ."

"Enough!" Senor Gomez's iron disdain snapped. He raised his sword in an elegant, smooth, terrible arc. "You killed Jeronimo, and yet we have been kind to you. That ends now." He swept forward in one quick, agile movement, the dance of the practiced duelist. In only a few blurred steps, he slashed out at Gerald, almost causing the gun to drop.

Gerald's face, so furious only an instant before, melted into panic. He raised the gun in a wild arc. "I am here to make you honor your agreement! I have worked too long for this!"

Senor Gomez shoved the older man to the ground. "You are the one who made an agreement you could not honor," he said, cold and calm. "Trying to pass off a useless girl as a rightful queen. I have managed to set things right with my uncle and the king, no thanks to you. And now I have no use for you, nor does my master King Philip. Once Lady Grey is married to a proper Spanish lord, we will make our case for a new queen of England." He took a deep, swift lunge toward Gerald, his sword raised high before it slashed down.

The girl screamed, and the gun in Gerald's hand

went off with a deafening explosion. The sharp, dark smell of burnt powder filled the air. For a moment, Kate could see nothing but a silvery haze, could hear only screams and shouts, a tangle of confusion and terror.

When the air cleared, she glimpsed Senor Gomez slumped on the ground, toppled to his side with a gaping, bleeding wound in his shoulder, the fine velvet and leather of his doublet ripped away. Gerald, too, was wounded, swaying on his knees, the gun fallen from his limp hand. Senor Gomez's sword lay in the mud, its shining steel stained bright red. The guards looked on from the other side of the road, unsure what to do next. Lady Catherine looked completely white, as if she would faint.

So many things flashed through Kate's horrified mind—Allison Finsley leading her by her hand through the garden as a child, the queen on her golden throne, Queen Catherine Parr with her head bent over her writing, Senor Vasquez lying dead in the garden.

Instinctively, Kate ran to Gerald's side, and caught him as he fell. He was alive, barely, his chest heaving with the effort of breathing, of holding on to the light. Yet she could hear the low, humming rattle of it, a sound she had heard too much in the last year. At Hatfield, at Westminster Abbey, at Nonsuch—the death rattle.

He stared up at her with faded, half-seeing

eyes. In that instant, he looked like the man she remembered from her childhood, the man who helped her with her music lessons, who laughed with her father and the Parks.

Yet he was a man who would concoct a treasonous scheme using an innocent girl as bait. What had driven him to such desperation?

"El—Eleanor?" he gasped.

"Nay, 'tis me, Kate. Eleanor's daughter. Oh, Gerald—why did you do this? My father would have helped you if you were in some trouble, given you money. . . ."

"Nay, not for money!" he cried. He clutched at her arm, surprisingly strong. "I only wanted to help—her."

"Mary?" Kate said. "You love her?"

"Not as a wife. I am not so—foolish as that. As a daughter, though I married her to protect her. She was alone in life after Allison and I took her from the Suffolk house, where she was sore neglected. I promised Queen Catherine I would protect her babe."

"Then she truly is Queen Catherine's child?"

"Aye, that she is, I promise on my dying vow. Allison and I raised her, we protected her, just as we promised the queen. Mary was meant to be a great lady, as her mother was."

"Queen Catherine would never have wanted her daughter embroiled with the Spanish," Kate whispered.

"She would have been a queen! Once Queen Catherine thought she might be pregnant with the king's child, not long before he died. It was her most precious hope. And when I realized that I alone knew Queen Catherine's code—the one she wrote in her music—I realized I could write another piece of music, one where the Queen bade me marry her daughter, at a certain time, a certain place, to keep her safe. A prophecy that could prove she was King Henry's when I showed Vasquez Catherine's letters from the days when she thought she carried King Henry's child. I knew she was not truly the king's, of course, but I knew I could find a way to pass her off thusly. But then I couldn't find the papers, the music Queen Catherine had kept when that night she feared for her life so long ago."

Kate thought of Queen Catherine's music lying on her desk, the one Queen Catherine had given her father for safekeeping that same night.

"The Duchess of Suffolk had no love for the child. In her household, it was easy enough to switch the baby for a peasant's dead child, and take her away to be raised by another family. Easy enough to bribe a priest to marry us. I wanted only to help her, however I could."

"To help her with a lie?" Kate said.

"To help her with what should have been the truth!" Gerald shouted with one last burst of energy. "I worked so hard on this scheme. When

I couldn't find the papers, I realized I'd have to resort to other means of procuring the throne. I tried to scare the queen into thinking her past had come back to haunt her, that she was not the true queen after all. I saw her behavior in the house of the Dowager Queen! I managed to leave the note in her royal chamber; I paid a beggar child to leave the doll at Greenwich. All for naught."

"The queen is too courageous for such cowardly schemes to frighten her—surely you must know that," Kate cried. "Oh, Gerald, how crazed your thoughts must have become."

"Not crazed! 'Tis the truth—what should have been the truth," he declared.

He fell back onto the ground, his eyes turning blank. Mary let out a wail and ran to his side, catching the attention of Gomez's stunned guards. They straightened to their feet, and Kate snatched up Gomez's fallen sword and held it out. She had no experience with such heavy blades, but she held the steel hilt with both hands, forcing her fingers and her mind to hold steady. Surely it had to be more reliable than a firearm that could explode in her hands at any minute.

Lady Catherine had no such doubts. She scooped up the heavy gun and waved it toward the guards. They froze in their steps.

"Your master is dead, so surely his traitorous bargains are at an end," Kate said in her own halting Spanish. "You must let us go now."

They still looked hesitant, but a thunder of noise in the distance seemed to make them decide. Horses' hooves pounded down the rutted road, growing louder and louder until a party of riders swung around the twist in the road, their own swords held high. At their head was Lord Hertford, and Lady Catherine cried out to him. The look on his face, sheer relief and fury, made Kate hope his feelings for Lady Catherine were true after all.

And riding just behind Lord Hertford, his own face filled with a panic and fury that even an actor's training couldn't disguise, was Rob. Kate tried to run to him, but her legs shook too much to hobble more than a few steps.

"Halt in the name of the queen!" Lord Hertford shouted.

Their Spanish captors immediately stepped back, arms raised.

"It certainly took you long enough," Kate said. She let the heavy sword drop, and swayed with the sudden wave of exhaustion and sorrow that washed over her. She turned away from the sight of so much blood, so much life wasted, and collapsed to the ground.

CHAPTER TWENTY

"The poor child," Queen Elizabeth murmured as she leaned over the bed where Lady Mary Seymour slept. She gently smoothed a wave of dark red hair from the girl's pale forehead. She had fallen into an exhausted sleep as soon as she arrived at the palace, her meager belongings fetched from the Rose and Crown. "How much she has been through."

Kate nodded. She still felt weary herself, aching all over her bruised body from the jolting carriage ride, but surely Lady Mary felt even worse, tossed from one world to another. Considered dead since she was an infant, raised secretly in the country, married at twelve— though the girl, through her tears, had assured the queen that it was not a *real* marriage, that Master Finsley had been as a father to her. A father who had kept her in isolation, used her for his own treacherous ends, and now had left her alone in the world, without a soul to care for her.

Kate thought of her own father, the way he had held her close when she stumbled back into the palace, his tender kiss on her forehead, and felt doubly blessed.

"What will happen to her, Your Grace?" she whispered.

"Mistress Park and her husband have agreed to go live with her for a time at one of my smaller manors. I will send her tutors, and one day we can find her a suitable true husband," Elizabeth answered. "None will need to know who she truly is, so she can have the freedom to find her own path. Perhaps one day she will be able to forget all this. Time can truly be a great healer, especially to one so young."

Kate thought of Tom Seymour and Queen Catherine, of young Princess Elizabeth, caught up in things she couldn't yet understand, feelings she couldn't yet fathom. "Has it helped to heal you?"

Elizabeth frowned, yet she said nothing. She took Kate's arm and led her out of the small chamber where Lady Mary slept so fitfully. "I know I need not say this, Kate, not to you. But you do know that no matter what Master Finsley's delusions were, Lady Mary could not have been the child of my father."

Kate nodded. She had told the queen all that she had learned of Gerald Finsley's actions, his attempt to convince the Spanish that Lady Mary could be the true heiress to the English throne, using the music as his "proof."

"I do know that, Your Grace. But I still feel so very foolish."

"Why foolish, Kate?"

"I could not see Master Finsley's true intentions. I think I was blinded by my childhood memories of him and his sister. It took me much too long to see what was really his scheme."

Elizabeth stopped next to the window at the end of the quiet corridor. She was silent for a long moment, as if her thoughts were very far away, and Kate studied the scene in the garden below. She glimpsed Rob walking with some of his actors, their brilliantly colored cloaks shimmering in the winter twilight. Kate suddenly found herself wanting to run down to him, to dance and laugh and revel in Christmas, and forget what she had seen.

But there was never any forgetting. She had learned that too well in her time at court.

"I hope that you will never lose that tenderheartedness, my Kate," the queen said softly. She, too, watched the actors, her dark eyes wistful. "Too many people here are hardened, their souls made brittle by what they have done to survive in this world. Perhaps I am the same way, and it makes me hard and suspicious. I need people around me who can remind me of the merry things in life. The important things."

"Important things, Your Grace?"

"Things like music, as I am sure you know well, Kate. Dancing, laughter. Family."

Kate gave a wry laugh. *Family* seemed to be what had led so many people astray this Christmas season. Master Finsley thought his wife, and there-fore he, should be part of a royal family. The queen's family schemed and planned behind her back—Lady Catherine for love, Mary, Queen of Scots, for more thrones. "Surely family has caused its share of problems."

"Especially of late? Aye," Elizabeth answered. "But such trials show us who we can trust. And teach us to take joy where we can, aye? So—let us have dancing tonight, and celebrate that it is Christmas once again."

Kate looked once more to Rob, whose golden hair shimmered in the emerging moonlight, whose laughter she was sure she could still hear. He looked up and caught her watching, and waved with a small smile just for her. "Aye, Your Grace. Let us have dancing indeed. . . ."

EPILOGUE

Twelfth Night

"Here comes I, old Father Christmas!" proclaimed the figure who strode across the stage of the great hall, his green velvet robes and false white beard flapping about to the merriment of the audience. "Christmas comes but once a year, but when it does it brings good cheer. Roast beef and plum pudding, and plenty of good English beer! Last Christmastide I turned the spit, I burnt my finger and can't find of it . . ."

Kate laughed along with the rest of the court as Father Christmas leaped about. She was happy to see the play for once from the audience side. She sat beside her father on one of the tiered benches that rose behind the queen's tall-backed chair. Queen Elizabeth smiled and waved her feather fan as her maids, arrayed around her in their bright satins, giggled.

Kate scanned the audience to take in the various groups in attendance. Lord Halton was there with the other Scots, though Lord Macintosh seemed to have absented himself. As had Bishop de Quadra, who claimed a slight illness. But every English family at court had crowded into the room, and the merriment seemed to burn even higher, warmer, after all that had happened to try to mar their holiday.

Lady Catherine sat with her friends and dogs on the other side of the queen, her pretty face still a bit pale against her black-and-pearl headdress, but Lord Hertford's "rescue" seemed to have revived her spirits, for she laughed with everyone else. She waved happily at Kate, and made her little spaniel wave its paw.

Kate waved back, and slipped her hand onto her father's arm. He smiled down at her, though she feared that he, unlike Lady Catherine, looked more wearied by the sorrows of finding out his friend's treachery. His eyes seemed a bit faded under his fine black velvet cap.

"I am certain I should not say it, Kate," her father whispered, "not with all the strangeness we have seen of late, but tonight is surely one of the finest Christmases I can remember."

"Is it, Father?" she whispered back. "Despite—everything?"

Matthew sighed. "Gerald Finsley *was* once my friend. 'Tis true. We both served Queen Catherine, whose learning and grace we admired so much. But anyone can be changed, twisted, by courtly ambition. They can be blinded by the sparkle around them so they no longer see to the core of truth. Human understanding and love are worth a caravel full of gold and emeralds. Your mother taught me that."

Kate studied the crowd as they laughed at the players' antics. It was a beautiful sight indeed. In the blazing light of the Yule log, the jewels of the queen's court glittered like a thousand stars, ropes of pearls, diamonds, and emeralds against bright velvets and rich furs. The crowd clustered around the queen, who was brighter than all the rest in her cloth of gold-and-white satin, her red hair piled high and wound with strands of rubies and topaz.

Elizabeth laughed behind her fan, and reached out to take one of her favorite cherry suckets from a bowl Robert Dudley held out to her. He whispered something in her ear, and she actually blushed, then tapped his arm with her fan. Robert's sister, the queen's lady-in-waiting Mary Sidney smiled, but several people frowned and muttered at the sight.

Kate realized her father was very right—she was in danger of being drawn too far into this world to turn back. Not because she longed for jewels or for the estates and titles that royal avor could bring—though she thought those might be nice enough. But because here, at the very center of the deceptive hive that buzzed around the queen, she felt as if she could be of good use.

She had work to do—her father and mother's legacy of music, aye, but also the vital work of keeping Queen Elizabeth safe and her throne secure. Without Elizabeth, England would be in terrible danger of being tossed back into chaos and darkness, as it had been too often in days gone by.

Kate knew well she was only one person, one young, inexperienced woman, who was still fumbling her way through the maze of court life. Yet every pair of eyes was needed to help guard the queen, and surely she could learn more ways to be of help.

If Elizabeth had never become queen, Kate knew she would have stayed in the country with her father, perhaps married a farmer or a village shopkeeper, helped run his business and home, had children she could teach a little music to. Not a bad life at all, and one that would surely have promised more contentment than a courtly career. But it was not a life that could ever contain all the things she was just realizing she had in herself.

"You taught me that as well, Father, and I promise I shall never forget," she said, squeezing his hand. "Courtly life does have its attractions for me, I admit, but not of the treasure sort. I am learning my way here."

"And you are learning it exceedingly well. You have the queen's trust. I am proud of you—as your mother would be."

Kate felt tears prickle behind her eyes, and she blinked them away. This was no night for tears. "So, tell me. Why is this a good Christmas after all?"

"Because I am with my daughter, of course! Any moment I have with my Kate is a good one." Matthew looked toward the stage, where Father Christmas had been joined by a chorus of angels, who danced in twining circles around him as they sang their final song. "But I must know one thing, my dearest, before I can go back contented to my little cottage."

"What is that, Father?"

"I must know whether you have forgiven me for keeping the truth about your mother's family from you. I meant no harm, truly. It merely seemed to be Eleanor's secret to keep. And I had to protect you."

Kate nodded. Secrets were the court's most valuable currency, and some connections were better unknown. "I know. To be a Boleyn was not a safe thing for a long time. Of course I forgive you, Father. I did long ago. You were truly only taking care of me." And, unlike Gerald Finsley's protestations that he was only trying to "take care of" Mary Seymour, or Tom Seymour's "protection" of a young Princess Elizabeth, her father's actions, his secrets, had been for the best in the end, Kate knew well.

She kissed his bearded cheek. "You have been the best of fathers. Surely Mother would be proud of *you,* as well. We have taken care of each other rather well all these years, I think."

Tears shimmered in his eyes, and it made Kate want to cry all over again. "Yet I will not be here forever. I do not want you to be alone, my Kate. I want you to find happiness such as I had with your mother." He gently touched the pretty little lute-shaped pendant she wore uncovered now, held on a string of seed pearls and garnet beads that had been the queen's Christmas gift. "This is a charming piece indeed, and most thoughtful. From Queen Elizabeth?"

Kate opened her mouth to tell her father about Rob, but something held her back. Her tiny secret hopes and ideas, that perhaps she had found someone who could truly understand her as her parents had understood each other, were still only her own.

At least for a little longer. She glanced at Rob where he stood by the edge of the stage, and found he watched her as well. How very handsome he looked that night, smiling his charming, careless grin, his hair shining like the summer sun against his violet velvet doublet. Yet she knew there was so much behind his beauty. There was a passion for art and life, a sense of adventure, that called out to her own.

But aye—that was her own secret for the moment. As was the letter she had received from Anthony that morning, asking if he could see her when next he came to London. She wondered, probably with far too much curiosity, what he wished to tell her. And what she would say in return. She could see why matters of the heart drove ladies like Catherine Grey, and even the queen, to distraction. They were even more baffling than deciphering Platonic musical codes.

She smiled at her father, and nodded.

The play came to an end in a show of silver sparkles and sweets tossed out into the audience. The queen's ladies rushed for them, and the actors lined up to take their bows. Elizabeth leaped to her feet, applauding, something she never did, and her astonished courtiers scrambled to follow her lead.

"I declare, my friends, that this has been the merriest night of Yule revelries I can yet remember," she said. "Now, while we still have the light of our Yule log, and plenty of wine and 'good English beer,' let us dance and make merry. Robin?"

Robert Dudley held out his arm to the queen, and led her from her chair as servants scurried to move the benches and musicians took their places in the gallery. In the light of the snapping, flaring Yule log, everything looked perfect.

For the moment.

AUTHOR'S NOTE

One of my very favorite things about the Elizabethan period (and there are many!) is the great number and variety of strong-willed and passionate women. Queen Elizabeth, of course, along with her mother and stepmothers, her cousins (Margaret Lennox; the Grey sisters; Mary, Queen of Scots), not to mention ladies of other countries such as Marie of Guise and Catherine de Medici, are all examples of the strong women I admire so much. The Grey sisters, ladies Jane, Catherine, and Mary, and their mother, Frances, Duchess of Suffolk, are fascinating and tragically sad in equal measure, and I loved getting to know Lady Catherine better in this story.

Not everyone (not even everyone who was a Tudor!) had an ambition to wear a crown in the 1500s, and this included the Grey daughters, though sadly their birth pushed them toward the throne anyway. Lady Jane's story is very well known—scholarly, brilliantly bookish beyond her years, dedicated to the New Learning of the Protestant church. But her younger sister, Lady Catherine, isn't quite as widely known. She was the "beautiful" daughter, the counterpart of Lady Jane—charming and known for loving a good party. Her ambitions were to be a wife (to a man

318

of suitable estate), and have a family, to live a romance like the ones in the French poems she would rather read than the serious philosophies and sciences her sister loved.

Catherine was born in 1540, and was the second daughter of Frances Brandon, who was the daughter of the famously beautiful younger sister of King Henry VIII, Mary Tudor (the French Queen, as she was always known, though she was married to the elderly French king for only a couple of months), and her husband, the Duke of Suffolk. Catherine was married off in 1553 in a political match to the son of the Earl of Pembroke (in the same lavish ceremony that married Lady Jane to Guildford Dudley). The marriage was annulled the next year, after the death of Edward VI and the collapse of the scheme to make Jane queen. Lady Jane and the Grey girls' father were executed, and Lady Frances was left to find a way to remake her position at court and take care of her two remaining daughters. Somehow she managed to do this impossible task very well. They were reconciled to Queen Mary, who gave them high positions at court, but Queen Elizabeth mistrusted and disliked them, especially Catherine. Elizabeth refused the desire of many (including her chief secretary, Sir William Cecil) to name Lady Catherine as her heir.

Catherine's best friend was Lady Jane Seymour, the daughter of the former Protector of England in the reign of Edward VI, Lord Somerset, and his equally formidable duchess Anne (another strong Elizabethan-era lady!). Catherine soon fell deeply in love with Jane's handsome, if unreliable, brother, Edward, Lord Hertford. Hertford seemed to return her passionate feelings, and the two were secretly married in December 1560 (about a year after *Murder at Whitehall* takes place). There were some rumors, especially in the summer of 1559, that Lady Catherine was becoming too friendly with the Spanish, and it's now known that the Spanish actually had some hopes of kidnapping her and bringing her to Spain, where she could marry a Spanish nobleman and eventually take over the English throne, though the extent of Lady Catherine's own involvement in the half-baked plan isn't known.

After Lord Hertford and Lady Catherine's hasty wedding (for which Lady Jane found the priest and was the only witness), the Queen sent Lord Hertford to France. After he left, Lady Catherine realized she was pregnant. She managed to hide it for many months, but of course that couldn't go on forever! When the pregnancy was discovered, and the secret wedding revealed, Queen Elizabeth was furious. Lord Hertford was summoned back to England, the couple was sent to the Tower, the marriage declared invalid, and the baby boy, Edward, rendered illegitimate.

(By this time Lady Jane had died and the priest could not be found.) Even the walls of the Tower couldn't keep the Hertfords apart, though, and the next year another son, Thomas, was born.

Lady Catherine was sent away to the country under house arrest, and died of consumption at age twenty-seven in 1568 (or of a broken heart at being parted from the family she had longed for). Lord Hertford was eventually released from prison and later married again and regained his place at court, though when he died he was buried with Catherine. Her sister, Lady Mary Grey, plagued with a deformed spine since birth, also went on to make a secret, disastrous marriage. But that's a story for another time!

Although Queen Anne is my favorite of Henry VIII's wives, I've always had a soft spot for Queen Catherine Parr. She had a rather astonishing life. Catherine Parr was raised by a strong, intelligent widowed mother, Maud Parr, lady-in-waiting to wife number one, Catherine of Aragon (who was possibly Catherine Parr's godmother). Maud had spirit, but not much money, and most of it went to securing a marriage for her son to the greatest heiress in England (a marriage that—spoiler alert—also did not go well). Catherine was married twice before she married the king, first to Sir Edward Burrough, who died very young, and then to John Neville, Lord Latimer, a widower twice her age with extensive landholdings in the isolated north. The marriage seems to have been reasonably happy, though, and Catherine raised his two children as her own. After his death, she joined the household of Princess Mary, where she caught the eye of King Henry. Henry had recently "lost" his unfortunate fifth wife, the young, pretty, giddy Catherine Howard, and was looking for someone steady and dignified. The widowed Lady Latimer, unfortunately for her, seemed to fit the bill, and the fact that she was being courted by Sir Thomas Seymour made no difference. Catherine married the king on July 12, 1543.

She was well suited to the role of queen, charming and stylish but also well read and practical. Even diplomats from France and hostile Spain sang her praises, and she brought Henry's three children together as a family for the first time. She especially encouraged young Princess Elizabeth, who had been mostly ignored up to that point, in her educational endeavors. But she also became deeply interested in the Protestant faith and the New Learning, as Lady Jane Grey had, and gathered a group of like-minded women around her for studies and discussion. She talked about her studies at length with anyone who would listen. She was the first English queen to publish works under her own name. These included works of prayers and philosophy (including *The Lamentations of a Sinner* in 1547).

Needless to say, this did not sit well with the more conserva-tive courtiers, including Stephen Gardiner, Bishop of Winchester. (It's true that one of Queen Catherine's best friends, the pert Duchess of Suffolk, named her spaniel "Gardiner.") Her increasing "radicalism" also did not sit well with her husband.

In the summer of 1546, Gardiner and his allies managed to turn the king's irritation against the queen, and an arrest warrant was drawn up against her. Luckily, Catherine was pre-warned, and managed to reach the king and appease him before she could be hauled to the Tower. By the end of the year, the king was dead, and Catherine was free for the first time in her life. She had an independent income as Dowager Queen, and moved to her house at the Old Manor in Chelsea, taking her stepdaughters with her. It was at this time that her old flame, Thomas Seymour, came back into her life, and they married barely six months later, without the required permission of King Edward and the council. Princess Mary was furious and moved out, trying to persuade Elizabeth to do the same, but Elizabeth stayed. She was thirteen, beautiful, headstrong, and devoted to her stepmother.

That devotion didn't serve her well at that time. Thomas Seymour, who it was rumored had hoped to marry Princess Elizabeth before "settling" for the Dowager Queen, took a most inappropriate interest in his young stepdaughter, and there were many scandalous reports of his behavior with her—trying to come into her bedchamber in the mornings before she was dressed, chasing her in the gardens, even cutting her gown off her. At this time, Catherine was pregnant for the first time at age thirty-five, a dangerous proposition in that era, and she sent Elizabeth away. Catherine gave birth to her daughter, Mary, on August 30, 1548, and died six days later. Mary was sent to live with Catherine's friend the Duchess of Suffolk, who complained of the expense of the child. Now, with Queen Catherine and his young daughter out of the way, Thomas decided to pursue his old ambition of marrying Princess Elizabeth. Thomas Seymour was attainted for treason for trying to marry Elizabeth without permission, and was beheaded on March 30, 1549 (and only Elizabeth's quick wit saved her from sharing his fate. Her household was questioned about her own intentions toward marrying Seymour, and her favorite servants, including Kat Ashley, were taken to the Tower, but Elizabeth talked her way out of trouble—as she would many more times in the future).

Mary Seymour's property was restored to her by an Act of Parliament in March 1550, to help the duchess with her upbringing, but the last that was heard of her was around the time of her second birthday. Most historians agree she died as a child, but there have always been rumors she survived to be married off in obscurity and raise her own family. (I would love to think this was true!)

As for the Scots—we will certainly hear much more about them in Kate's next adventure, *Murder at Fontainebleau*, when she visits the French court of Mary, Queen of Scots! In this story, we see the aftermath of July 10, 1559, when King Henri II of France died after a terrible jousting accident, leaving his teenage son, Frances, husband of Mary, Queen of Scots, to rule France and press his wife's claim to the English throne. In December 1560, a group of Scots Protestant lords who sought to take up arms against the French Catholic Regent, Queen Mary's mother, Marie of Guise, came to Elizabeth's court under the support of William Cecil. Sir William was eager to be rid of the thorn of Queen Mary, but Elizabeth, as usual, was cautious. She knew the English treasury was empty and war was expensive, and how would it look to support the overthrow of another anointed queen—even if she *was* a nuisance?

The Scots Protestants pressed their claim for aid, saying military reinforcements were due to arrive from France to crush the rebellion—an army that could then easily be used to invade England. Elizabeth finally agreed to send a fleet to Leith to block the French arrival, and ordered the Duke of Norfolk northward "for the preparation of the army to be sent into Scotland." On February 27, she officially took the Scots Protestants under her protection with the Treaty of Berwick, and on April 6 laid siege to the French garrison at Leith. Peace was negotiated with the Treaty of Edinburgh in July, where both England and France withdrew from Scotland—but Mary, Queen of Scots, refused to ratify the treaty. It was only the beginning of decades of conflict between the cousin queens—and I can't wait to delve into the lives of the two queens!

If you're interested in looking deeper into the time period, here are a few sources I loved (and relied on heavily for the history behind *Murder at Whitehall*).

D. M. Ashdown, *Tudor Cousins: Rivals for the Throne* (2000).

Tracy Borman, *Elizabeth's Women* (2009).

Hugh Douglas, ed., *A Right Royal Christmas* (2001).

Marie Hubert, ed., *Christmas in Shakespeare's England* (1998).

Susan E. James, *Kathryn Parr, The Making of a Queen* (1999).

Leanda de Lisle, *The Sisters Who Would Be Queen: Mary, Katherine, and Lady Jane Grey* (2008).

Janel Mueller, "A Tudor Queen Finds Her

Voice: Katherine Parr's *Lamentations of a Sinner*," in Heather Dubrow and Richard Strier, editors, *The Historical Renaissance: New Essays on Tudor and Stuart Literature and Culture* (1988).

————, "Devotion as Difference: Intertexuality in Queen Katherine Parr's Prayers or Meditations (1545)," *Huntington Library Quarterly* 53 (1988).

Stephen Pincock, *Codebreaker: The History of Codes and Ciphers* (2006).

Linda Porter, *Katherine the Queen: The Remarkable Life of Katherine Parr, the Last Wife of Henry VIII* (2010).

Evelyn Read, *Catherine, Duchess of Suffolk* (1962).

Simon Thurley, *The Royal Palaces of Tudor England* (1993), and *Whitehall Palace: The Official Illustrated History* (2008).

Center Point Large Print
600 Brooks Road / PO Box 1
Thorndike, ME 04986-0001 USA

(207) 568-3717

US & Canada:
1 800 929-9108
www.centerpointlargeprint.com